An Independent Woman

To look back for a while is to refresh the eye, to restore it, and to render it the more fit for its prime function of looking forward.

Margaret Fairless Barber
English Christian Writer
1869-1901

An Independent Woman

A Regency Novel

Peggy Lovelace Ellis

Faraway Publishing
Black Mountain, N.C.

Peggy Lovelace Ellis
76 Wagon Trail
Black Mountain, NC 28711-2565
https://www.peggyellis.com

First Edition
2025

Cover Design: Raney Day Creatives LLC

Scriptures in the Author's Note are taken from the *King James Version (KJV)* of the Bible.

Published by Faraway Publishing
125 Spring View Drive
Black Mountain, NC 28711

Printed in the United States of America

ISBN-13: 979-8-9881761-9-0

Library of Congress Control Number: 2025931495

An Independent Woman
by Peggy Lovelace Ellis

1. Historical Romance, 2. Regency Romance, 3. Regency Morals and Manners, 4. The Regency *ton*, 5. Napoleonic Wars, 6. Wellington, 7. Regency Nobility, 8. George III, 9. The Prince Regent, 10. Regency Slang, 11. Metaphysical/Visionary

For Ruthie

Acknowledgements

Some people are irreplaceable in my life.

First and foremost is my husband, James T. Ellis. He has been my support in uncountable ways throughout our fifty-six-year marriage and especially during those times when my mind was so busy with characters vying for my attention that I didn't hear him.

No one produces a book without considerable help from others. I'm fortunate to have known and worked with people who willingly listened as I droned on about my stories.

My sister and our niece, who prefer to remain anonymous, always have my back.

Two authors with long publishing histories of Regency novels have been generous in sharing their knowledge. My special appreciation to Dawn Aldridge Poore (https://www.amazon.com/Books-Dawn-Aldridge-Poore) and to Gail Eastwood (https://www.amazon.com/Books-Gail-Eastwood/).

Randolph Shaffner shared his publishing expertise in this book's publication.

My endless appreciation to all.

Table of Contents

Author's Note

Many publishers will not accept manuscripts containing guardian angels as characters, and with good reason. The existence of guardian angels is scriptural as we find in the following verses, among many others: *Psalms* 91:11—For he shall give his angels charge over thee, to keep thee in all thy ways; *Hebrews* 1:14—Are they not all ministering spirits, sent forth to minister for them who shall be heirs of salvation?; and *Hebrews* 13:2—Be not forgetful to entertain strangers: for thereby some have entertained angels unawares.

The problem arises because humans cannot know the extent of angels' capabilities, so we give them the attributes that fit our story. As you read *An Independent Woman,* sympathize with Susanna's difficulties with her charge, but remember both are figments of my imagination.

Prologue

Hampshire, England, October 1801

The seven-year-old ragamuffin kicked off her half boots, laughing with delight while she wiggled her toes among dead leaves. The earthy smell rising from beneath the top layer made her nose crinkle. She sneezed and wiped her nose on her sleeve, then tucked her skirts into the top of cotton drawers and climbed the tree until she stood on a broad limb. There were many trees around, but this one had limbs near the ground. Mattie didn't let her climb trees.

The little miss sank small teeth into a juicy red apple, delighting in the noise. Mattie would frown about that too. Eating whole apples is beneath your social position, she would say. What would she say about all the smudges on her charge's face? The child didn't want to know. She didn't want a governess, but Father insisted she needed lessons Nanny couldn't teach her, so Miss Matthews had moved into Ainsley Park.

Susanna's scolds are different. After all, she is an *angel* and whispers into her small charge's mind.

Horse's hooves interrupted the child's thoughts about the ridiculous whims of her elders. Probably a groom from Ainsley Park looking for her. She didn't want to give up these few minutes of stolen freedom. The child peeked through the leaves.

Reining his gray horse to a standstill beneath the tree, the rider reached for an apple. Not an Ainsley groom, but a young gentleman she'd never seen before. Relief bubbled into a mischievous impulse. She tossed her half-eaten apple toward him. It hit the horse, which reared, white-stockinged feet clawing the air.

The unexpected movement sent the rider backward off his mount. His brimmed hat flew in one direction, his apple in another. He scrambled to his feet and soothed the mare. "Sorry, old girl. That apple chose a bad time to separate itself from the tree."

The girl couldn't control her giggles, which brought the man's frowning gaze upward. Afraid now, she lost her footing, tumbling unceremoniously toward the ground. He jumped forward and caught her. They landed in the leaves, barely missing the horse's hooves.

She rolled off him and scooted backward, staring into the prettiest face she'd seen outside her storybook about Greek gods. Glittering green eyes beneath fair curls that tumbled over his forehead stared back at her.

"Did you throw the apple?" He smoothed his face into a superior smirk. "Oh well. You're only a little girl, not old enough to know better, but don't throw apples at horses again, understand?"

The voice of the Greek god in her storybook must sound like his, light, not a deep rumble like her father's voice. "Little hoyden, your face is filthy." He stood, hauling her up beside him. Without warning, he kissed the tip of her nose. "There, I'll wager that's your first kiss—also your last if you don't wash your face."

"My name's Judith," she blurted. "What's yours?"

"Richard." He rescued his hat from a low limb, then swung himself onto the saddle and spurred his mount.

She shouted after him, "I'll marry you someday, even if you are prettier than I am!"

His laughter floated back until his mount's long strides carried him from her sight.

"I *will* marry him," she muttered, "or my name is not Judith Elizabeth Ainsley."

Don't make rash promises. They might come back and haunt you someday. Now, you must return home.

Judith trudged toward Ainsley Park: Susanna telling her what to do again.

One

Somewhere in France

June 1815

Jagged lightning split the night sky, giving the mounted man a brief glimpse of a traveler plodding on foot, his head bowed under the rain's onslaught. Slipping into the deep shadow of a hardwood, which bordered the muddy lane, the rider slid from the saddle and laid a hand over the horse's muzzle. There he stood until the other traveler passed from his view.

He must be on his way if he wanted to meet the brig that would carry him to English shores. He might have to hole up at Calais for a day or so, but at least he would be there when the storm passed. A few nights in a comfortable bed would be welcome before continuing home. His journey had been long, filled with more than ordinary discomfort, not only physical but mental also. He was glad the end was near.

Early in this trip, he realized his age counted against him for this job. He would never admit this failing to anyone. Instead, he would let his superiors realize they needed a younger man. The work had been exciting in earlier years, outmaneuvering friendly authorities as well as adversaries. He could smile in retrospect at some of his narrow escapes. However, now the thrill had gone. Besides being a wearisome job, traveling kept him from normal pursuits too often for too long a period.

He had done his assigned job—delivering papers to the right hands. Now he was ready to go home. The weather made this a good night for spies and smugglers alike—which was the man he had seen?— albeit not for horses carrying a load. He would walk awhile. Apollo needed a rest. They had traveled a far distance that day with still farther to go. He stepped from the shadow with thunder rolling overhead.

Two

Dreadful News

Hampshire, England, June 1815

Judith grimaced at her companion when the sitting room door opened. "Ruthie, I'm having a difficult time with the scene between the governess and the curate. They refuse to behave as they ought. Perhaps we should give only one a strong personality."

Writing novels under the name of 'Mrs. Blaylock' was Judith's initial way of earning funds. She did the major writing, while Ruth's job was curbing her flights of fancy. Ruth also wrote the clean copy for the publisher. Judith admitted she was too impatient to mind her penmanship.

For a moment, her musings reverted to the day she'd overheard the conversation between her parents. On that same day, Daniel had brought the news Mr. Davison wanted to publish the book she and Ruth had written. They had kept their writing a secret because Lady Monford did not allow them to read gothic novels, so how could they admit they'd written one? At that instant, Judith decided their novel would be the beginning of her quest for independence.

Now, Ruth Edgecombe eyed the crumpled sheets of foolscap littering the floor around the writing table. "I can see your struggles, which we'll deal with later." She took a deep breath. "I've just come from Lady Monford. Prepare yourself, my dear. I have dreadful news."

The quill dropped from the other's hand, splattering ink on her gown as she rose. "What is it, Ruthie? Has something happened to Mama? Is she ill? Should I go to her?"

"Not Lady Monford. The news is about your father."

"What happened?" Judith sank onto a low, armless chair, her hands clasped together.

"A courier from London brought a message from Whitehall . . ."

"*Whitehall*? What do they have to do with Father? He's past the age for battle."

"I agree the obvious connection is absurd, but there must be one." Ruth perched on a chair across from her. "The message revealed that Alexander Ainsley died in France . . ."

"*France*? We're at war with France. Why would Father be there?"

"Please allow me to give you the little information I have without further interruption."

Judith clamped her lips shut and listened.

"The message simply said Alexander Ainsley died while traveling on the continent. He apparently stabled a horse in Calais, and it returned to the stable without him. Several days later, searchers found his body. The authorities delivered his mount, saddlebags, and signet ring to Monford House in London. He's buried in the French countryside."

"Why didn't they send his body home? I don't want him buried so far away!" Judith's voice broke, and tears streamed down her face.

Ruth handed her a handkerchief edged in lace. "All things considered, I didn't expect this reaction."

Judith wiped her eyes. "I didn't want him dead. I wanted to confront him and declare my independence, then leave Ainsley Park."

"I do understand, Judith. However, for now, you must be brave. The next several days will be difficult for everyone, especially your mother. You must give her the support she needs."

"Ruthie, do you truly believe she will want support from me? You're closer to her than I am."

"Perhaps your father's death will ease the strain between you and Lady Monford."

"I hope you're right. In any event, I must go to her."

<> <> <> <> <>

Wearing deep mourning a week later, Judith gripped the burgundy drapes in her father's study, her mind in turmoil as she stared out the window toward the rain-soaked park. The ticking of the mantel clock was the only sound in the book-lined room that overlooked the front drive. She had come here to be alone, collect her thoughts, and mourn not what was but what might have been. She ignored the jagged lightning that split the sky.

At age fifteen, she'd lost respect for her father, the father who people believed doted on her. Grief for the love she had for him during childhood tugged at her heart, even while pain almost overwhelmed her when she recalled his deceit. She'd fought this battle many times in the intervening six years.

The pain Judith felt at fifteen was agony even now. She had begun making plans the same day to thwart him. She learned she had a head for business, and she'd used her brain, difficult though she'd found absorbing financial details in the beginning. At times, her love for her father conflicted with her determination to outwit him. Today, after talking with their man of business, she would put her carefully made plans into action. Judith had eagerly awaited independence. Now when freedom was within reach, her mood was as somber as the clouds hanging over Ainsley Park.

Between thunder rolls, carriage wheels on the gravel drive distracted Judith. Ruth came into the room and chose a straight chair near the door. Moments later, Lady Monford entered and sat near the fire.

Judith chose a chair opposite her mother, her back ramrod straight, her face devoid of expression.

After a light tap on the door, the butler ushered two gentlemen into the room. Judith nodded at Mr. Sizemore, the family solicitor for many years. The other gentleman, a heavyset man of about sixty, had a red nose, indicating he enjoys spirits too well. He was bald on the top of his head with a fringe of stringy, gray hair from above his ears reaching his shoulders. Revulsion gripped her.

Relax, Judith. Calmness will carry the day. Trust me.

Judith rested her shoulders against the chair's high back. She was not always aware her guardian angel was close, but any time she'd needed help, Susanna had been there. The first encounter was when, at the age of four, she escaped Nanny and ran across the lawn. Gentle hands had pulled her back from the lily pond, holding her until she was steady on her feet.

The guilty child had turned around, thinking Nanny had caught her, but no one was there. When she demanded to know who had stopped her, a soft voice in her head had given her name: Susanna. She'd never seen the angel, which didn't matter because Susanna's voice had been a constant in her life, although grown-up people, even Nanny, had laughed at the idea. Judith had learned early to conceal her encounters with the angel.

With a mental thank you, she turned her attention to Mr. Sizemore.

"Lady Monford, Lady Judith, Miss Edgecombe, this gentleman is Lord Harold Robert Ainsley, cousin of the late earl."

Lady Monford waved him toward a chair. "Many years have passed since we last met, my lord. Ainsley Park welcomes you."

"I rarely leave my Kent estate." He bowed before Lady Monford and turned toward Judith. "If my memory serves, you were still in the nursery during my last visit."

She rose and dipped a slight curtsy. "That explains why I don't recall seeing you, my lord. May I introduce my companion, Miss Ruth Edgecombe?"

"My pleasure, Miss Edgecombe." He nodded at her curtsy, then sank into an oversized leather chair with a muttered, "Gout," and lifted his left foot onto an ottoman. Squeaking sounds broke the silence as he settled his large frame in a chair.

When he quieted, Judith turned her attention to Mr. Sizemore.

Seated at the desk, the solicitor delved into his jacket pocket for spectacles, which he wiped with a large white handkerchief. He cut his glance toward Judith a couple of times, then cleared his throat before speaking in a dry, official voice.

"I am here to read a document titled, 'The Last Will and Testament of Alexander Elliott Ainsley, the seventh Earl of Monford.' The document, executed ten years ago, is simple but quite clear. I won't read the individual servants' legacies. They're routine. I'll meet with those persons later."

During the hush following those words, Sizemore took a deep breath and glanced once more at Judith. Her face a careful blank, she listened while he read in a toneless voice.

"The monies which I received upon my marriage to Catherine Mary Ainsley *nee* Burwell are returned as her jointure. I direct Lady Monford to occupy the Dower House at Ainsley Park. Her jointure is insufficient to support her elsewhere. Further, I direct that Miss Ruth Edgecombe will always have a home at Ainsley Park with income sufficient for her needs."

The solicitor rattled the pages he held. After clearing his throat, he continued. "The Monford estate with all properties, real and personal, which I hold are entailed upon my heir, Lord Harold Robert Ainsley of Kent, now the eighth Earl of Monford."

"To my daughter, Lady Judith Elizabeth Ainsley, I leave the following instructions. I direct you to continue management of Ainsley Park. I trained you to take proper care of the estate, and I can trust this property to no one else. To accomplish this, you will marry my heir, Lord Harold Robert Ainsley, by special license, within fourteen days of hearing these instructions. If you refuse my instructions, you must leave Ainsley Park within the said fourteen days, with no inheritance. You will have no claim on the Ainsley estate. Furthermore, you can never return to Ainsley Park."

The ticking clock on the mantelshelf was loud in the otherwise quiet room. Judith sensed her mother's stare as she recalled the conversation she had overheard between her parents when she was fifteen.

"Does she still think you'll choose a husband near her age?"

"I'm not sure what Judith thinks, but it makes no difference to my intention."

"You indulge her to the point you'll have a hard time convincing her to obey you on this point."

"Oh, Judith will do what I say," the earl stated with his usual arrogance. *"True, I indulge her in small things, but I have complete confidence in my control over her. She'll marry the man I choose, never fear."*

"I don't understand why you chose Harold Ainsley anyway. He does not appear to be a suitable choice. His age

counts against him for one thing. Producing an heir could be a problem."

"It wasn't a matter of choice. Harold is my heir. As his wife, Judith will continue to manage the estate. He's still hale and hardy and has offspring scattered hither and yon, so producing a legitimate heir won't be a problem."

"I don't understand. You've always said our daughter is your heir because, through the special dispensation of somebody or other generations ago, the title can descend through the female line."

"That was a necessary subterfuge. She might not otherwise have taken such an interest in the estate."

"I'm not convinced of her obedience. She has already shown she has a mind of her own. How can you be sure she will obey you?"

"Judith will either marry Harold or she will leave Ainsley Park with nothing. However, I have no fear on that score. Judith will come around, even if she's stubborn at the outset."

"And she will be," Lady Monford said.

"Oh yes, without a doubt our daughter will be obstinate. She'll obey me, though, because she loves me—also this place— too much to leave. I made sure of that. Why else would I have carried her over every inch of the estate, even before she sat her first pony? Why else would I have her present at my business meetings with Sizemore? She has a better head for *business than anyone I know. Excluding myself, of course."*

"Your arrogance will catch up with you someday, mark my words."

His arrogance had, indeed, caught up with him. Setting aside her thoughts, Judith spoke, her words clipped without emphasis, her face turned toward her mother. "I've long known you only tolerate me, Mama, for which I realize I am much at fault. I ask your forgiveness for my many shortcomings. However, I believed Father loved me. I was wrong." She forced down a threatened sob and turned toward the solicitor. "Sir, is there anything more I should hear?"

Rather than answering her question, Sizemore said, "I tried to talk him out of this, Lady Judith. He was adamant. Nothing I said swayed him. His intention was the protection of the estate's future, you see."

"What I see is that property was more important to my father than his daughter's well-being. However, what he failed to see was that he would force me into a miserable marriage for naught. Instead of keeping me immured on the estate, he could have found me a husband from my generation, one both of us approved, thus allowing me to produce an heir in the direct line. How my father could be so illogical on such an obvious point is beyond my understanding."

The callous indictment fell into silence until Judith continued. "Do I understand I may take my personal possessions with me when I leave?"

"Leave?" her mother protested. "You cannot leave! You must obey your father. Now, you'll learn he simply used you like he did everyone else."

Lady Monford's outburst brought horrified silence, into which Judith's quiet words fell like stones.

"I learned that at fifteen, Mama, when I overheard the two of you discuss his plans for my future. I've had six years to accustom myself to the fact the father I adored was a man without honour."

After listening without comment, the new earl chose this moment to speak. "I don't believe I would go so far as to say my cousin was without honour, don't you know. He knew you would be safer in my keeping than with a young buck. I believe we can make a go of this marriage."

"I appreciate your view, my lord, however I decline. I do not intend disrespect, but I refuse to marry a man who is three or four decades older than I. When I was thirteen years old, my friend's father forced her into just such an abhorrent marriage. Father promised me, then, he would choose for me a husband near my own age, a promise he didn't intend to keep, judging by the date on the document which Mr. Sizemore holds. My father's behaviour toward me was reprehensible and beyond forgiveness."

Sizemore forestalled Lady Monford, who started to speak. "To answer your question, Lady Judith: yes, you may take with you any possessions provably yours. However, perhaps you should give this matter some consideration. Where will you go? How will you live?"

"Sir, there are some words not in my vocabulary. Impossible is one of them. I have known my father's plans for six years. I'm a realist. I knew from the beginning I couldn't wait until the last minute to thwart his intentions toward me and, therefore, made my own plans. You know my investments because you carry out my instructions. I also possess a considerable amount of valuable jewelry, which I can sell if I need additional funds. Do you doubt I can support myself?"

"I must question your assumptions, my lady." Sizemore's voice was gentle. "Are you sure those investments and possessions are yours? Did the earl use estate funds for the purchases? I know the original investment monies were estate funds, because I have a clear recollection of that transaction. His lordship told me he was satisfying one of your whims."

"That was not a whim but a carefully constructed plan." Judith's strained laughter filled the room. "I learned when I was fifteen that I can be devious too. I inherited deviousness from him, even though he told Mama he held me in complete subjection. I intended to leave on my twenty-first birthday, which was three weeks ago. However, I decided to await his return to prove my independence. My only regret is he will never know how I outwitted him."

The last bitter statement fell into another silence, which the solicitor broke after a long moment. He repeated his earlier words.

"Yes, you may take your personal possessions, if you can prove your ownership of what you claim. However, I must verify the authenticity of your proof."

Judith turned to her companion, who had remained silent. "Ruthie, will you bring the ledgers, please?"

Lady Monford reprimanded her. "Must I remind you, Ruth is family, not a servant? You have no business ordering her about. Besides, ledgers should be kept in this room."

The two friends shared a smile before Ruth slipped out the door.

"Mama, Ruth is not only family: she's my dear friend. Only she and I know where I keep my ledgers. You can't think me so stupid I would leave them lying around where Father could destroy them once he understood their significance."

Silence reigned until Ruth returned, handed two leather-bound books to Judith, and reseated herself, all without speaking.

Judith grasped the ledgers. "After hearing my parents discuss my future, I decided to leave rather than be forced into a marriage with an elderly gentleman. I realized I would need to prove ownership of everything I intended to accumulate. Therefore, I persuaded my father to list his gifts as my personal property, not part of the Monford estate. You will notice this list includes my horse, Gypsy. At my insistence, he recorded them in his handwriting. In his arrogance, he didn't question me about why I wanted him to write the items."

She handed the red-bound ledger to the solicitor. "You will note among the receipts inside the front cover that I repaid the five hundred pounds, my original investment, together with interest. Therefore, the investments I've made since that date are my own."

Sizemore studied the handwriting, which he compared to the document before him. "There can be no doubt this is his lordship's hand. I have a great many samples in my office, should anyone inquire."

"I never doubted for a moment you would verify my father's handwriting."

Glancing down the pages, the solicitor looked at Judith. "This is quite an accumulation."

Anger filled Lady Monford's voice. "I don't care what you planned, the fact remains you must stay here and marry this man. I cannot stay here alone with him, and I refuse to live in the musty old dower house.

Judith steadied her breath. "Times without number you said Father indulged me with too many presents. You never took into consideration that, every time during the past six years he gave me a gift, he also gave one to you. At my insistence."

"But those things are part of the estate."

"No, they aren't. I kept a ledger for you too." She held up the other ledger. "I also persuaded Father to execute a conveyance deed giving you ownership of your family home in Warminster. I don't understand why he did, because, legally as your husband, he still owned the property. His way of humoring me, I suppose," she added. "He probably called it satisfying another *whim*."

She handed the black-bound ledger to her mother. "You described the set of diamond jewelry I chose four years ago as the most hideous thing you had ever seen. I agree with you. However, they will support you comfortably for an appreciable period, should you choose to sell them."

Lady Monford glanced through the ledger without speaking.

"You are an independent woman," Judith told her. "You don't have to depend on me, or the earl, or your jointure."

With that flat statement, Judith left the room, with Ruth close on her heels.

Three

Change of Plans

When the young women left the room after he finished reading Ainsley's instructions, Mr. Sizemore waited for Lady Monford to speak. The quietness reigned for only a few moments.

"What did she mean, I'm an independent woman? If I understood her, this ledger lists several items, which are mine, but they by no means add up to the wealth she implied."

The solicitor cleared his throat. "Lady Judith commented earlier about the investments she left in my care. She also invested funds on your behalf. I can't tell you the exact amount without checking my records. I imagine, though, she can tell you to the last penny piece what funds you have."

"Does this mean I can afford to live in Warminster? I'm not an expensive person. I can be frugal, if I can be near my friends."

"The late earl had the house renovated when he executed the conveyance deed. Upkeep should be at a minimum for several years. Yes, I believe you can live quite comfortably on the investments which your daughter made on your behalf."

Mr. Sizemore's City acquaintances considered him an astute man. He appreciated their opinion but doubted he had earned their regard since learning of Lady Judith's business sense. At sixteen, she had already displayed more acumen than most men had, including her father. Now at only twenty-one, her understanding of business matters was almost frightening. She was shrewd and level-headed, two attributes he had never expected he would use to describe any female.

He had followed her advice through the years for his own investments. As a result, he had become a very wealthy man. Only once had he not followed her example, resulting in the loss of considerable funds on a fraudulent canal scheme. He never again deviated from her investments with the result he could live out his days in comfort. This current situation would push him into retirement except for one circumstance. His son needed a few more years of experience before taking over the business.

Sizemore pulled his attention back to Lady Monford. "Your daughter has an uncanny grasp of financial matters despite her extreme youth and being a female. You might ask her advice on investing your jointure too."

Lady Monford rose. "I'm not so unfeminine as to have a head for business matters, so I shall leave the investments in your hands."

The gentlemen had risen when she did. Sizemore sketched a bow. "Thank you, my lady. Shall I report to you on the same basis I have for Lady Judith?"

"You have my permission to consult with her, if you choose. I don't concern myself with business."

With that parting shot, she closed the door behind her.

Sizemore watched her leave the room, sighed, and blessed his lucky birth. He was grateful for aristocratic business, yet he would never understand nobility. He shook his head at the obtuseness so many people demonstrated. Exchanging glances with the earl, they regained their seats.

The earl broke the silence. "Lady Monford and her daughter do not appear to have a close relationship."

"I've never witnessed their verbal interchanges before now," Sizemore answered with caution but continued with a burst of candor. "However, to say truth, Lady Monford is an embittered woman, jealous of her own daughter."

"I imagine we can lay her spite at my cousin's door. Alexander always had an eye for females who were no better than they should be. He didn't bother hiding his shenanigans either. Quite the autocrat, he was. All females must do his bidding. The document you read proves his arrogance, had there been any doubt. Now, tell me about Judith's companion. She's an attractive chit."

Sizemore considered the possibility his lordship did want so young a bride. True, old age took some men that way, especially when there was no heir. In this instance, there wasn't, not legitimate at any rate, so there was no son eligible to inherit the title and the entailed estate.

"Miss Edgecombe, a few years older than Lady Judith, is Lady Monford's relation on her maternal side. Old Edgecombe gambled away every cent he had before blowing out his brains fifteen years ago. Mrs. Edgecombe died when her daughter was a small child, so Miss Edgecombe was alone after her father's suicide and dependent on distant relatives who had their own plans for her. When Lady Monford learned of Edgecombe's death sometime after the fact, it is to her credit that she insisted upon her cousin living here."

"Perhaps that explains why the two young ladies are so close." After a moment, the earl continued. "I know we must dress for dinner. First, however, can I trust the agent here to maintain the estate for me without constant oversight? I much prefer to live on my smaller Kent estate."

"Daniel Sherwood has been the agent here for several years. I know Ainsley had complete confidence in him, so I'm sure you can too, my lord. I'm not thoroughly familiar with Sherwood's ancestry, but I do know he is the son of a Yorkshire vicar whose brother is a bishop."

"That relieves my mind. I'll leave the estate in his hands, and yours, also, if you're agreeable. Consult Lady Judith on my behalf too." Receiving the solicitor's agreement, the earl rose painfully to his feet. "We'd best change for dinner, else we'll rouse Lady Monford's ire."

<> <> <> <> <>

Judith's calmness deserted her when she reached her sitting room after hearing her father's instructions. Fighting tears, she paced the room while Ruth sat quietly watching her.

"You knew what to expect, Judith, so pull yourself together."

"Oh, Ruthie, regardless of what I said, I did hope Father might have changed his mind before he left." She flicked a tear from her eyelashes and heaved a deep breath. "The first thing we must do is visit London to find a house."

"I agree. Perhaps those houses we viewed after your father left on his last trip are still available. Did you have a favorite among them?"

"The small Georgian in Wimbledon was nice." It had not been easy to give a reasonable excuse for a visit to the metropolis, one that would not raise her mother's suspicion. They had managed without too much subterfuge. "The immediate grounds appeared well-tended, and fifty acres are sufficient for us. We didn't inspect the stables, which we can do on our next visit."

"Perhaps we can ask Mr. Sherwood to inspect them for us."

"Why would we? I'm quite capable. I don't need a man to do anything for me."

"Oh." Ruth's strangled voice drew Judith's attention.

"Is something wrong, Ruthie?"

A long moment passed before Ruth answered. "Mr. Sherwood asked me to marry him, but I said I can't leave you."

Judith stared at her. The idea Ruth might want a different kind of life, one with a husband, had never occurred to her. She could even want a life that did not include being a companion of her younger cousin. Judith hadn't known Ruth had more than a nodding acquaintance with the estate agent. Swallowing her chagrin, she rushed to embrace her friend.

"You've been keeping secrets from me, you naughty creature." She strove for a light tone. "You must marry him, if that's what you want."

"I can't leave you," Ruth repeated, her tones firm, yet moisture clouded her eyes.

"Yes, you can. I can live alone."

"You'll do no such thing! How could you even think so?"

For the first time during their acquaintance, Judith spoke to her cousin in icy tones. "I'm independent. I can and will do as I please."

"I know you're independent and can accomplish anything you choose. The investments you've made at such a young age attest to your financial acumen. However, since your father never permitted you to enter society, or have friends who did, you cannot know living alone will put you beyond the pale. If you want to take your rightful place in the *ton* after your mourning period, you must obey society's dictates."

Judith continued to glare for a moment, then capitulated. She knew an earl's daughter had a place in Society. Although naïve to most Society rules, she did realize she must have a respectable chaperone. When that day came, she would need someone who could introduce her to the right people. How to find such a person when the time came was beyond her present plans. Meanwhile, she must behave in an acceptable manner. Susanna would advise patience.

"You must stop pacing," Ruth said. "This Aubusson carpet you finagled from your father will be worn through before you set up your own home."

Judith settled into her favorite low, armless chair. "Ruthie, I had not considered asking Sherwood to leave Ainsley Park because I don't need an agent. However, I not only need *you*, I *want* you with me, so I will ask him to be my steward. Instead of taking London by storm, I shall purchase an estate, which he can manage. You and he will have a suite in the house."

Tension eased from Ruth's face. Judith watched her closely as she continued. "That is, if you will risk your future with me. He might not want to leave here because this is an ideal place for an agent."

"I realize that, but I believe Daniel will agree to go with you."

"I can't afford a place the size of Ainsley Park." Judith pushed the wistfulness from her voice. "Perhaps, I should lease a place until we see how well things go. Talk to Sherwood now."

Ruth glanced toward the carriage clock on the mantelshelf crowded with books, riding crops, and leather gloves. "He's in the estate office at this hour, so I can see him before we dress for dinner."

"I prefer a tray here."

"Do you want the others to know how upset you are?"

"No, I don't," Judith agreed, suppressing a deep sigh. Someday, she wouldn't have to concern herself with others' opinions. On that, she was determined.

After Ruth left the room, Judith resumed her pacing, breathing in the scent of the applewood fire. Her thoughts darted around like leaves in autumn until Susanna's voice interrupted.

After all Ruth has done for you, was that the right way to speak to her? God sent her to be your friend, to help you through these difficult years.

Judith appreciated Susanna's help, but she had long since grown tired of the scoldings. She'd learned early in life to carry on mental conversations with Susanna. Nanny had said some people would believe she was insane if she talked to an unseen person. Somebody might lock her in the attic when no one was looking. She had ventured up there once. The dark place was scary. Probably monsters lived there, or at least spiders.

I'm independent. I don't need anyone to do anything for me. I've managed quite well for myself these past six years.

If you have, why did Daniel Sherwood carry your manuscripts to the publisher? Why was it necessary he take your business instructions to Mr. Sizemore while you stayed at home?

Yes, he acted the role of courier for me, but I kept a close watch. I don't trust him. He's a man.

Not all men are the same. Your argument doesn't convince me you're independent. Why did you involve Ruth in your schemes? If you could manage on your own, why was it necessary to be devious and draw others into your cunning?

Before Judith formed an answer, Susan continued.

Pride gets in your way, Judith. You deceive yourself when you take credit for all you have accomplished. The fact is God gave you the abilities you need for success, and He gave you two humans along with me to guide you.

Judith wanted to rebel against Susanna's interference. She didn't answer the questions but did admit the angel was right. She never lied to herself, no matter the lies she had lived over the past few years. *I'll apologize to Ruth when she returns., but I still don't trust Daniel Sherwood or any other man.*

After taking the headstrong girl to task an hour earlier, Susanna nestled among the dining room ceiling ornaments. Flickering candles cast shadows on the table heavy with silver and crystal. When the servants left the room, the only sound was the clink of utensils on china. She eavesdropped on the thoughts swirling around the dinner table. They were enough to make any self-respecting angel give up all hope for humans.

Lady Judith pushed the food around on the plate. After a struggle with her conscience—why should she mourn the blackguard?—she had changed into another unrelieved black gown. Except for a pleasant greeting upon entering the dining room, she refrained from speaking unless to answer direct questions. She occupied her mind with what she must do before leaving her childhood home, never to return. When her father's face intruded, she shoved his image away.

Ruth sat lost in thought, occasionally reminding herself to eat something. The possibility of marriage was a dream coming true. Females in her position rarely had the opportunity. She even had a dowry, thanks to Judith's investment acumen. She was not wealthy, by any means. Still, she need not worry about her future. The knowledge comforted her when she heard of indigent females who must tolerate any abuse just to stay alive. That was not now a consideration, for which she must thank Lord Monford. Even if marriage were not possible, she would always have a home where she would be well-treated.

She and Daniel could marry with clear consciences. He'd agreed all of them living together was an excellent idea. They would have a quiet wedding in London with a special license. Their leaving would create a nine-day wonder but wouldn't dim her happiness. She kept her exultant emotions to herself. No one looking at the serene face she presented could guess her true feelings.

Lady Monford picked at her food. The tiny lines at the corners of her gray eyes, the high cheekbones, and hollowed cheeks gave her an air of fragility. On the contrary, she was quite strong, although she had enjoyed the illusion of ill health for several years. At last, she could go home to Warminster, so near yet so far away. Monford had never wanted her to visit there.

Never again would he criticize her friends. Never again would she keep silent when her husband spoiled their daughter. However, most importantly, she would never again silently hold her head high while people discussed her husband's infidelities. They'd snickered behind their hands for the last time. She would think twice before even considering another marriage.

The new Lord Monford eyed Judith, wondering anew how anyone so lovely could have good brains. Perhaps he should ask her advice about his Kent estate. Too many sure investments had failed over the past several years. He was by no means destitute. However, he could not deny this inheritance was welcome. His life would be better if he could sell this huge place.

After a few efforts at conversation, Geoffrey Sizemore sat in silence concentrating on his food. The Monfords always set a plentiful table.

Susanna followed the ladies into the drawing room after dinner as each continued her meditations. The rattle of teacups was loud in the otherwise silence, which remained unbroken, because the gentlemen didn't join them for tea. The evening ended when each lady departed for her room soon after the footman removed the tea tray.

Snuggled inside the blue brocade bed curtains, Susanna watched her charge relax into sleep. Judith had absorbed much of her efforts to draw the girl into God's plans for her, but there was considerable work still ahead. The girl had conducted herself well on this trying day. How long would it last?

Susanna often regretted that God allowed humans free will. The angels' work would be easier if He had not. However, He is the Supreme Being. Who was she to question? Her work on earth was temporary. She could then go home until God chose another earthly job for her. She admonished herself to remember the angels who had defied God. They could never go home again.

Four

A New Day

The following day was hectic. After their early breakfast, Judith asked to speak with Mr. Sizemore in the morning room.

Waving him toward a chair, she said, "I'm now able to take care of business directly with you."

"My pleasure." He rose from his chair in a half bow. "I had hoped on this occasion we could discuss your investments."

"I, too, wished for this opportunity. These past years seeing you here and not discussing my interests have not been easy. My first concern is that we have heard nothing about our three cargo ships returning from the West Indies."

"Their late return concerns me, also, but we need not be overly alarmed yet. An East India Company ship arrived three days ago, several weeks later than the expected date. The captain reported calm waters had slowed their return."

"We can hope the same is true of our ships, although piracy is always a concern in those waters." She made a note. "If I remember correctly, the next coal deliveries from Newcastle-on-Tine are only a few weeks away. The same for Whitehaven. Do we have sufficient storage space available?"

"I leased the newly renovated warehouse situated beside ours, so, yes, we do, my lady."

They continued through Judith's investments until she was content her business was securely in her own hands. When they finished, she said, "Sherwood, Miss Edgecombe, and I will consult you in London in a few days about leasing an estate."

"I will have possibilities ready for your perusal."

Judith led him toward the front door where his carriage awaited. There, she bid him goodbye with an extra thank you for his diligence.

Before his carriage left the drive, Lady Monford ordered packing boxes delivered to her rooms. She gave orders for the estate carriages to move her and her possessions to Warminster within the week. Then, with only a glance toward her daughter, she returned up the stairs.

Judith shrugged. She could not recall her mother's ever leaving her bedchamber so early. "Mama will require all the estate vehicles, Ruthie, yet I don't want to postpone our trip. Do you have a suggestion?"

A carriage was the one item her father had refused her—his way of keeping her here. Throughout the years, she had only left the estate grounds with him.

"Perhaps Daniel can borrow the vicar's extra carriage."

"Perfect. The carriage we commissioned in London should be ready for us when we arrive there. Will you approach Sherwood?"

Ruth nodded and turned to go but stopped when the earl approached.

Lord Monford limped toward them as they crossed the entrance hall. "Ladies, how are you this morning?"

"We're well, thank you, my lord." Judith spoke for both. "We go to London tomorrow to begin our search for accommodations, so I will be away from here within the specified fortnight."

"You're welcome to stay here for whatever length of time you need, your father's wishes notwithstanding." He shifted his weight off his left foot. "Yet if you leave, you are also welcome to take anything you want from here. Ainsley Park has been your home all your life, so there must be many mementos you wish to have. They would mean naught to me."

"No thank you, my lord. You are quite generous. However, I will take only what is mine. Please appoint someone to see that we don't pack anything extra."

"M'dear, that won't be necessary." Exasperation coloured Lord Monford's voice. He spoke across his shoulder as he hobbled toward the study. "I have already said you can take anything you please."

They watched him until he closed the door before Judith spoke to the hovering butler. "Stewart, I will take only those items provably mine. Please instruct the other servants. Please, also, check off each item in the ledger as the others pack the boxes."

Her heart ached at the sadness in his eyes. He had always been there, indulging and correcting her equally, which only old retainers could do.

"Yes, my lady. May I know when you plan to move?"

"That depends on housing circumstances. We'll stay at Grillon's Hotel for a few days while we consult Mr. Sizemore, after which we will return here and collect our possessions before going to our new home." She paused a moment, struggling for calmness. "At any rate, we'll be gone within the fortnight the late lordship ordered."

"What time tomorrow do you wish to leave for London?"

"We will leave quite early with the expectation of reaching London by nightfall. My maid will attend us, with Mr. Sherwood as our escort. The under-coachman will drive unless Mama has requested his services."

The study door opened, and Lord Monford's head appeared around the lintel. "Lady Judith, may I speak with you a moment, please?"

Standing just inside the study door, she gazed at him across the room for a moment but lowered her eyelids. Her heart lurched, seeing another man occupying her father's chair.

His tone had moderated to hesitancy. "Ah, m'dear, can I say or do anything to change your mind about marrying me?"

Judith gaped at him. She hadn't expected this, but her answer left no room for doubt. "No."

"Ah, I thought not."

Was that a flash of relief in his eyes? The flicker was gone too quickly for her to decide. He must realize he'd find life uncomfortable married to a young wife with decided ideas. She didn't tell him she would never marry anyone, never give another man control over her life. Her father's perfidy precluded the possibility.

He lowered his gaze. "I've mulled over this matter and concluded there is no reason you cannot stay here and manage the estate for me. Your father believed you are capable, so the estate is safe in your hands."

At her gasp, he glanced up but then returned to fiddling with the quill-pen on the desk. "There's no reason to leave your home. His instructions only bind me not to break the entail, nothing else. I cannot be punished if this marriage doesn't happen. Nothing can stop me from installing you as my agent either."

Judith fought to steady her temper. Imagine being subject to someone else in her own home, *her* estate, were the truth acknowledged. However, she managed a polite answer. "My father made his intentions clear. He has turned me out of my home. I have no desire to stay under any circumstances."

"Well, I tried to obey your father's wishes," he said with a shrug. This time, his relief was unmistakable.

"I do appreciate your offer." With that prevarication, she left the room. She must prepare for the trip to Town.

Five

Good News, Bad News

Vienna, Austria, June 1815

"Yes, Cam, I'm aware Congress has reconvened to finish drawing new boundaries for the European continent after the years of Napoleon's rule." Richard Chadwick had returned to Vienna, seeking the excitement he enjoyed during the Congress the previous autumn when the countries affected by Napoleon's actions first met to divide the spoils of war. "However, no, I don't intend to participate, even on the fringes."

Joseph Cameron shook his head. "The parties, Chad, the parties! You can't miss those! Remember Madame Bouchet's parties which lasted for days?"

"Too well. The last one I attended erupted into a political brouhaha, which lasted almost as long as the party." They stopped before an imposing limestone building. "I'm renting rooms here. Come join me in a drink."

"I'm already a day late joining Madame Bouchet, so I'll decline. Are you sure you won't come with me? She made a fuss over you last year, and she's sure to ask about you."

"I'm sure." With a wave, he watched Cameron turn a corner. Cam had pulled him into the excitement last autumn. He'd appreciated the attention during the first weeks in this strange city, even though they had little in common. As for Madame Bouchet, Richard had no interest in over-rouged, gimlet-eyed dowagers who pretended to be much younger.

The crowds, the carriages, the shouted greetings between old friends had been exhilarating after long years of war. They still were. Perhaps he would stay a while and revisit the places he'd enjoyed the most. The Spanish Riding School, for instance, was a fascinating place well worth another visit.

The constant suspicion and tittle-tattle surrounding Congress had soon bored him, although, during the early weeks, he found the intrigue interesting. Even the Allies hadn't trusted each other. The smaller countries accused the four major countries—Britain, Russia, Prussia, and Austria—of taking more than their rightful share. The larger countries each demanded the lion's share. The resulting infighting was enough to make any sensible man avoid politics.

Richard climbed the steps and sounded the brass doorknocker shaped like a lion's head. He curbed his inclination to run his fingers over the mane, which he had done at the entrance of Chadwick Park when he was a child and had to stretch on his tiptoes to reach the knocker.

"Good afternoon, *Herr* Chadwick. You had a—ummm—joyful outing, *ja*?"

He smiled at the blue-eyed schoolgirl, who opened the door at his knock. Her broken English amused him.

"Good afternoon, *Fräulein* Gretchen. Yes, I've had an enjoyable morning." He swept her a deep bow, bringing forth giggles. He had already learned that Austrian girls giggle the same as the English ones at home. He could tolerate them for limited periods only, here or there.

She stepped back, allowing his entrance, then closed the door after him.

After Napoleon's confinement on Elba the year before, Richard had traveled rather than return to his father's roof. He had enjoyed Italy, especially Venice. He'd pondered visiting Greece. Perhaps he would go to Germany, instead, or Verona. He could renew his fencing lessons there. He had all the time in the world to choose, he reflected, as he ascended the broad sweep of carpeted stairs to his rooms.

Richard would never admit this, but Napoleon's escape from Elba earlier in the year had been a relief, despite the long days in the saddle and the gut-wrenching fear when bullets whistled around his head. He had rejoined Wellington for continued battles until the final confrontation at Waterloo a few weeks earlier.

There were regrets, though. He'd left too many men lying on the muddy battlefields. After a week of identifying those who fell at Waterloo and writing letters to their families, he'd asked Wellington for some leave time to consider the future. Now, he would enjoy a few months of leisure before he returned to England and reported to Whitehall for his next assignment. He was happy to be back here, the most beautiful city he had visited in his earlier travels.

He shrugged out of his dark green morning coat and then stood beside the open window. The sweet scent of flowers rose on a slight breeze. The combination of tinted gravel and blooming shrubs produced a riot of color in the gardens below. Everything about Vienna was colorful from the flowers to the flamboyant décor reflected by floor-to-ceiling mirrors. These abounded in every room, making the rooms appear much larger.

Richard already felt at home after only a few days back. This was where he belonged. He ignored a sharp tug in his chest when a vision of Wiltshire's rolling hills slid through his mind. He wouldn't be lonely. With Napoleon's defeat, Englishmen would travel again. At least until Napoleon raised another army, which he surely would attempt and go on the rampage again. He, Major Richard Chadwick, would stay alert to the possibility.

He strode across the room to answer a knock on the door.

"A message for you, Herr Chadwick."

"Thank you, Gretchen." He stood at the door watching her scurry away, her clogs loud on the tiled floor. Another schoolgirl with blue eyes, eyes the colour of water on a sunny day, tugged the edges of his mind as she did too many times to count over the past few years. She didn't giggle.

Richard closed the door and scanned the missive from the family solicitor. Stunned, Chadwick sank into a high-backed chair, then read Coleman's letter again, scarcely absorbing its meaning. His father was dead. The estate was in deplorable shape. The duchy had been wealthy for several generations, so how could it be destitute now? Times without number, he'd wanted to learn how to manage the estate. The duke had resisted his every effort, insisting his heir must develop an interest in ancient writings.

Instead, Richard had begged permission to join the army. After a tirade about undutiful sons, Rochdale granted permission. Richard believed his father didn't care what his heir did so long as he was elsewhere. He didn't know what he could have done to block his father's depletion of the estate—but he would have tried.

When Richard purchased his commission, his mother had cried over his leaving, which he had known she would do. Her tears, however, did not bother him. His father's indifference did. Being the heir of a peer was not the perfect life lower classes believed.

Reading the letter a third time, he accepted the obvious. Regardless of how the duchy had become destitute, he must correct the situation.

Now, Richard called for Pierce, his batman, to pack his baggage and arrange passage for England.

<> <> <> <> <>

The newly elevated Duke of Rochdale arrived at Whitehall for a conference with Colonel Staples. That was how the lackey had styled him—His Grace, the Duke of Rochdale. Richard shuddered. He refused to consider himself as anything except Major Richard Chadwick. He'd soon have to forego the military title, but he'd never be Rochdale. His father would always own the civilian title, at least in Richard's mind.

He had accepted the obvious—pain him though it did—and now explained his circumstances. "I must resign my commission, Colonel. The estate requires my presence."

"I am indeed sorry, Major Chadwick, uh, Your Grace." The colonel rubbed his lined forehead. "Napoleon remains a problem. He abdicated again at Rochefort where he's negotiating his future residence. The underground rumour says he's trying to put together another army. I doubt he will succeed, but we need to stay alert until the new French government finally puts a stop to his shenanigans. Even then, the army will need men of your caliber."

"I agree with you about Napoleon's intentions. His arrogance will not permit him to live quietly for long, and I wish I could assure you that I would be available. My future lies in a different direction."

"Are you convinced you must follow this course?"

"Unfortunately, yes. The problem is my father left the estate in deplorable condition. I must correct the situation. There's no one else."

Exactly what he could do was not clear even to him. The lowest stable hand knew more about managing the estate than Richard did. Nevertheless, duty called, and he couldn't ignore it. He dreaded the return home, believing he should have returned sooner and tried harder to become closer to his father. Now he was too late, forever too late.

In truth, he'd enjoyed his years in the Peninsula despite the hardships and the deaths of his men. He had led a charmed life, although he'd made a point of leading his men into every battle. Staying in the background like some others of his rank did not set well with him. Besides, he hadn't cared whether he lived. This *derring-do* led to rapid rises in rank. Those years of battle horrors had matured him considerably. He would return home a far different man from the one who had left there six years earlier.

After meeting with the colonel, Richard returned to his townhouse. There, he sprawled in a leather chair in the dimly lit study, a glass of brandy cradled in long fingers. A fire crackled in the huge fireplace giving warmth that did not penetrate the chill in his bones.

Rather than brooding over the future, he considered finding some feminine company but shook his head. He was not in the mood for the twitter his presence would cause. He would stay home and be comfortable here where the atmosphere did not reek of his father's presence. Never had he been so pleased that his father had spent little time in London. Satisfied with his decision, Richard grew pensive and stared into the fire, allowing his thoughts to wander back to conversations with his father. The opening door interrupted his painful memories.

"Your Grace, you have a caller." Handing him a small square of pasteboard on a silver salver, his butler inquired, "Shall I admit him?"

Richard glanced at the card. Mr. Thomas Hinson. Ah, here was a welcome distraction. He couldn't ask for a better one. "Certainly, Nicholls, show him in."

"You're just what I need, an old friend to help me pass the evening." With an outstretched hand, he met his guest at the study door, his observant eyes noting the additional weight on the once-lanky frame. They had been schoolboy allies in all sorts of endeavors. Richard had missed their close companionship in recent years. There had been many times on the battlefield when he would have been more confident if Tom had been beside him. A later friend, Charles Sanderson, rode beside him through battle after battle from Portugal on through the Spanish campaigns and at Waterloo. He couldn't take this old friend's place, however. No one could.

"It's a pleasure to see you after so long. Yes, I will have some brandy, thank you."

"How did you know I'm here? I left Vienna in such a rush I didn't notify anyone of my return."

"I saw you earlier today going into the City. My appointment was in the other direction, so I couldn't greet you." Tom sipped his brandy. "I was sorry to hear of your father's death. Influenza has taken its toll this season."

"Thank you." Richard cleared his throat. He was not yet ready to deal with sympathy. Perhaps never. "Now, tell me about your family. When last we met, you had inherited Longview Park at East Leah and married Hope. Are there any little ones creating havoc about the place?"

Laughter greeted this question. "Oh, yes, Tommy is four now and into every kind of mischief he can conjure. We call him Tommy Trouble. I often ask if I got into the many scrapes he does. My old Nanny assured me he doesn't hold a patch on me at that age."

"I'm not surprised, considering the scrapes you got into at school." Fearless best described Tom Hinson from early childhood. "Do you remember the time we walked along the humped-back bridge railing in a heavy rain while the stream was in flood stage?"

"If I tell the truth about that escapade, I must admit to quaking in my boots."

Stunned, Richard said, "You can't be serious. You practically ran across the railing."

"Yes, I'm serious. I didn't dare let a future duke know I chewed my tongue more than once."

"For my part, I didn't dare let my best friend know a future duke was a coward. There were times I was not sure my own tongue would survive my teeth."

"Two of a kind, were we not?"

"I won't tell anyone what cowards we were if you won't. Is Tommy the only little one at your house?"

A wry grin crossed Tom's face. "No, we also have Anne. Two years old. She already has me wrapped around her little finger. Hope warned me doting on my little darling would be my undoing, as she gets older. I can't help myself. She's adorable."

"You wouldn't be prejudiced, would you?" Richard teased as he passed the brandy decanter again. How would it feel to have a son to follow in his footsteps? A daughter to idolize. He sighed. The time was not far distant when he must address that, little though he was inclined to find a mother for his offspring. Blue eyes the colour of water on a sunny day passed through his mind.

He and Tom reminisced while the fire turned to glowing embers, hardly noticing when a footman came into the room.

"Your Grace, Mrs. Nicholls asked me to ascertain if you will be in for dinner."

Richard returned to the present with a blink. "No, tell her I will dine out."

With a bow, the footman quit the room, and Richard turned toward Tom. "I didn't realize so much time had passed. I must change from my riding clothes. Then we can find a place for dinner: one of the clubs, perhaps, and possibly some entertainment afterward. Does that appeal to you?"

"I'm agreeable to the idea, but I, too, must change. Suppose we meet someplace. Your choice."

"I don't recall you have a townhouse. Where do you stay in Town?"

"Grillon's Hotel. They set a good table if you care to join me there. We can decide about entertainment afterward."

"Perfect."

Later, Richard leaned back in his chair with a smile for his host. "This is my first time to dine here. I assure you it won't be the last."

He glanced toward the open door into the lobby. Then his gaze became fixed.

"Who is she?" Tom asked.

"I don't know." Richard shoved back his chair, colliding with one occupied by an irate gentleman who spilled his beverage down his shirt front and sputtered about the manners of the younger generation.

Nodding an apology without taking his gaze off the beauty in the lobby, Rochdale strolled toward the door to get a closer view of the delicate profile turned toward him. She wore her raven hair in a chignon low on her neck. Her camellia-like complexion stood in bold relief against the shadow of her bonnet. His breath caught when she turned magnificent blue eyes toward him. Eyes the colour of water on a sunny day. He held her gaze until she flushed and looked away. Then he returned to his table in a pensive mood.

"Did you recognize her after a closer scrutiny?"

"Her face was not familiar, yet I've seen those eyes before," Richard answered. Those bewitching blue eyes had invaded his dreams throughout the war. It would be embarrassing if people knew a schoolgirl dominated his dreams.

Tom rose. "I would like to hear more when you remember where you saw them before. But, in the meantime, the waiter wants this table."

"What? Oh, the waiter. We'll go to my club for a drink before we call it an evening."

Six

Lingering Memories

"I never want to make another such journey in one day." Judith collapsed onto a chair in her sitting room at Grillon's Hotel while she waited for tea.

During the journey, she'd been quiet, remembering her father. On their few trips to London, they stayed overnight at the Ramsgate Inn, where the people treated the very young Judith as though she were an adult. Today, when they passed the inn, she tightened her lips, her gaze forward.

Judith had roused herself when their carriage reached Grillon's Hotel. In the lobby, she turned at a sound and stared into admiring green eyes. Richard.

The curls that had tumbled over his forehead when she first saw him at the apple tree were gone, but his hair still feathered around his neck below his ears, just as it did when she saw him two years later. Her father had taken her to the theatre after a business meeting. Richard had the audacity to kiss the top of her head when she lost her footing on the stairs and fell into his arms. At least he had aimed higher than her nose. He hadn't recognized her though, and that had irritated her. Now, one thought drummed through her brain. Regardless of crinkles in the corners of his eyes and the lean planes of his face, he still looked like a Greek god.

Now, she and Ruth relaxed in their private sitting room while Alice unpacked their baggage.

Judith gazed around the room. "I had forgotten how nice these rooms are."

"I gather you didn't consider staying in Monford's townhouse."

"No." Before she could explain her blunt answer, Daniel came in on the heels of a maid, who carried a tea tray. He closed the door after she left the room.

Sipping the hot brew, Judith changed the subject. "The most important thing is meeting Mr. Sizemore and the property agent. Afterward, we'll know how much time we have for other things. Perhaps the theatre."

"I must meet with the bishop," Daniel said with a smile at his betrothed. "I lived with him for a year while I considered my future—whether to enter the Church. It will be a pleasure to see him again. Perhaps my being his nephew, he will speed up the process for me to obtain the special license."

Judith brought their attention to her. "I'm excited about meeting Mr. Davison at last. He was not available when we came some weeks ago. Just think, he published seven books for us yet would not know us if we passed on the street."

"He's an amiable gentleman," Daniel assured them.

"Does he know she's two people?" Judith refilled her teacup. When Daniel admitted he had not given Mr. Davison that information, she said, "Won't he be surprised when we walk into his office."

"Perhaps he should come here, if you mean to continue concealing your identity." Daniel glanced from one lady to the other.

"I believe we should, Judith. Privacy has always been important. Not only because of the late earl but for the day when you enter Society."

"Yes, when I set the *ton* on its ear, I don't intend for them to know they're harbouring a novelist in their midst. Such an admission would assuredly deny me entrance at Almack's Assembly Rooms, would it not?"

"Several other places, also," Ruth agreed.

"I'll miss dealing with him on your behalf, but it will be interesting to see how he reacts when he sees the two of you." Daniel placed his teacup on the tray. "I will arrange dinner here for you ladies and have my meal in the public dining room, if that's agreeable with you, Lady Judith."

"Daniel, I recognize the difference in our positions dictates you use my title in the presence of servants or outsiders. However, I implore you to address me by name when we're alone. Both of you are my friends, not employees. I would prefer to dispense with my title altogether, yet I realize that cannot happen."

"As you wish, Judith" he concurred.

Later, Judith stared at the canopy above her bed. A male face crossed her mental vision. Chuckles erupted as she recalled her first encounter with him: falling from the apple tree, knocking him to the ground. Passing years had not dimmed her memory of his godlike face.

<> <> <> <> <>

Susanna hovered near Judith in the lobby and watched her blush, knowing she recognized the gentleman. Her charge had been an exhausting responsibility from the moment she arrived, kicking and screaming into this world. Susanna had guided her toward what she needed for happiness. The child fought every inch of the way with amazing strength. After learning about the earl's deviousness, she'd forced herself into fierce independence.

The angel had sent Ruth to guide the strong-willed adolescent into an acceptance of her appointed place in life. That had not worked, so she must try a different way to guide the stubborn young woman. A smile settled on the angel's face when she remembered the dirty-faced child shouting, "I'm going to marry you even if you are prettier than I am!"

The earl had made a shamble of rearing his daughter. Changing her determined belief that all men were untrustworthy would not be easy. Susanna sighed as she acknowledged that truth.

<> <> <> <> <>

The following morning dawned bright and clear, despite the rumours London weather was always dismal.

Mr. Sizemore welcomed them into his office, where he introduced Mr. Clarkson, the property agent whose books showed several estates available for sale or lease. After a moment, the latter covered his surprise when a female led the discussion.

Judith was accustomed to that reaction because such was common when she attended her father's business meetings. With an inner smugness, she hid her satisfaction that another male had to accept her intelligence—even though she was a female.

Three hours later, their heads in a whirl, they left the business office.

"I had no idea there would be such a large choice," Judith exclaimed. "We should postpone meeting our publisher until we settle the property situation."

Daniel admitted the possibilities were greater than he'd expected. "We have enough to consider before we meet Mr. Sizemore tomorrow morning."

Over a light meal in their private parlor at Grillon's, they discussed the various estates. Judith decided to visit two properties, others later if necessary. One was southwest of London at East Leah, the other several miles beyond East Leah. She didn't want to be either too near or too great a distance from London but did want to be some distance from Ainsley Park. Southern Hampshire sounded ideal.

The following day, they stood before a small thatched inn fronting on East Leah's High Street. Judith had little knowledge of villages, but this one seemed pleasant. A small church stood next to a general merchandise store. An apothecary, a greengrocer, and a blacksmith's shop lined one side of the street while, on the other side, cottages ringed a small open space where children played.

After tea at the Traveler's Inn, they met the local land agent and rode to the Manor. An Early Georgian house of red brick mellowed with age stood at the top of a circular crushed-stone drive. Lush ivy framed the entrance from the ground to the eaves. A stable block stood off to one side and toward the back, a short distance from the house.

With the others around her, Judith stood inside the front door. The scent of beeswax permeated the large hall. Her glance swept up a circular staircase of highly polished wood. She led the way through the rooms, some wood-paneled, others hung with drapery. Judith peeked behind one, expecting dampness. Instead, she found a plain board wall, unpainted. A sniff told her there was no mildew problem. They spent the balance of the day inspecting the house from attics to cellars. The estate, some two thousand acres, mostly pasturage but some planted, impressed Judith. Sheep, a primary income source at Ainsley Park, would work here too.

Back at the inn, Judith stepped through the doorway and collided with a solid mass. Richard again. When she met his green eyes, she saw doubt, then dawning recognition, creep into his eyes.

"Pardon me, Miss. I trust I didn't startle you unduly."

Amusement lurked in the voice she had never forgotten. His youthful laughter echoed down the years. His voice, deeper now, still thrilled her.

The denial forming on Judith's lips died when she gazed into his twinkling eyes. Embarrassment made her toes curl. Unable to speak, she backed further away. This time he recognized her, but was it only from their encounter at Grillon's Hotel or from years ago?

<> <> <> <> <>

Richard turned to Tom. "We see the beauty again, this time in East Leah. She does move around."

"How fortunate you agreed to visit me for a few days." Tom's lips twitched. "Such a shame dark hair is unfashionable this year. One would hardly dare be seen with her, would one?"

Tom laughed aloud at the other's disgusted glare. However, before Richard could utter a well-calculated set-down, he continued. "I've never seen them before, although I've lived here several years. They must be passing through the area."

"Such a pity. Those blue eyes could tempt me into paying an extended visit. I remember where I've seen her, but the memory doesn't tell me who she is." With a grin, he answered his friend's raised eyebrows. "She has fallen into my arms twice."

"You rascal, you can't stop there. If you held such a beauty in your arms, how come you don't know her?"

"I knew that would get your attention. The first time, she was a schoolgirl with curls tumbling down her back. She stumbled on the stairway at the theatre a few days before I went to Portugal. Then, when I was in England before returning to Spain three years ago, I caused her to lose her footing at the Royal Academy. She fell into my arms again."

"You didn't learn her identity? How remiss of you."

"She was only a child. I had older feminine company in mind. She isn't a child now."

"I noticed. Has Cupid's arrow finally pierced your armour after all your avowals to the contrary? I never expected to see the day."

Richard left the inn without replying. In truth, he refused to consider such an absurd idea. He was years away from being leg-shackled. Even then, he didn't expect Cupid to involve himself. The Duke of Rochdale would do what his ancestors had done: find a proper young lady of his station, marry her after a decent period, and set up his nursery. A shudder passed through his body. It would be a cold, bloodless union like his parents' marriage had been. A bleak future faced him because his moral code would not allow him to set up a mistress, common among gentlemen after marriage. The prospect gave him even more reason to postpone the inevitable until well into the future.

Judith sat in the first chair she found in the sitting room. If they were going to continue meeting Richard, she must admit her recognition.

"Ruthie, I remember where we saw that gentleman before."

"Which gentleman do you mean?"

"The green-eyed one downstairs, the same one we saw at Grillon's Hotel."

"Tell me about him. I only glimpsed him downstairs and missed him at the hotel."

"I keep falling into his arms."

"You do *what*?" Sherwood stared at her.

She tossed him a saucy grin, then turned to Ruth. "Do you remember going to the Royal Academy three years ago?"

"Yes, I do. We went to an art gallery while your father tended to business. You fell into a gentleman's arms when you stepped backward, if I remember correctly, although I don't recall his features."

Judith didn't reveal she knocked him flat on his back the first time she saw him. Her companions didn't need to know. "He's the same person."

Ruth continued her reminiscences. "I remember the exhibit of J. M. W. Turner's works, yet I cannot call to mind what caused you to fall."

"I commented on being cold simply from looking at Hannibal's army crossing the Alps. The gentleman we saw downstairs stood behind me. He laughed. I whirled and fell against him. Embarrassed me no end."

"Are you certain he's the same gentleman?" Ruth cradled her teacup. "It was my first trip to a large city. I'm sure I gawked like the veriest rustic."

Judith avoided the entire truth. "Oh, yes, I'm sure. He's older, but I remember his voice, which hasn't changed."

"I wonder who he is," Ruth mused.

"We might never know since Judith falls on him. He might run when next he sees her." On that teasing note, Daniel suggested an early dinner during which they discussed the Manor.

"The house itself is in surprisingly good repair, considering it has stood empty, except for a caretaker, since Mr. Woodall died more than two years ago," Judith commented. "Do you agree, Daniel?"

"Yes, I do, and admit to curiosity. Why has the estate not sold before now?"

"Perhaps other prospective buyers wanted more acreage," Ruth suggested.

This is the place for you. Susanna whispered in Judith's ear. *Purchase it.*

Can I afford the purchase without depleting my investments?

Yes. Trust me.

I'm still concerned about the overdue cargo. Three lost ships could bankrupt me.

Trust me.

Judith's memories slid back to her being ten years old, the first time Susanna had said 'trust me.' Up to that time, the disembodied voice had said 'Trust God.' The inquisitive child had demanded to know why she should trust somebody named God when He wouldn't talk to her. She'd said she would trust Susanna who talked to her most days. Now an adult, she hid a smile at her childish refusal to trust God. Putting the past away, she announced her decision.

"The Manor satisfies my needs. I see no reason to inspect the other estate. Unless either of you foresees problems, I will purchase the Manor outright. Do the two of you care to be my companion and agent?"

"Yes," Daniel spoke for both. "I'll send a message canceling our other appointment."

"This calls for a toast," Judith said. "Will you request champagne, Daniel?"

Moments later, the three lifted their glasses in a salute to each other.

"To our new home," Judith said. Her calm words didn't reflect her internal jubilation: *My* home. *My* property. *Mine.* She had spent six years waiting, planning, yearning for her *own* estate. Now she would have what she wanted, paid for with her *own* funds. No one could take this one away from her.

<> <> <> <> <>

They returned from East Leah to London in high spirits. Their final few days there passed in a blur. Mr. Sizemore agreed to expedite the paperwork, leaving Judith and her companions free to enjoy themselves. They began by inviting the publisher to tea.

Mr. Davison appreciated the humor that 'Mrs. Blaylock' was two young ladies. "From the beginning, I envisioned a little old lady with spectacles perched on the end of her nose. Your readers are clamouring for another book. When may we expect one?"

Judith explained their situation, promising a book at the first possible date. When the door closed behind him, she commented, "This has been a long, tiring day. I suggest an early evening."

"I shall order your meal sent up and see you tomorrow." Daniel's gaze connected with Ruth's while he lifted her hand to his lips. "Our wedding day, my love."

Judith wondered about the hollow feeling deep inside.

<> <> <> <> <>

Late the next morning, the two ladies and the maid were in frenzied activity. Ruth struggled to fasten the wrist buttons of her wedding gown. "I'm so nervous I don't believe I can do this."

Alice's excitement at being part of the wedding preparations hindered them, but she managed to fasten the tiny buttons marching down the back of Ruth's deep-green gown adorned only with tiny embroidered white flowers scattered on the bodice.

She then turned her attention to Judith, who had chosen a blue-satin gown the colour of water on a sunny day. The folds dropped straight from the high waist. Small pearls decorated the hem and the round neckline.

The shopping she and Ruth had done on their visit to London after the earl left on his last trip had been pure joy. She had limited her greediness, though, rather than arouse her mother's suspicions. They'd been fortunate to find a modiste who had gowns commissioned by a lady who later declined to purchase them. Only minor adjustments had been necessary, so now Judith could enjoy the gowns without censure.

The bridegroom arrived, handsome in black trousers with a cream-colored waistcoat under a deep-gold jacket. A small topaz nestled in the folds of his exquisitely tied cravat.

"You're a surprise, Daniel!" Judith was accustomed to seeing her agent wearing loose-fitting work coats and riding leathers.

With a laugh, he ushered them to the waiting carriage, which the builder had delivered earlier that day. Judith relaxed against the squabs, reveling in her ownership—another proof of her independence.

Mr. Sizemore, who agreed to serve as groomsman, had located a small chapel in Kensington whose vicar agreed to perform the ceremony.

Judith tried to concentrate on the proceedings, but her mind slipped back to the other wedding she had attended: that of her only friend. She had watched Sybil, deathly pale, cringe away from her new husband who jerked her to his side, holding her close. The bride was thirteen. The groom was fifty-four. Judith never saw her again. Some years later, she learned her childhood friend had died in childbirth, her third delivery within three years. At Sybil's wedding, Judith's father had promised to find her a husband near her own age. That conversation, too, was forever entrenched in her memory.

Her father's perfidy on that long-ago day overwhelmed Judith. How could he have lied to her? She forced her attention back to the present. The ceremony had passed without her hearing one word, and they were soon in the private sitting room at Grillon's Hotel.

Leaving home was not what Judith had wanted. Quite the contrary. She already knew life didn't imitate dreams, which didn't bother her. Anything was better than the alternative, she reminded herself. A vision of stringy, gray hair flashed before her eyes. She straightened her shoulders, stared at her mirrored reflection, then ordered a smile to appear as she joined the dinner celebration. With one final toast to the bride and groom, Judith went off to her lonely bed.

During her younger years, she daydreamed about Richard, the pretty boy she met at the apple tree. That changed when he didn't recognize her in their later encounters. Seeing him twice within the last few days renewed her childish dreams. Would she like being the wife of a man who resembled a Greek god? Every female in the kingdom would clamour for his attention.

No, she would never allow any man to have control over her. Those childhood dreams were before she learned she couldn't trust her father. If she couldn't trust him, how could she trust any man? She pushed Richard's image away with another vow, this one that she would not marry him or any other man.

Judith turned from the window when Ruth, her eyes large with excitement, rushed into their sitting room late the following morning.

"Daniel has obtained a box at King's Opera House for this very evening—Lucia Vestris, no less—and the theatre tomorrow evening!"

"Wonderful, but who is this paragon?"

"A singer who has come into prominence since Catalani left London two years ago. Vestris is only eighteen, so she can look forward to a long career. I'm happy—no ecstatic—we get to hear her."

The conversation moved to the topic of what to wear. Each had brought three gowns. Now, they spent a happy hour discussing their merits.

When Daniel joined them for dinner in their private sitting room, he was wholehearted in his admiration of both ladies, although his glance lingered longest on his wife. She had chosen rose satin with a spider-gauze overskirt in a lighter shade.

Judith made her entrance in a deep-green, moiré silk gown. After much discussion, each lady had decided to wear a diamond pendant hanging from a thin gold chain with diamond studs adorning her earlobes. Judith felt grown up at last. And in fashion, not like the gowns her father had demanded cover her from chin to toes. She hid a satisfied smile as she gazed at her mirror image.

Their carriage seemed to crawl to Covent Garden. Indeed, when they neared the Royal Opera House, the driver inched forward, deposited his passengers, and moved away. If Town were thin of company now as the Season waned, what would the crowds be like during the height of the Season?

They worked their way through the crowded lobby at a snail's pace. Judith didn't remember the grand staircase from her childhood visit, only her fall. In their box, she gazed with wonder through the parted deep-red drapes at the richly dressed ladies and gentlemen. She ignored masculine eyes observing her from nearby boxes.

No one approached their box during intermission, but the buzz of interested chatter reached them. Judith hid a smile while she listened to their speculations.

The following evening, Daniel took the ladies to see the great Edmund Kean in his now-famous role of Richard III. The crowd at the Theatre Royal in Drury Lane paid more attention to his party than the stage.

"I don't know why some people go to the theatre," Judith said while they awaited their carriage. "They don't listen. Their chatter is distracting. It was the same last night at the opera."

Daniel answered, "They go to see and be seen."

"Speaking of being seen," Ruth interposed, "did you notice the fair-haired gentleman in the adjoining box? Is he not the same one we've seen before?"

"Yes." Judith grinned. "At least I didn't fall into his arms this time."

"Ladies, you have been the center of attention of half the *haute ton* for the past two evenings."

"Only half?" Ruth teased.

"The other half has departed for their country houses," he answered with aplomb. "Don't let the attention go to your heads, however. We return to Ainsley Park tomorrow."

"Must we?" Judith asked. "I had hoped we could visit Hatchards for the latest books."

"Checking out Mrs. Blaylock's competition, Judith?"

"Now that you mention it . . ."

Ruth joined their laughter, but before she could speak, Judith rushed on.

"I would like to visit a modiste too. My riding habits bear no resemblance to the ones I saw earlier today. And you know how much time I spend in the saddle."

"Perhaps we should wait until your mourning period has passed. You can then have a modiste come to you. Fashions will probably change before then."

"You're right, Ruthie, as always! We can visit Hatchards and then leave quite early the day after tomorrow."

"Sensible suggestion," Daniel agreed. "We'll do that."

Among the theatre crowd, who had stared at the unknown beauty, was one who recognized her. Richard had returned to London from East Leah before going home to Wiltshire. The few days with Tom had relaxed him enough to look up some old friends. The estate problems would wait another day. He had little hope of leaving Chadwick Park anytime soon after he arrived there.

His friends' dinner chatter about the latest high-flyers bored him almost to the point of pleading a headache and avoiding the theatre. However, what would he do with the balance of his last evening of freedom? Nothing interesting occurred to him, so he accompanied the others. They arrived minutes before the lackeys opened the curtain. After a glance at the adjoining box, he looked closer. Was she the same raven-haired beauty? Without doubt, he decided after a moment's covert study. Thereafter, the stage failed to hold his attention. His friends quizzed him when they observed his preoccupation with the adjoining box.

"Rochdale, you dog, who is she?"

He must submit to hearing others call him by his title, otherwise his friends would call him a paper skull. "I have no idea, but you should know. After all, you haven't been out of the country for years as I have."

His friends studied the beautiful profile, shaking their heads. They agreed they had never seen any of those people before.

Richard turned his eyes toward the stage with many glances to his left. He managed once to meet the blue eyes before she turned away. A flush covered her face. At the intermission, he avoided staring at the box but watched from the corner of his eye. No one approached the box to visit with the occupants, who remained seated talking among themselves.

When the play ended, he again gazed into the bewitching blue eyes, which turned stormy gray when she caught him staring. He'd never seen eyes change colour. Blue was blue, and gray was gray. Another fascinating facet about this mystery woman. Hurrying from his box, he waited at the bottom of the stairs while she descended. He stepped in front of her when she neared him. With a broad smile, he stretched his arms toward her as if expecting her to tumble into them. His chuckle followed her while she crossed the lobby and out the door.

There was no one he could ask for an introduction, so he returned to his townhouse, still in the dark about the mystery woman. He vowed to ignore the proprieties. The next time she was near, he would simply introduce himself. An introduction would be easier if she fell into his arms again. More pleasant too.

His recollection of the child who had tripped on the stairs all those years ago was dim, but his recollection of holding her at the Royal Academy was clear. Something about her eyes nibbled at the edge of his brain. If he could bring forth that information, he was sure her name would follow. Richard drifted into sleep with her vision emblazoned on his eyelids.

<> <> <> <> <>

The return trip to Ainsley Park, the last she would make, passed in a haze. She kept her mind firmly on the future—her own estate—the Manor at East Leah. When they arrived at Ainsley Park, the butler opened the door and, with proper majesty, welcomed them home.

"Good afternoon, Stewart. Is Lady Monford still here?"

"No, my lady, she left with her possessions yesterday."

Judith bit her lip. Why would she expect her mother to wait for her return before leaving? Lady Monford's failure to say goodbye before they left for London did not bother her, because she expected her mother would remain at Ainsley Park several more days. Now, however, when they would meet again was uncertain. She set aside her reflections of her mother. "Our travel wagons will arrive tomorrow. We will leave three days later."

Daniel cleared his throat, causing Judith to exclaim, "Stewart, please wish Mr. and Mrs. Sherwood happy. They married while in London and will leave Ainsley Park with me. For now, please have rooms in the house prepared for him."

The stooped butler raised his eyebrows but offered his best wishes to the newlyweds.

"Thank you, I've waited several years for her," Daniel said. "Due to our short time here, I won't change my living quarters. Now, I must speak with his lordship."

"You will find him in the study, sir."

"May we have tea served in an hour, Stewart?" Judith turned toward the door. "I need to shake my fidgets with a walk first."

A short while later, Judith reached the huge apple tree, her favorite childhood hideout, a haven when life's uncertainties had threatened to overwhelm her. The past six years had produced many such times. This was another. What would she do without this tree during the future uncertainties she was sure would occur?

Without a moment's hesitation, the now adult 'little hoyden' tugged off her half boots and climbed to the first sturdy limb. How many times had she sat just so? She relished the rough bark as she stroked the limb beside her head. The dull pain behind her eyes was on the verge of becoming a horrendous headache.

This was the last time Judith would sit here brooding over her father's actions as well as her plans to thwart him. Another last experience changing her from father's daughter at Ainsley Park to an independent woman owning her own estate. Only Susanna knew about this hiding place. Sometimes just knowing the angel was near comforted her. Other times—when she was tired of the interference—Judith was impatient with the disembodied voice, wishing it would go away. She could use some comforting right now.

Struggling with the onslaught of tears, Judith didn't hear the approaching horse.

Seven

Somewhere in France

An old man opened his eyes slowly. Dim light came through a window high on the opposite wall. He moved his head restlessly on a hard pillow and glanced around the small space: an attic with slanting walls rising toward a low, but sharp, ceiling. He raised his head but gasped when a sharp pain shot through his right temple.

He lifted a trembling hand to the side of his head. A bandage? He probed gently, finding an egg-sized knot. He lowered his head to the pillow as the room swirled around him, slowly settling as he lay still.

When footsteps approached, the old man shifted to his side. This time, bile rose in his throat, almost choking him. He swallowed hastily and closed his eyes, facing the wall while he waited for whatever happened next.

The door opened. He sensed two people leaning over him. A man's deep voice spoke.

"He's still asleep."

"Henri, five days have passed. What will we do if he never awakes?" The trembling voice verged on tears. "I could almost regret you brought him here."

"We'll face any problem when the time comes, Maria. I couldn't leave him lying in the mud, even if we had trouble later. We talked about that."

"I know, but still . . ."

"Have any strangers come by inquiring for him?"

"No one."

"If anyone does or even any of our acquaintances come to visit, don't even hint we're harbouring a stranger."

"I won't," she assured him.

Their footsteps receded. The door closed. The old man waited a few moments, then turned onto his back, being careful not to lift his head. Puzzled, he mentally replayed their conversation. They spoke French, but his thoughts were English. He would have to think about it later. He drifted into sleep.

Eight

Homecoming

Chadwick Park, Wiltshire

A frown marred Richard's countenance. He had this instant arrived home. The view meeting his eyes from the top step made him cringe. He'd sent word of his arrival, so he couldn't turn tail and flee—his first inclination.

The vista from the steps had always been pleasing. It didn't compare with Capability Brown's designs but pleasing all the same. Smooth lawns and formal flowerbeds led to a small copse of silvery birch trees toward the left. A dense grove of hardwoods stood to the right. Graceful black swans caused hardly a ripple, drifting along a small lake straight ahead.

That's how the landscape was during his youth. Not now. The lawn was no longer smooth, and weeds smothered the flowerbeds. Green scum covered the lake. What had happened to the swans? The trees still stood, for which he was thankful.

Unnerved at the sight but with a fixed smile in place, Richard turned toward the opened door where his butler stood waiting. "Good afternoon, Wilson. I trust I see you well. Mrs. Wilson?"

"We're both well, Your Grace. May I say how pleased we are to welcome you home?"

"Thank you. Under the circumstances, I can't say I am particularly pleased to be here." He handed his hat and cane into the butler's waiting hands. "Where will I find Her Grace?"

"She awaits you in her sitting room." Wilson hesitated a moment. "Mr. Guthrie asked I tell you he would like to see you when convenient."

"Ah, yes, the estate agent. I don't imagine he has anything pleasant to tell me. Be that as it may, ask him to join me in the study in half an hour." Richard took a deep breath, then, with squared shoulders, climbed the curving staircase. He tapped on the open door of his mother's sitting room.

"Hello, Mother. You're your usual beautiful self." She didn't give the appearance of being in straitened circumstances, if he knew anything about female clothing. And he did. On her, widow's weeds did not resemble mourning.

"Richard, darling, you're home at last!" She clung to him for a moment before stepping back to study his face. "You certainly appear well."

"I am well, Mother. You don't seem happy about my appearance, if I may say so."

"You know that wasn't my meaning," she scolded before embracing him again. "Have you left the army?"

He set her aside and strode to the window, which reflected his bleak expression. "Yes."

"Then, you will stay here?"

"For a while. I will have a better idea about the estate's condition after I've seen Martin Guthrie this afternoon."

"You do realize your father's failure to maintain the estate is your fault?"

He swung around. "*My* fault? How did you reach such a conclusion?"

"If you had stayed home, you could have persuaded him to maintain the estate."

"Persuade my father to part with a penny piece for the estate? Persuade him to allow me a hand in managing the property?" Richard's bitterness hung in the air between them. He ignored having had a similar thought when he learned of his father's death. "I tried numerous times, only to hear I should mind my own business. He would not acknowledge Chadwick Park was my business."

"You could have stayed," she insisted. "He might have changed."

He shook his head but knew the uselessness of arguing with her. He had never encountered a more stubborn female. "Over many years—not just the years I've been gone—Father allowed the estate to deteriorate to an alarming degree, so I must deal with his neglect."

"You can ignore everything. He did."

"Ignore the condition of my inheritance? My home?" The very idea appalled him. "I dread riding around the acreage, if the rest is in the same shape as the front."

"Then, don't," she replied. "You can clean up the front. That's all you need to see when we drive out to visit the neighbors."

He stared at her in disbelief. Could she possibly be serious? She was. His opinion of female intellect was admittedly low, yet she should at least understand the longer this neglect continued, the harder it would be to correct. Unless recovery was already past hope, which wouldn't surprise him. "I can't do what you ask, Mother. Now, I must see Guthrie. We'll meet again at dinner."

Moments later, mentally asking permission to enter, which his father had always insisted upon, he opened the study door. The wiry old gentleman waiting for him didn't appear to have aged a day since the first time Richard saw him long years ago. "Guthrie, I'm glad you're still here."

The agent studied his new master from beneath bushy brows. "Your Grace, I don't know where else I would be, considering I've been here, man and boy, for nigh on sixty years."

Seated at the desk, Richard glanced at the books covering every available surface, even stacked on the floor. Could this be where the money had gone? *Books*? He directed the agent to clear a chair and sit.

"Guthrie, you know His Grace never permitted me to learn anything about the estate, but I'll strive to understand whatever you tell me." Richard nodded toward the window. "I suppose the late duke neglected the entire estate to the same extent as what I saw between here and the road."

The agent confirmed Richard's worst fears. "Mind you, the property can be fixed up, right and tight again. Just needs blunt, that's all."

"That's all," Richard repeated. "Is there any money?"

"I don't know. The late duke generally paid the wages on time, for the few workers who remained. He didn't spend any gold on the farms, though." A grimace settled on Guthrie's face. "He kept a tight rein on the books. Never let me see them. Not like the old duke, your grandfather. He left the books to me, just checked behind me regular like. Never found anything wrong with them either, he didn't."

In effect, Guthrie had not been an estate agent at all but a lackey. "The first thing I must do is have a look at the books. I will start that chore first thing tomorrow, then consult you when I see how things stand."

After Guthrie closed the door, Richard dropped his head into his hands. Record-keeping was a mystery to him. Too late to start learning now, though. He must change for dinner.

Her Grace, every bit the Duchess of Rochdale, was in her element presiding over dinner with a handsome man who didn't have his nose in a book. Her son could appreciate that, yet the knowledge didn't prepare him for what was coming.

"Richard, dear, since you've come home, we must begin entertaining."

"Entertaining?" He pulled his mind back to the dinner table. "What do you have in mind?"

"Oh, a small dinner party to welcome you home. We will open the formal dining room, which seats fifty." She babbled on, unaware of his stupefaction. "Then we must have a ball . . ."

"Mother!" His astounded tone brought her attention to him. "Have you forgotten our mourning period?"

"No, of course not," she blustered. "Surely under the circumstances, we can ignore the usual customs."

"What possible circumstances can excuse such gross disrespect?" Richard could hardly believe her attitude. He realized his parents' marriage had been one of convenience, the fate of their generation. However, his mother had always kept up the pretense her marriage was all she could desire. He'd believed she would tie her garter in public before allowing anyone to think otherwise.

"You've been gone for the better part of ten years. The neighbors will understand we want to celebrate your happy return."

"In the first place, I don't find anything happy about my return. Furthermore, over the next several days, I will be busy determining the condition of the estate, the depth of ruin, and the amount of debt. Perhaps, then, I will know how to reclaim it. Entertainment must wait."

"We must eat, Richard. We can do so as easily at a dinner party as with only us"

"Mother, you're willfully refusing to understand. I will be in the saddle a large part of each day. During the evenings, I won't want to hear the neighbors' inane chatter. You continue with your usual activities, but remember, you're a recent widow. Don't involve me. Do you understand?"

"You're obstinate like your father." She changed her tactics. Raising her napkin, she touched the corners of her eyes and allowed her lips to tremble. "You must not neglect me the way he did, Richard. I couldn't bear more disregard, truly I could not. You cannot know how alone I've been all these years."

Dismayed, he was ready to comfort her, until multiple scenes from his childhood flashed into his mind. She had produced tears all those times he had wanted to play with the neighborhood boys. He had submitted, which was easier than seeing her cry. When he entered Eton, she produced tears in abundance, pleading with Rochdale to hire a tutor for their delicate son. His father had rightfully stated the boy was not delicate, only pampered. Richard had suffered terrible guilt, not because he was leaving her but because he was so happy to get away from her.

He spoke now with wry irony. "I see you can still do it."

"Do what?"

"Produce tears at a moment's notice. Crying won't work anymore. I'm a grown man now, not the schoolboy you could make feel guilty for wanting to be like other boys." He held her gaze until she lowered her eyelids and then changed the subject.

"Does Amelia visit often?"

His mother's answer was much as he expected. His sister and mother had been at odds as far back as he could remember, and neither would give an inch in their disagreements. Like mother, like daughter. Was this true of all mothers and daughters? Or fathers and sons for that matter.

"Rarely. She's much too busy with her two girls and her husband. No time for her mother. How I could have given birth to such an ungrateful . . . ?"

He'd heard enough. "If you will excuse me, I've had a long day. I believe I will take a turn on the terrace before seeking my bed."

<> <> <> <> <>

Chirping birds announced dawn. A slight breeze moved the curtains. When his batman tapped on the door, Richard opened his eyes, wondering what the day held for him.

"Good morning, Your Grace. Will you ride this morning?"

"Pierce, I do not want to hear that title come from your mouth. Ever. Do you understand me?" Pierce had attached himself to Richard soon after the latter joined the regiment in the peninsula and had stayed with him throughout the campaigns. When Richard had tried to send him home after the Waterloo battle, Pierce had answered his only home was with the major. Richard was too appreciative to send him away.

"Yes, Your . . . um, what should I call you?"

"Major will do." Richard had earned that rank after the battle at Toulouse, which they wrongly believed ended the war. "Yes, I'll ride." Being a slugabed wouldn't help matters, so he swung back the covers. At the window, he took a couple of deep breaths, then dressed for a ride, leaving Pierce to pick up yesterday's soiled garments.

"Good morning, Bolton." Richard greeted the grizzled stable hand. He'd avoided looking around when he left his mount and curricle here upon his arrival. Now, while Bolton saddled Sheik, he wandered through the derelict stables where the only inhabitants were a broken-down nag and the pair of grays that pulled his mother's carriage. He could almost smile at the image of her pitching a tantrum when his father wanted to sell them, which, without doubt, he did. He had sold off a fine stable. With a shrug, Richard accepted the reins from Bolton. "We must do something about this."

He returned after a short ride, slumped in the saddle. How could he ever put this place to rights? Make the duchy profitable again? He took a deep breath. The ledgers awaited him.

A few hours later, Wilson opened the study door. "Your Grace, the duchess is inquiring for you."

Raising weary eyes, Richard struggled to comprehend the butler's words. He ran his hands through his already mussed hair. "Tell her I'll be with her in twenty minutes, Wilson."

He had spent the morning sorting through the desk drawers. He found more bills than seemed possible considering the neglect. The most recent ledger indicated his father had made the last entry three years before, soon after he, himself, had returned to Spain. The brandy decanter across the room tempted him. Never a heavy drinker, his problems were almost enough to change the vow he made after the only time he'd attempted to match drink for drink with a fellow first-year student at Oxford. Almost, but not quite. The decanter remained untouched. He would struggle through the problems in dreary sobriety.

In his chambers, he splashed cold water on his face, tidied his appearance, and with squared shoulders approached his mother's door.

"I trust I see you well, Mother."

She chose to act the loving, helpless, female. The duchess had never yielded easily. He hid his smile.

"Where have you been all morning? I've missed you."

"After an early ride followed by breakfast, I've spent the morning in the study." He hesitated. "I haven't finished, but I am appalled at the outstanding debts Father left."

Her Grace stiffened before she visibly wilted. Looking upward through her lashes, she said, "Darling,

I don't know anything about *debts*. Let us talk about something interesting. I need your escort for calls this afternoon."

"I don't have time for afternoon visits, Mother." He struggled with his temper as he repeated his earlier words. He would rather deal with an entire company of subalterns than this one female. "The estate will take all my time for several days just learning the extent of debts. Deciding how I can pay them will take longer."

"Darling, I can't make calls on my own when everybody knows you're here. People will say you neglect me. You can't want that. Besides, the vicar will want to see you about parish concerns."

He took a steadying breath before replying. "You must understand, I came home to put the estate in order. Socializing with the neighbors is out of the question. They know the condition of this property— how could they miss the neglect? Without doubt, they expect me to correct the estate's deplorable condition before I do anything else."

A tap sounded at the door, followed by Wilson, who announced their meal was ready.

"Perhaps you will have time to join me, Rochdale, before you return to your *important* concerns." She used his title for the first time, which alone showed her displeasure with him.

He bit back a bitter smile.

"Yes, Mother, I will join you." He bowed her out the door. She must learn she could no longer lead him around by the nose. He managed a light conversation throughout the meal of cold chicken and fruit, although his mind was never far from the task before him.

When he excused himself from the room, he hesitated outside the door, rubbing his forehead. Perhaps a ride away from Chadwick Park would ease his tension.

Astride Sheik, Richard ambled throughout the countryside byways for a few hours. He had spent little time in his home county since early childhood yet felt at peace here like no other place. Most estates were in good heart. None showed the horrible neglect of his own. He didn't recognize where he'd wandered when he saw an apple tree and, feeling a trifle peckish, decided fruit would help. Nearing the tree, he saw a female perched on a limb. She hugged the trunk, her stocking-clad feet hanging free.

"Hello there," he called. "Do I see a damsel in distress? You appear to be in a precarious position."

"Go away," a muffled voice called. "I don't need assistance."

"Perhaps not, but the age of chivalry is not dead," he assured her. "Surely you will not deny me the opportunity to be a gentleman. I'm not a knight in shining armour. Still, I fancy I can get the job done."

The muffled voice repeated, "I don't need rescuing."

"I always wondered how the knights of old could do anything while wearing so much armour," he confided. "Must have been cumbersome."

"Will you please go away?"

"Just think of me as a Good Samaritan. I truly cannot pass you by."

"Yes, you can. I don't need assistance."

"Are you a person, or are you perhaps a tree fairy? You must understand I cannot leave here until I know which."

There was a moment of silence from the tree. "I can jump down if you move back. You'll see for yourself I don't need help."

"Sounds fair enough." He dismounted and drew the horse back a couple of steps. He soon saw feet and some well-turned ankles descending. When the girl dropped toward the ground, he sprang forward pulling her against his chest, her feet dangling between his ankles.

A pair of bewitching blue eyes, wet with tears, stared into his face. Her lips formed a silent O.

"Ah, my bewitching blue-eyed beauty, you fall into my arms again. Grown up this time." He couldn't resist her luscious mouth. Clasping her waist, he lowered his face and brushed his lips across hers, then captured them in a brief kiss.

After a stunned moment, she struggled to free herself, opening her mouth to protest, which was all the encouragement he needed. The kiss deepened.

When he released her lips, he smiled with amusement into her startled face. "Never been kissed either."

With a gasp, she wrenched herself free and ran as fast as her bare feet could move until she was inside the home wood.

He laughed with sheer exuberance. "I'll find you again, my bewitching beauty! Someday, somewhere, I'll find you."

<> <> <> <> <>

Judith leaned against a tree to catch her breath. How dare he kiss her? A rogue, that's what he is, going around kissing innocent females.

You enjoyed the kiss. Admit you did.

Susanna, again.

He laughed at me. It isn't my fault Father never allowed me around men, so how could I learn how to kiss?

Kissing comes naturally. Susanna chuckled. *You'll have more opportunities. Trust me.*

She ignored the angel as she had so many other times through the years. Judith had been shocked when she gazed into the green eyes that had persisted in invading her dreams since she was seven years old. His voice had changed, deeper now, yet she would recognize the cadence anywhere. She touched her lips. At least this time, he didn't kiss her nose or the top of her head. She peeked through the trees to be sure he was gone, then retrieved her boots.

On her return home, Judith spotted the vicar's carriage at the front steps. She slipped around the side and up the back stairs. After changing into an afternoon gown of sprigged muslin, Judith entered the drawing room with a smile pasted on her face. She dreaded this encounter.

"Good afternoon, Mr. Lacey, Mrs. Lacey. I trust I see you both well."

"Lady Judith," he answered with a knee dip. "Lord Monford has explained the circumstances. We regret we won't have your presence in services hereafter."

"Thank you, sir. I'll miss your well-thought-out messages." *See, Susanna, I can be gracious.*

Yes, I see. Now pay attention to your guests.

Boring! Nevertheless, she obeyed. The requisite half-hour visit passed pleasantly enough with Mrs. Lacey exclaiming over Daniel and Ruth's marriage. Such a surprise. The new earl regretted he must live in Kent rather than here, but the vicar was sure he would make suitable arrangements regarding Ainsley Park.

When the door closed behind the Laceys, Judith told Ruth she hoped the East Leah vicar would have a more pleasant voice.

During her last two days at Ainsley Park, Judith kept her mind on the details of moving and believed she managed the situation well. However, after the house grew quiet on her last night in her childhood home, Judith descended the stairs for one last pilgrimage. Walking from room to room, touching the much-loved items, she reached the study. There, she held the candelabra high for one last look. She'd spent so many happy childhood hours here with her father that she couldn't bear to enter the room. No papers on the desk, the ledgers stacked on shelves. The sight of his riding crop on a table near the door was her undoing. She returned to her bedchamber with tears streaming down her face.

Sleep would not come. Instead, Judith paced the floor. Years earlier, she'd made up her mind to take control of her life and had endured many sleepless nights. At times, her conscience had bothered her, but she persevered. Her father had been the center of her life. She'd ached to deceive him even while rejoicing she could. Why did he tell her falsehoods? She loved him above all others yet, for the last six years, had fought her love until she believed the adoration had died. Her childhood had been happy, but, now, she recognized the sham.

Judith's emotions were under control when she descended the stairs for breakfast a few hours later. Her mirror had revealed dark shadows under her eyes, giving notice of a sleepless night. Her hand trembled when she lifted the teacup.

The servants, who chose to accompany her to East Leigh, had left hours earlier with the loaded wagons traveling directly to the Manor. Now only one carriage stood at the front portico. The new head coachman sat proudly on the box. A stable hand stood nearby, the reins of Mr. Sherwood's gelding in hand.

Judith stood on the top step for a long moment. Her gaze moved slowly over the beloved vista. The lily pond at the foot of the garden had pink blossoms lying on water that reflected the blue sky. On the left was the maze where she got lost when she was seven. Mattie vowed that escapade had taken ten years off her life.

Father had been on a trip but would have laughed had he been there. He'd always laughed at her mischievousness. Her gaze lingered longest on the path through the home wood which led to the infamous, as she now considered it, apple tree. Shutting out her memories, she allowed Daniel to hand her into the carriage. Judith sat with her eyes staring forward as she left her childhood home for the last time.

Nine

New Home, New Adjustments

"Welcome home, Lady Judith, Mrs. Sherwood, Mr. Sherwood." Kenneth, the footman, had become Taylor, the butler, gaining new dignity in the process. The remainder of the servants, led by Mrs. Butterfield, the Manor housekeeper for many years, lined up behind him. They bowed and curtsied when their new mistress greeted them by name. Judith dismissed them to their duties after a cordial greeting.

"Taylor, we need thirty minutes to remove travel stains, after which we will appreciate tea in the drawing room," Judith said as she started up the staircase. At the top, she turned toward the right and smiled across her shoulder at the Sherwoods, who turned left into their wing.

<> <> <> <> <>

In her sitting room, Judith kicked off her slippers and sank into a small armless chair. Wiggling her toes on the plush carpet, she remembered one occasion when she kicked off her shoes before climbing a tree. Her dog had carried them away, so she'd returned home barefooted. Mattie scolded, but Father roared with laughter and called her his little hoyden. Glittering green eyes appeared in her vision. He called her a hoyden, too, all those years ago. Her lips tingled at the memory of his recent kiss. That proved she couldn't trust any man to respect her wishes. She ordered herself to put both men from her mind.

To avoid thinking of men, she stared out the window toward a nice view overlooking a wide expanse of lawn leading toward a small formal garden where sculptured boxwoods surrounded stone benches. Not home, though, not what she wanted to see from her sitting room window. The perennial beds at Ainsley Park were a riot of color from early spring well into late autumn, leading to the rose gardens beyond. Their indulgent gardener had allowed Ruth full control there. Perhaps marriage made leaving the roses easier for her.

Judith pushed away the memories. Moments later, she swept into the drawing room where the Sherwoods awaited her.

Daniel relaxed into an oversized chair with a teacup in hand. "We must discuss my estate responsibilities. Is this a good time?"

"Also, mine about the house," Ruth inserted.

"Yes, this is a good time before the tenants become too concerned regarding their future. About the estate, Daniel, let's continue the schedule we maintained at Ainsley Park."

"Ruthie, I suppose I should be in this house more than I was there. I regret Monford will leave only a skeleton staff at Ainsley Park. They'll never be able to maintain the estate, neither indoors nor outside, as it needs. I admit, though, I'm pleased so many of the staff came with us. I also admit absolute ignorance about directing them."

Her moue of distaste brought a quiet laugh from her companion. "Perhaps I can help you with that."

"Ruthie, I must depend on you to teach me about household matters, if I'm not to appear abysmally ignorant in Mrs. Butterfield's presence. We're fortunate she chose to stay on as housekeeper. You do know about such things, Ruthie? Although I don't know when you had an opportunity to learn anything, considering how I've kept you busy dealing with my behaviour." Owning her own home has responsibilities she hadn't considered.

"I learned under Lady Monford's guidance while you were busy with his lordship. She never suspected my reason."

Judith stared at her. She'd never inquired what her cousin did when they were not together. Was there no end to her own self-centered behaviour? Susanna had admonished her about selfishness times without number, but had Judith ever paid attention? No. Her comment now was humble. "I'm pleased you had the foresight, because I did not."

"I enjoyed it, Judith. Learning the correct way of things in a large house is quite different from the smaller houses where I had lived."

"Oh, and Ruthie, you must find time to plant the rose cuttings you brought from the gardens at Ainsley Park. The rose garden here is quite small, so your cuttings will be a great addition."

"I know we discussed this, but I'll ask anyway. May I enlarge the rose garden here as much as I like?"

"You can enlarge the rose garden to your heart's content," Judith assured her, then added with a twinkle, "however, leave enough room for the sheep Daniel plans to purchase."

On that merry note, Judith rose. "I believe I'll get settled into my rooms until dinner."

Judith glanced around her rooms. Her furnishings graced their new premises well. The blue, cream, and gold colour scheme of the sofa complemented the cream-colored drapery. Three chairs picked up the gold shade. The Aubusson carpet boasted cream and yellow flowers surrounded by a deep blue shade.

She busied herself filling shelves with her favorite books, including the ones written by Mrs. Blaylock. She also wrote a letter to her mother, carefully including her return address. Perhaps the distance between them would encourage a better relationship.

Judith watched the post for several days, but in the end, she admitted her efforts to reach a better understanding with her mother were futile.

She fought tears. *Susanna, are you here?*

I'm always with you.

What can I do about Mama? I miss her, although I never expected I would because we were ever at odds. Mostly my fault, I admit.

That's part of maturing, which was something your father denied you in many ways.

You've told me many times I should honour my parents. I don't remember the exact words, but they had no meaning until now. I don't know how I could have honoured Father, especially in the last few years, but I should have honoured Mama instead of ignoring her. Another thing to regret.

Angels don't see into the future, so I don't know if you and your mother will ever be close. I can only say God is in control of your life and hers. The pain of your loss will diminish in time, though. Trust me.

<> <> <> <> <>

Within days of taking up residence at the Manor, their first visitors were the vicar and his wife, Mr. and Mrs. Downey. Opposites certainly do attract. Judith viewed the tall, thin vicar with his cadaverous face and hawk nose. A short, almost rotund woman stood by his side.

"The Manor has been without ladies for several years, so you'll find you're most welcome. We were a giddy group until Mrs. Woodall's death nearly ten years ago." Mrs. Downey became quiet when her husband cleared his throat.

There followed a recitation of parish needs. Mr. Downey settled his teacup into a saucer. "We hope each of you will find a place to participate in our various activities."

"We will," Judith assured him. "Our gardens are available to your flower committee, for instance. The grounds have been amazingly cared for, considering the lack of an interested owner."

"We don't have a flower committee since Mrs. Woodall passed on," Mrs. Downey confessed. "I do the best I can with what we have, which isn't much. The ladies here are more familiar with kitchen gardens than with flowers."

"I enjoy working with flowers and place myself at your disposal," Ruth said. "Is Saturday morning the usual time?" Assured on this point, she promised she would be there. "I'll bring an assortment of blossoms."

"You may call on me when you need someone to read the lesson," Daniel said. "I realize that's the prerogative of the local squire, which I'm not. However, I will substitute when you need me."

The vicar nodded. "We do have two men who volunteer their services in the absence of a squire, but I'll call on you when the need arises."

"Mr. Sherwood has excellent carpentry skills, in the event the church needs them," Judith said and asked if they have a village fête or harvest celebration. The earl had never opened Ainsley Park to the villagers.

"Not in recent years, I regret to say."

Judith exchanged glances with Daniel and Ruth. "We'll discuss the possibility, if not for harvest this year, at least next year here on our grounds."

She knew she should offer some personal help, but her mind was blank on that point. The church didn't need her knowledge of estate work, her only accomplishment. Regretting anew how restricted her life had been, Judith turned the subject to other neighborhood activities.

When the Downeys rose to leave, Judith nodded toward Daniel to escort them out, Then she listened as the murmur of voices reached her. Daniel explained her situation.

"Ah, Vicar, there is just one thing. Lady Judith's father died a short time ago. Although he didn't believe in deep mourning, she chooses to respect his memory by living a quiet life for a while."

At their expressed sympathy, Daniel clarified the situation. "She doesn't want to distress our new friends by flaunting her grief, so she will do some entertaining. Teas, perhaps small dinner parties for several months, I imagine."

"We understand and admire her decision."

Daniel returned to the drawing room. "Judith, in accordance with your wishes, we are neither keeping your title a secret nor bruiting it about. I daresay little time will pass before the vicar or his good wife spread the word."

She assumed a mulish expression but laughed when Ruth spoke. "I wonder who joined Mrs. Woodall in her giddiness. We didn't see other residences that might house women of the same social standing."

With a grin, Judith said, "Comparatively speaking, Mr. Downey's voice is almost musical!"

They settled into a daily routine, which carried them through the first days of change. They became acquainted with their acreage on early morning rides, which Judith enjoyed but Ruth endured. The ladies accompanied Daniel on his formal visit to each tenant farmer. Thereafter, Judith kept herself busy in a futile effort to keep memories at bay.

A small girl with a mass of fiery curls tumbling around her face caught Judith's attention on a morning ride. The child stood beside the road, a finger in her mouth, her big brown eyes never blinking.

"What's your name?" Judith had little contact with children at Ainsley Park and couldn't even remember ever talking with them. "Take your finger out of your mouth, so you can talk to me."

"Susie."

"Susie, I'm pleased to make your acquaintance. May I come see you sometime?"

The child's eyes grew wider as she nodded in a quick jerky motion.

"I'll visit again in a few days."

True to her word, a few mornings later, Judith tucked a battered copy of *Aesop's Fables* into a basket containing sweet biscuits from the kitchen. When she arrived at the Tucker cottage, she spotted Susie gazing out a window. By the time Judith tethered Gypsy, the child was at the door waiting. Stepping inside the cottage, Judith removed the book and handed the basket into Mrs. Tucker's hastily dried hands.

"I believe Susie might like one of these while I read her a story."

Judith settled down on the doorstep with the child close beside her. After reading *The Fox and the Cat*, she rose to leave but succumbed to Susie's pleading eyes by sitting down again. "One more story, but then I must go. Would you like to hear my favorite fable?"

"Oh yes, please."

Changing her voice for each character, Judith launched into *The Boy Who Cried Wolf* while Susie's eyes grew wider. Closing the book again, Judith called goodbye to Mrs. Tucker.

Susie gazed at the fabulous book. Smiling, Judith gently placed the volume in her hands. "Will you take care of this for me? I will come again in a few days. We can read another story then." Mounted, she glanced back over her shoulder. Susie clutched the book in both arms, a smile spread across her face.

Judith rode away, an unexpected hunger tugging at her heart. Would she ever have children to read to, or cuddle? That was out of the question. No children unless she married—something she had long since decided against. Her parents' marriage had been a disaster. What other kind was there? He had ignored his wife and lied to his daughter. She would not risk such treatment.

Sleep continued to elude Judith. One morning, she headed for the stables after staring at the darkened windows for hours. A sleepy-eyed groom saddled Gypsy, while Judith struggled to contain her impatience. After accepting a toss into the saddle, she urged her mount into a trot across the park, then up a hill. Pausing at the top, she glanced over the cottages tucked among cultivated fields, the pastures waiting for sheep, before turning toward the forested area behind her. Elation flooded her being.

"Mine," she said aloud. "All mine."

You once accused your father of believing property was more important than his daughter. Do you not realize you're the same way? You put more importance on land ownership than anything else. Try to develop other aspects of life. The Manor is only property, which you will leave someday.

Judith scoffed at Susanna's question. *I know this estate is only property, but it's my property. Can you not understand? Mine, earned by my own efforts. No one can take it away from me. I don't intend to leave this place. Ever.*

I understand your reasoning, but when you die, you will leave it behind, so why place great importance on ownership?

Judith struggled to explain. *This isn't just land but my independence, my proof Father doesn't have me under his command, even though he believed he did.*

Yet, to a certain extent, he still exercises control over you through your memories. Standing here, you looked out over this acreage the way you once did with him at Ainsley Park. If he were not on your mind, at least subconsciously, you would not have exulted over your ownership.

Susanna was right, much as Judith wanted to believe otherwise. Her heart lurched at the memory of the many times she'd sat her pony, then later Gypsy, on another knoll looking out over what she expected would be hers someday. She was not alone but with her beloved father. A dim memory flitted into her consciousness.

She was so tiny her short legs stretched over the front of the saddle. Father's arm tight around her was security. That was even before her pony. The last time they sat together on the knoll was the day before he left Ainsley Park on his last journey. They sat quietly, he on his stallion, Turk, she on Gypsy. She looked at him, silently screaming for him to tell her the truth so she could stop deceiving him. He hadn't. The following day she told him goodbye, wondering if he noticed the word.

They never said goodbye, but with a hug and "I'll see you soon" he would mount his waiting horse and ride away. She had always waved until he disappeared from her view around a curve in the drive with one last turn toward her, hat lifted in farewell.

This time was the same, but it was truly goodbye. She would never see him again. She'd done what she had determined to do six years ago, so why did a lump clog her throat?

Judith found attending to estate matters difficult at the Manor. The idea of doing what she had done on a regular basis at Ainsley Park intensified her hurt. The Manor estate hands avoided her when she was among them, never looking her in the face, increasing her unease.

Daniel assured her their reaction was a temporary matter, but she used their attitude as an excuse to spend more time visiting the tenants. This was one of her responsibilities, she told Susanna when the angel scolded her for not helping Daniel. Those visits helped keep her mind off the kiss too, and the green-eyed rogue who caught her unawares.

Richard returned to Chadwick Park after kissing the girl with the bewitching blue eyes. His earlier musing nibbled at the edge of his mind again. Something to do with her name, yet he clearly remembered the two times he met her when she was younger, and he never heard her name.

Slipping in the side door, he reached the study without anyone's knowing. There, he spent another hour separating bills and receipts into various stacks, matching some with the other. The unpaid bills far outnumbered those marked paid. An immediate visit to the tradesmen was in order. He shuddered at the embarrassment that would entail. He'd rather face Napoleon's army again.

Richard sat staring into the distance, his thoughts in turmoil, trying his hardest not to condemn the late duke, when Wilson entered the room.

"It's time to dress for dinner, Your Grace. Hot water has been delivered to your rooms."

"What did you say, Wilson? Oh, dinner. Thank you." With one last glance at the desk, he left the room, dragging one booted foot after the other. Pitched battles had never tired him this much. He remained quiet while he changed from riding leathers to evening wear and accepted a fresh neckcloth from Pierce, who helped him shrug into a dinner jacket.

Over dinner, he talked to his mother when the servants were present but sat in silence otherwise. She ignored him, eating without comment except for directing the servants.

Her reserve didn't bother him. He would rather have her aloofness, even the sharp edge of her tongue, than her tears. Nevertheless, he would not submit to her stratagems.

Excusing herself, she reached the door before turning. "You seem determined to be a martyr, so I suppose you will want the bills from my writing desk." She left the room before he could speak.

There were more bills? He gulped his cold coffee, then hurried to her sitting room. Pulling open the desk drawers, he found them stuffed with bills. Stunned, he carried them to his study. Modistes, milliners, glovers, all waiting for funds. How could one woman wear so much clothing? He spent two hours organizing her bills, then trudged off to his bedchamber. There, he allowed Pierce to remove his jacket and boots, then dismissed him with a nod.

Morning came too soon. The rattle of drapery rods roused him when Pierce flung back drapes revealing a sunny day.

"'Tis another fine day, Your Gr . . . um, Major."

Richard nodded and swallowed the almost scalding coffee Pierce handed to him. He'd slept little, but a ride before breakfast would clear the cobwebs from his mind. His mother never left her rooms in the mornings. Had her habit been otherwise, he was not sure he could control his temper. He summoned the butler to the study. "Wilson, I've organized the bills in my father's desk and those in my mother's writing table. Do you know if there are others?"

"The kitchen bills are in my pantry, Your Grace. Shall I bring them to you now?"

Richard dropped his head into his hands with a groan. "Yes, please. Wilson, I understand from Guthrie that the servants' wages are current. Am I correct?"

Wilson hesitated. "They were current at the late duke's death but are due to be paid again."

Moments later, Richard accepted a sheaf of papers from his butler. Heaven only knows what he could do if the family solicitor was in ignorance of the money situation. He penned a letter to Samuel Coleman, requesting his presence at the first possible moment and for whatever time he could spare from his other business.

Mid-afternoon found Richard busy adding columns of figures when Wilson entered the study. "Your presence is desired in the drawing room for tea, Your Grace."

"Tell Her Grace that I can't join her today. I'd like a tray here, please."

The butler left, closing the door, which burst open within minutes admitting his mother with a frown on her face. "We have guests, Rochdale. I told them you will join us for tea, so make yourself presentable." She exited the room without waiting for a reply.

Muttering with annoyance, he quit the room after straightening his clothing. The drawing room appeared to be full of females. He greeted each while he distributed the teacups, and the moment they left, he escaped to the study. Ledgers, little though he still understood, were of more interest than chattering females.

Rebellion came after the third afternoon of hearing inane chatter among women enjoying cup after cup of tea—females with nothing on their minds except neighborhood tittle-tattle. They were enough to turn any man against women for all time. Under other circumstances, he might consider joining a monastery.

Confronting his mother over their midday meal, he stated he would not join her for tea that afternoon or any other day until after the estate was in order.

She glared at him. "When will that be?"

"Not in the immediate future, for certain. I can't say further than that. I'm waiting to hear from Mr. Coleman, who, I hope, can tell me whether the estate has any funds. Funds, I might add, which are imperative to pay all the debts accumulated over the past few years."

"Don't talk to me about debts!"

"I must, for the simple reason Father failed to do so." He shook his head in the face of her determined obtuseness. "Understand this, Your Grace. Father paid no bills for at least three years. I have no idea whether there is money to cover even a portion of those outstanding. The safe contains no money, not even for incidentals that might occur. Therefore, we will not incur further debts until these are paid. *All* of them, do you understand me?"

"I must have my modiste come for a few days! I don't have a decent rag to put on my back. When we start entertaining . . ."

He interrupted with icy tones. "We will not entertain anyone in the foreseeable future. Considering the clothing bills you accumulated, your closets should be overflowing."

"But, but . . ."

Richard ignored her sputtering and excused himself from the table with one final admonition. "No shopping, Your Grace, until the estate is in order. No shopping until I specifically say you can summon your modiste."

He had to leave the house. His nerves would not tolerate another minute shut up inside. At this point, dealing with bills was beyond him.

He ordered his horse saddled, then wandered for an hour before seeing a familiar figure.

"Anthony!"

"Richard! I mean, Your Grace." Anthony Guthrie broke into a grin at the reply.

"Oh, stow it, you ninny. Anyone who led me into the scrapes you did can't address me by my title." He clapped his old playmate on the shoulder.

"I deny I did the leading, although I do admit to participating in a fair number with you. Still, I must address you correctly, Rochdale, or my father will nail my hide to the barn door, even at my age."

"Wouldn't surprise me, if he did, but I implore you to avoid 'Rochdale' if at all possible."

Anytime Richard had managed to escape both his nurse and his mother, he had searched for the estate agent's son, who became his friend before he reached school age. Anthony was a year older so could teach the younger child about climbing trees, fishing, and the other activities that children enjoyed. The pampered boy decided early in life the scolds he received when he returned home dirty were endurable, if he'd had some pleasure beforehand.

"I could use some company, if you have the time."

Anthony nodded. "I'm just gawking at this stand of trees, remembering our adventures there when we were boys."

"They were huge even then, at least in my eyes."

"Do you remember when you broke your arm falling from a beech tree?" Anthony chuckled at the memory. "At the time, I was sure you were dead. I had visions of hanging from the highest limb for murdering the future duke."

The friends reminisced while they ambled around the acreage. "Do you have plans for the estate, or must you report back to the army? I can't imagine they would want to lose your services, based on the times I read your name in war reports, especially your battlefield promotions. Not common, I believe."

"Of necessity, my army career is over. I came home to learn how to manage a neglected estate. The reality has thrown me for a loss."

"The estate has changed. Your father didn't believe in spending money. I apologize. I should not speak so."

"You can't say anything worse than I've said the past few days. However, to answer your question, I do intend to restore the estate to what it was before I joined the army. How to accomplish the herculean task is beyond me. I face years of work, but I *will* return the duchy to solvency."

"I believe you. Chadwick Park can be a thriving estate again, but it will take considerable money."

"That's what I don't know—how much, if any, money there is. Father bought books instead of paying bills. The funds I inherited from my godfather are not sufficient to support an estate this size. I must dip into my assets for wages now and may well do so again."

"The tenants have suffered only during the last three years. His Grace ignored estate needs after you returned to Spain."

Richard nodded at the reminder of that trip. No matter the ending—his mother's tears, his father's temper—that had been an interesting trip, a break from the battlefield with an opportunity to purchase new uniforms and boots. The trip also allowed him the opportunity to see what Tattersall had to offer. He leaned forward and patted his mount's neck.

"I found Sheik there. He proved to be an excellent battle mount, never shying even when bullets whistled by us."

"I heard Parker had to sell off his stable to pay his son's gambling debts."

"His problems were my good luck, yet I abhor what he's doing to his son. He needs to stick the boy in the army. A couple years as a subaltern would correct his attitude."

"You're right about that. I saw some interesting broadsheets around Town a few days after you left." A wry grin crossed Anthony's face. "I didn't understand them but chose not to ask strangers. They were close to treasonable."

"What did they depict?"

"The Prince Regent dressed in a splendid uniform surrounded by soldiers wearing rags. The soldiers had their hands over their mouths."

Richard chuckled. "I don't know about treasonable, still I wouldn't risk Prinny's ire by discussing them in public. I've been witness to his set-downs enough to avoid them. I wish I had seen the broadsheets though."

He paused. "The official reason for my trip to London was to attend the ceremony at Whitehall Chapel honouring the capture of some French eagles. I was part of the contingent which escorted them from Spain. You know the Prince Regent is overweight . . ."

"To say the least!"

". . . and it was comical to see him strut into the Chapel wearing full military regalia while we stood in our well-brushed but worn uniforms."

"Oh, so those little figures portrayed on the table in the broadsheets were the eagles."

"Yes. Wellington's troops captured five that year: two at Salamanca, two at Madrid, and one at Ciudad Rodrigo." Richard shifted in the saddle when Sheik sidestepped a rabbit hole.

"Those were all great victories for England, as the Prince Regent stated. However, his claim to have been at Wellington's side, leading the charge, caused some hastily controlled merriment. Everyone there knew our future king had never set foot in the Peninsula or on any other battlefield."

"I recall hearing King George had forbidden his heir to join the military. One could sympathize with Prinny, even excuse his excesses."

"I agree."

Anthony spoke after a long moment of silence. "I regret my mother's health kept me from joining you. I simply couldn't let her worry about me."

Richard tapped him on the shoulder. "I would have done the same thing, had I been in your situation, so don't let staying home bother you."

"Some people around here believe differently. To my embarrassment, they don't hesitate to let me know their feelings." Anthony reverted to the eagles. "I understand to capture even one is extraordinary."

"True, because under normal circumstances the regimental leader will destroy the eagle rather than allow the statuette to fall into enemy hands."

They had crisscrossed the estate. On the top of a small knoll overlooking the home park, Richard's glance swept the area. Swallowing a sigh, he said, "Her Grace holds me responsible for the problems here. She believes Father would have relented if I had stayed home."

"Preposterous! No one could sway your father from his purpose."

"Talking with you helped me a great deal, Anthony. I appreciate your confidence. I expect the solicitor any day. When he comes, will you give us the benefit of your opinions?"

"My father will meet with you."

"Yes, but I want you to be there too." Richard met Anthony's direct gaze. "If you will have the job, I want you to be the agent here when your father is ready to retire. Please understand, I'm not putting him out to pasture. I'll make sure he understands, because he is far from being ready to do nothing. The thing is, I don't want you to take his place as uninformed as I am in taking my father's place."

Their gazes connected for a long moment as understanding flowed between them. They parted with a nod and a handshake.

Ten

Out and About

Richard stood at the study door to welcome his solicitor to Chadwick Park, a Chadwick Park he was ashamed for anyone to see.

Coleman stepped past him. "Thank you, Your Grace. Your father's death was a shock. I've never written a more difficult letter than the one I sent to you in Vienna. Again, please accept my condolences."

"Thank you." He pointed to the stack of papers on the desk. "You can see I need your help. I believe all the outstanding bills are here, but there are no estate entries in the ledgers for the last three years. I have no idea how much, if any, money the estate has. Guthrie can't tell me because my father never trusted him with any information either."

"The late duke was particular about maintaining his privacy. I found it difficult to deal with him. I understand my father had some difficulties with your grandfather although not to the same extent."

"Rest assured the chain is broken with me. I need all the help you can give. Can you stay for a few days to go over estate matters? I must warn you—I am deplorably ignorant."

Coleman didn't bother to hide his elation. In an exuberant voice, he assured the younger man he was at his disposal.

Richard prepared himself to listen and learn. After two days in the study with the solicitor, he believed he had a reasonable grasp on the ledger contents. Coleman had brought some good news. An investment made years earlier, long forgotten, had reaped some benefits when a trading ship showed a profit on its second trip to China. Those funds, together with the little they discovered available in the ledgers, meant the estate was not destitute. Part of the burden lifted from Richard's shoulders. There were enough funds to pay the most pressing debts, so he could hold his head high again.

"Your Grace, have you considered selling your father's books or manuscripts?" The solicitor's tone reflected his hesitancy.

Richard glared around the room with distaste. "To put the matter in a nutshell, I don't care if I never see either again. Do I understand there's hope someone would purchase them?"

"Oh, yes, I know several collectors who would be interested. You might not sell the entire collection at once," he cautioned. "Still, there is no doubt you can find buyers in a reasonably short time."

Richard breathed a sigh of relief. "That's good news indeed. My father kept a meticulous list of books and manuscripts, which should help find buyers. I will place those ledgers in your care, leaving the situation in your capable hands. Meanwhile, I'll pack everything in crates and hope I don't damage anything."

"You are wise to do the packing yourself rather than entrust it to the servants. I advise you to wrap foolscap around each item for protection."

"Thank you. I would not have thought of doing so. Now, about tomorrow. Will you ride over the estate? I would like you to see the overall condition."

Coleman nodded. "I assume the agent will ride with us."

"Yes, he will. Guthrie has been with the estate in one capacity or another since boyhood. I intend for his son to become the agent when Guthrie retires. I've known Anthony since childhood. He's agreeable to being my future agent, even though he could better himself at a larger estate, so he will ride with us also."

The men spent long hours in the saddle over the following few days, making notes of the most urgent needs. Thus, on Coleman's last evening at Chadwick Park, Richard faced the future with optimism for the first time. A tight rein on spending over a few years would see the duchy in good order again.

To Richard's relief, his mother ignored the gentlemen during the day, but at dinner she insisted they observe the proprieties. To this end, she bombarded their guest with queries about the latest Town *on dits*.

Arriving at the drawing-room before dinner on Coleman's last night with them, Richard stood in appalled silence at the sounds penetrating the door. Yet inside the room, he did not indicate by even a raised eyebrow he had not expected to see the Downeys, or Squire Odom with his wife and two daughters. He shook hands with the men, bowed to the older ladies, and spoke briefly to the two simpering girls.

During dinner, the duchess decreed that, with such a small group, the conversation should be general. She avoided meeting her son's eyes.

A smile stayed on his face despite the chatter surrounding him while course followed course. When the local visitors said their farewells, he turned to his houseguest, suggesting a brandy with their coffee.

Mr. Coleman declined, saying he would retire with the expectation of an early departure on the morrow.

Scarcely waiting for Coleman to enter his bedchamber, Richard entered his mother's sitting room. "I wish to speak with you, Your Grace."

"At this hour? I'm preparing for bed."

He opened the sitting room door, standing aside for the maid to leave before closing it. Without speaking, he leaned against the door, crossed his arms, and eyed his mother. She was unable to withstand the silence.

"I suppose you intend to berate me for having dinner guests."

"No, not for having dinner guests, but why did you not advise me beforehand? I struggled to hide my surprise when I saw them. And, why on earth did you invite those Odom chits?"

She glared at him. "I didn't tell you because I knew you would object. I invited the girls to introduce them to you. Why else?"

His next question was deceptively mild. "Why would you introduce giggling schoolroom misses to me?"

"They are respectable young ladies, ready to make their come-out next season."

"I repeat my question."

"You owe it to the family name to marry and set up your nursery. Who better than a local young lady well known to your family?"

Despite his anger, he managed even tones. "I will choose my own bride when I'm ready. She will not be a schoolroom chit who is unable to string three words together without a giggle. Furthermore, this is not the time to consider marriage."

She continued to glare at him without speaking.

He straightened his lanky frame. "Mother, by some judicious work and careful spending for a few years, I can save the estate from bankruptcy—bankruptcy, I emphasize—which would mean losing our home and moving into digs someplace. To avoid leaving Chadwick Park, you must accept your normal life is over for an appreciable time."

"The estate can't be that bad," she protested. "Your father never mentioned a problem."

"My father never had any interest in Chadwick Park. He never spent a farthing on the acreage, if he could avoid doing so. He practically depleted the estate to buy ancient books."

"Such cannot cost so much. You're still at fault if the estate is bankrupt. Your father spent the funds on your army career."

"His Grace never spent one penny on my army career, nor anything else for me since I left Eton at sixteen and received an inheritance from my godfather. I used some of that to purchase my commission." He passed a weary hand over his face. "Father insisted I go up to Oxford, which I did for two years, yet he refused to pay the fees or provide even a minimum allowance."

She maintained a tightlipped silence.

"Now, we will stop this wrangling. Mr. Coleman leaves tomorrow morning. I will leave within a few days."

"You just got here!"

"I know. However, by the time I get to Town, he expects to have possible purchasers for Father's books, which I must deliver to him. If he can sell them for any reasonable amount, the money will go a long way toward getting the estate productive again."

Her lips tightened again, but she didn't speak.

Stubborn woman. With an audible sigh, Richard continued. "Your Grace, you must accept the fact I'm not the child you manipulated, nor am I my father with his total lack of interest in this estate. I *will* bring Chadwick Park back to what it was for many generations until Father came close to destroying his— and my—inheritance. You could help by being reasonable. Nevertheless, I will do what I must, with or without your assistance."

He stared at her until she dropped her gaze, then he left the room.

Richard stared out his study window at heavy gusts of rain blowing against the glass panes. He didn't envy Coleman's traveling in this weather. The storm had been like this since early morning with no sign of letting up. No ride today, but at least the weather should keep visitors away.

He had spent the morning crating his father's books and manuscripts. Now, he needed to stretch his legs after the stooping and bending. He climbed the stairs to the long gallery where he had played throughout his childhood. He smiled at the memory of mocking the dour faces depicted in the paintings, which lined the walls.

His stride took him halfway down the dimly lit room before something registered in his brain. Aghast, he drew back the window drapes. The additional light confirmed what he didn't want to believe. The walls were bare. The carved niches were empty. The Old Dutch masters were gone. Rembrandt, Rubens, Vermeer: gone. The Botticelli: gone. Even a small Titian, his favorite, was gone. In one corner, he found the only artwork left, a Gainsborough too new to be valuable.

Richard cursed long and silently, words he didn't realize he remembered from his battlefield years. His father had sold everything of value. His grandfather's collection had been small, no comparison to those of many great houses, but he had been selective. Now, nothing left.

He strode across the gallery until his temper cooled. The art collection had not entered his mind. His brain had been too full of debts. He should have known, though, that there would be nothing of value left in the house.

Should he ask his mother? No. She wouldn't know or care. He would write Coleman. With something definite to do, he returned to the study.

<> <> <> <> <>

"I've counted enough sheets," Judith announced over breakfast. "If I look at any more menus, I won't ever want to eat again. Furthermore, the mere thought of sheep leaves me cold."

Ruth exchanged a smile with Daniel over their coffee cups. "We appear to have a mutiny on our hands."

"Perhaps both of you need a respite."

"Yes," Judith agreed. "Let's do something frivolous."

"What do you have in mind?"

She hesitated only a moment, then laughed at her own absurdity. "Go to the village. You can always use more thread for your beloved embroidery, Ruthie. I will even help you choose some."

"That sounds like a real jolly time." Daniel shot them a wry glance. "However, I have a better suggestion. Tomorrow, I want to talk with some farmers near Amesbury, northwest of here. It's a small village, but you can shop or look at ruins."

Ruth asked about the ruins.

"There is an odd arrangement of stones nearby, called Stonehenge, for one thing. Also, every English village in existence has a church of some antiquity."

Judith paid little attention to the conversation around her. Although in a different county, Amesbury was not far from Ainsley Park. Could she bear to be so close yet not go there? Could she bear not seeing if the new earl was caring for the estate, the way she would have done? She might even see people she knew. She couldn't stay confined at East Leah forever.

"Yes." She interrupted Daniel's explanation of how the farmers near Amesbury had improved their barley crop production by more than half. He wanted to know how to do the same. "We'll go with you. While you learn their secrets, we'll occupy ourselves with whatever is there."

Daniel asked, "Rather than be rushed, shall we plan to stay in Amesbury overnight? I seem to recall the George is a comfortable inn."

With agreement reached, the ladies went about their packing while Daniel informed the butler.

The following day, Judith glanced from side to side when she stepped from the carriage in Amesbury. She didn't see anyone she knew. In this instance, she could appreciate her previous confined existence.

"Why did you sigh?"

"It's foolish of me, I know, Ruthie, yet I dreaded seeing anyone from home."

"Home? Why would anyone else from East Leah—oh, I understand. You meant Ainsley Park. I forgot it's in this general area. I apologize. I wasn't thinking."

"There's no need to apologize. I shouldn't still think of Ainsley Park as home, yet I do. Now, shall we have tea at the George before shopping?"

Refreshed, they made their way to the mercantile store. Ruth hadn't dared hope for such a large yarn selection, she confessed to Judith an hour later.

"I admit needlework does not interest me . . ."

". . . because you resisted Lady Monford's efforts to, in her words, civilize you."

Judith joined her laughter. "Even though I have no interest in needlework, I do admire your embroidery. Would you consider making some cushion covers or wall hangings, or both, for the breakfast parlor?"

"Oh, yes, I would enjoy embroidering them, if you're sure you want them."

"I'm definite about this even if I appear undecided on other things. While you were poring over your choices, I admired the flowers in the window boxes. Our breakfast parlor is so nice and sunny that I believe cushions with bright flowers would be a great addition, especially during the gloomy days of winter."

"I'll stitch some with the understanding you will tell me if you decide you don't care for them. I can always find a place for them in our rooms."

"Agreed. Now, Alice can carry our parcels to the inn while we visit St. Mary's Church, which I see just across there." Moments later, she asked Ruth what she knew about old churches.

"Not much, I admit. I do recall something about this one. I lived for a few months with a distant cousin near here at Stapleford."

"I knew you lived there when Father brought you to us when I was fourteen, but I don't know where else you lived."

"After my parents died, I lived with various relatives until Lord Monford asked me to be your companion— the luckiest day of my life."

"Mine also! Since you lived near here, I imagine you have also seen those rocks Daniel called Stonehenge."

"No, and the oversight puzzles me, because I lived so close by for almost a year. Now, about the church. I never went inside, but the vicar was leaving when I passed it one day. He talked with me for a few minutes, pointing out the amenities of his cruciform church. I imagine he rarely found a new audience."

Judith tilted her head first one way, then the other. It simply looked like a church. "Cruciform?"

"Yes. That means in a cross shape, although you can't see the outline from here. However, you can see the square tower, which sits in the middle of the crossing."

"It isn't very impressive: too squat, like a little old man who is as wide as he is tall."

Ruth's lips twitched, but she didn't reply to Judith's outrageous comparison. "The church was once part of an Abby. William of Normandy . . ."

"Who?"

"Perhaps you've heard of William the Conqueror?"

Judith admitted she had but just barely. "French, I believe."

"I should have set you to studying history instead of continuing with Miss Matthews's deportment classes! Anyway, William the Conqueror invaded England from Normandy. Did you know that's in France?"

"Ah, I see. You're talking about only one William. What's his connection with this church?"

"He had this one, and many others throughout England, built like the churches in his native Normandy."

"That's enough history for one day," Judith said with a mock frown.

Ruth's voice grew reminiscent. "I wandered through the cemetery while my cousins dealt with business. Afterward, we took our basket of food to the riverside. Fish hid in the shadows, and I wanted to do the same when my cousins started their never-ending bickering."

"Bickering?"

In a burst of confidence, Ruth said, "The lack of arguments was the first thing I noticed during my early days at Ainsley Park. The house was peaceful and serene: no yelling, no quarrels. You have no idea how much I appreciated the quietness."

Here was something else Judith had not known about her companion, her one friend. She smothered a sigh. More self-centeredness. Was her own self-absorption endless? She lightened the mood by giving Ruth a quick hug. "I don't remember any arguing at our house, yet I warrant I gave you enough problems to make you rue the day you came."

"Ummm, at times . . ."

Laughing, they returned to the inn to await Daniel for dinner.

The following morning, Daniel suggested they visit Stonehenge before beginning the journey home.

"Rocks! Just tall rocks," Judith exclaimed later. "Nothing interesting that I can see."

They stepped from the carriage and strolled closer.

Ruth agreed. "I don't recall hearing anything about them when I lived at Stapleford. Why did you believe we might find something interesting here, Daniel?"

"The origin makes them interesting, or rather the lack of known origin. Why are they standing on end? How deep are they underground? What do they represent? One account I heard as a youth held it was a place of ancient religious rituals—sacrifices. They don't stand in a particular design, however, which would be reasonable if they were part of rituals. Another account maintains they are merely house remains. Some people believe there would be engravings if the rocks were of any significance. No one has found carvings."

The rituals idea intrigued Judith. She tucked away the idea for Mrs. Blaylock's consideration, but another possibility flashed into her mind. Could these have been *people,* giants, judging by their size, turned to stone for disobedience? Susanna had told her someone in the Bible had turned to salt when she persisted in looking back at her home. If salt, why not stone? She returned her attention to Ruth's prosaic comments.

"A house makes sense, a grand house suitable for an important personage: a king perhaps before recorded history. Lesser structures would not have such large pillars. We have seen no structures around here which would need a foundation this massive. Even the Amesbury church, which is quite sizeable for such a small village, is not this large."

"Well, ladies, should the question ever arise over teacups, you can impress your listeners with your visit to Stonehenge. Meanwhile, let us refresh ourselves with food at the George before we return home."

An hour later, replete with baked chicken with fruit, Judith stood at the door awaiting the carriage. Glancing to her left, she saw two men riding into the village. One was a stranger. The other, in a green jacket and buff leathers, cut a dashing figure on a magnificent roan. She didn't recognize the breed. She did the rider: Richard. What was he doing in this tiny place? Perhaps he lived nearby, which explained his presence at Ainsley Park, not far across the county line.

Stepping into the shadows, Judith touched her tingling lips in memory, then followed his gaze toward an attractive fair-haired female strolling toward the apothecary shop, a basket swinging from one hand, the other hand holding a parasol. Judith kept her head turned away from him as she hurried into the carriage. Why should she wonder about him or any female? He was nothing to her except the rogue who stole a kiss. Her reaction upon seeing him notice another female was not jealousy. Admitting it would be tantamount to admitting she wanted a man in her life. Never.

"Care to ride into the village with me, Anthony?" After the latest example of his father's despicable behaviour, Richard had sought respite from estate responsibilities. He feared the artwork was gone forever. He wouldn't mind the rest so much if he could obtain the Titian. He issued the invitation when he met his childhood friend on an early ride.

"That's just what I need. Do you have anywhere in particular in mind?"

"No, just a getting re-acquainted visit," Richard replied, although he intended to reassure the local tradesmen about his good intentions.

They rode companionably, reminiscing about bygone years. Nearing Amesbury, Richard's sharp eye spotted a fair-haired female strolling along the road, a basket swinging from one arm. He asked her identity.

Anthony followed his nod, then quirked an eyebrow in his direction. "That's Eleanor Ingram, a widow who moved into the old Manchester house a year or so ago. Shall I introduce you?"

"Do you have an interest in her direction?"

"None whatever," Anthony assured him. "She's a touch above me. My purse too."

"Probably above mine too, but, yes, by all means, introduce me."

They dismounted and approached the apothecary shop as she came out the door.

"Good morning, Mrs. Ingram. Allow me to present Richard Chadwick, the Duke of Rochdale, newly returned from the Peninsula."

Richard bowed in answer to her curtsy. She lifted her soft brown eyes to meet his scrutiny. They talked for a couple of minutes before she took her smiling leave. Richard stared after her for a long moment. Becoming better acquainted with her might be worth his while, at an afternoon call perhaps.

The following day, Richard found planning an afternoon visit easier than accomplishing one. For three days, he tried to contrive a meeting with the widow, finally succeeding on a day when he had not prepared for it. On an early morning visit to consult the blacksmith, he saw her standing outside the greengrocer's shop.

"Good day, Mrs. Ingram."

They talked a few moments, ignoring covert glances sent their way, until he tipped his hat and turned toward his horse.

"Would you care to come for tea this afternoon, Your Grace? Or do your estate duties keep you too busy?"

He turned back toward her and accepted the invitation, hiding his satisfaction. His day was looking up already.

On this day, Richard managed to avoid his parent. He sat with Mrs. Ingram the requisite half hour, then he stood. Finding a way to approach her about another meeting proved difficult, a rarity in his life. She seemed quite proper, yet he had glimpsed a light in her eyes revealing less than proper possibilities sooner rather than later. She solved the problem for him.

"Do you dine out in the evening, Your Grace?"

"I've been here for such a short time I have not yet become re-acquainted with my neighbors. However, I'm open to invitations."

"It would please me if you came here for dinner tomorrow evening, if that's convenient."

He bowed over her hand with the assurance he would be delighted.

Tooling his curricle toward his rendezvous the following evening, he refused to dwell on the scene with his mother. Tears, recriminations, even demands followed him out the door, despite the presence of his servants. They would have a lively conversation over their meal.

The evening was pleasant. Also, completely proper. Richard had assumed they would dine *tête-à-tête* but learned his mistake when he found others there before him. After greeting him, the two couples quizzed him about the latest area *on dits*.

"I suppose you've heard Monford died in France," Frederick Underwood said. "And his daughter has disappeared."

"No!" Edward and Jean Benson glanced at each other. "We have only today returned from visiting family in St. Ives, so do tell us," Jean urged.

"The official report is that he died while traveling on business. However, there's some speculation he was a Napoleon sympathizer."

"I don't believe a word you say." Edward rattled his cup into its saucer. "I've known Alexander Ainsley all my life—my father before me. We have only the deepest respect for him."

Frederick handed his cup to Mrs. Ingram for a refill. "Perhaps so, but both Nancy and I heard the rumour."

Nancy wiped her mouth on a napkin. "Considering his reputation with women, I don't know how you can respect him."

"Being a womanizer doesn't mean he would be disloyal to his country."

Richard had a brief recollection from his youth that Monford lived across the county line in Hampshire. He had never met the earl, so he let the heated verbal battle go on around him. He raised an eyebrow toward Mrs. Ingram, who shook her head. She didn't know the man either. Standing, he bade the others good evening and followed Mrs. Ingram to the door.

Before bidding him goodbye, she invited him to tea for the following afternoon. He didn't make the mistake of expecting he would find her alone. To his delight, he discovered the less he expected the more he would receive.

She was indeed alone. The half hour stretched into an hour before he rose. Holding her hand longer than was strictly proper, he let his gaze wander over her face, lingering on her full, inviting lips. He lowered his face toward hers as she leaned toward him. Just before their lips met, brown hair turned raven, hazel eyes turned deep blue—the blue of water on a sunny day—before they turned stormy gray. Straightening abruptly, he blinked away the vision.

He ignored the disappointment in her face when he wished her a pleasant evening.

Why had another face invaded his mind? The owner hadn't entered his thoughts since he kissed her under the apple tree. Her eyes had turned from blue to stormy gray that day. He would tolerate no interference from those eyes again, he vowed, if another such occasion arose.

Eleven

Neighborly Visits

Neighborhood visits permitted Judith little time to dwell on Richard and the fair-haired woman in Amesbury.

Ladies came in groups, sometimes with daughters in tow. Judith took an instant liking to Hope Hinson, who sat quietly while the other ladies chattered over teacups. Sitting near Mrs. Hinson, Judith inquired about her family.

A smile lit Hope's eyes. "Oh, yes, Miss Ainsley, I have two children: Tommy, who is four, and Anne, who is two."

"Please call me Judith. I will call you Hope, if I may. I would love to meet your little ones. Perhaps you will bring them the next time you come?"

"I will, if you won't be bored."

"Children never bore me." She'd known so few, how could she be sure? Nevertheless, if spending time with Hope included children, so be it.

Conversation became general when Mrs. Moore raised her voice. "Did you hear about the robberies in the neighborhood?" She nodded in complacency when she had everyone's attention. "And not only in this neighborhood. I understand there have been instances all over the area."

"Is it house burglary or highway robbery?" This could be the basis for their next Mrs. Blaylock book. Judith welcomed the possibility. "Highwaymen, I wouldn't wonder, wearing masks."

Mrs. Peterson's quiet voice filled the void left by Judith's unexpected enthusiasm. "I understand both, so everyone should be careful. There have been no injuries yet, and we must pray there won't be."

The talk centered on the robberies until the ladies left with promises of return visits, preferably with more pleasant news.

One particularly fine afternoon when Richard's face persisted in her mind, Judith sought company. At the Manor's western boundary, she rode through a stand of poplars coming out at Longview Park: the Hinsons' home.

Riding along the curving drive, she heard joyous laughter coming from her right. She looped Gypsy's reins over a convenient limb, then strolled around the house until she reached a small garden surrounded by low shrubs. She watched the children's antics until her chuckles became laughter. This drew Hope's attention.

"Judith!" Hope pushed her disheveled hair from her face and started to rise.

"Don't get up. I will join you on the ground." She greeted the children with a smile. "Riding piggyback is fun, is it not? May I play too?"

Tommy giggled. Anne, who mimicked her brother in all things, joined him. Soon the ladies were on their hands and knees, each with a child on her back. They tired of the game before the children did, much to Tommy's dismay.

"Come, Judith, we'll deliver these little urchins to Nanny, then have tea. Tommy, Anne, thank our visitor for playing with us."

Tommy stuck out his lower lip but capitulated when Judith winked at him. He executed his best bow. "Thank you, ma'am, for playing with us. You make a nice horse."

Not to be outdone, Anne bobbed a curtsy that almost landed her on the ground. "Nice horsey!"

Relaxing over teacups on the terrace, Hope apologized for her husband's absence. "You still haven't met my husband. This afternoon, Tom has errands in the village. He will be sorry he missed you yet again."

"I'm sorry I missed him too. However, I can meet him at a small dinner party I plan for next week. A footman will deliver the invitations—when I sit down long enough to write them. In the meantime, please accept my verbal invitation for an informal Tuesday evening."

"I believe you avoid your desk the way I do. I look forward to the dinner party with great anticipation. I'm sure Tom will too."

Half an hour later, Judith found Ruth in her sitting room. Upon hearing Judith's plans, she lifted startled eyes from her embroidery frame. "You're going to do *what*?"

"When I visited Hope Hinson this afternoon, the invitation just tumbled out."

"Will you invite others?"

"I considered only the Hinsons, but I suppose we should include the Downeys. The numbers won't be even, but I shouldn't think that would matter for an informal dinner."

"I understand from Mrs. Downey that the vicar's nephew is visiting, so we'll invite him too. As I recall, his name is Rupert Jackson. Interested in antiquities, although she was not specific."

After a discussion with Daniel at dinner, they added Mr. and Mrs. Peterson to the list.

"Now, Daniel, I do hope you won't huddle with Mr. Peterson in a corner talking about sheep all evening." Ruth didn't understand why Judith went into whoops.

"You sound like an old married woman." Judith's laughter circled the room.

Ruth stared from her to Daniel, whose grin spread across his face. "Oh, both of you behave yourselves. I *am* an old married woman."

Standing at the open drawing-room door on Tuesday evening, Judith greeted her guests. "Hope, it's such a pleasure to see you again. This must be Mr. Hinson. Welcome, sir."

His eyes widened when he gazed at her. "Meeting you at last is my pleasure, Miss Ainsley. My wife has mentioned you several times."

The evening was lively—even the vicar chuckled his way through a funny story.

Judith endeavored to include the vicar's nephew in the conversation. "Mr. Jackson, I understand you have an interest in antiquities. We recently visited a place called Stonehenge near Amesbury. Have you been there?"

He stammered a negative reply and then sat in blushing silence.

Judith took pity on him and lightly told him she didn't think he had missed much by not going there. "Just some tall rocks, as far as I could tell. Not interesting at all."

The only grim note was a comment by Mr. Peterson that the burglars had hit again. This time they had injured the homeowner.

"He will survive, though," interjected Mrs. Peterson. The conversation turned toward more pleasant subjects.

When their guests left, Judith murmured to Daniel, "Not even one mention of sheep. Congratulations."

"If not sheep, what did you discuss with Mr. Hinson at such length at the door?" Ruth asked.

"Hinson said he has a friend who will visit from Wiltshire soon and would like to introduce him. I said they should bring him to tea."

"Ah, a newcomer to liven our lives," Judith said with satisfaction. She'd been sheltered so long that new faces were always welcome.

<> <> <> <> <>

Riding through a copse on his estate one afternoon, Richard pondered how he could contrive to see Eleanor Ingram again. His answer came when he spied an elegant female sitting on the bank of a small stream. "Good afternoon, Mrs. Ingram."

With a startled gasp, she jumped to her feet. "Your Grace! I was so deep in my thoughts I didn't hear you arrive."

Looping the reins around a tree limb, he motioned for her to resume her place, then sat beside her. He drew one knee toward his chest, clasping it with laced fingers. "I apologize for startling you. I don't normally see a beautiful woman sitting here."

"Do I trespass?"

"Not at all. Feel free to come here whenever you please." He glanced around. "I fished in this stream when I was a small child. I didn't often catch one, ended up in the water more often than not, but I enjoyed every minute of my stolen pleasure."

"How did your nanny react to wet clothing on her little angel?"

He roared with laughter. "Little *angel*? She most often called me a little imp." He grew sober. "Nanny was the love of my life. She always held me when thunder woke me, and she never revealed my misdemeanors to my parents. A distinct twinkle accompanied all her scolds. I still miss her, although she's been dead these fifteen years."

His companion laid her hand on his arm, recalling his attention to her. He raised a hand to caress her smooth cheek. He leaned closer when she stared at him through widened eyes.

With a feather-light stroke, his lips touched the dimple cornering her mouth and moved across her lips before centering. Suddenly, he became still, then stood.

"My apologies, Mrs. Ingram. I don't know what came over me. Forgive me, if you can." He mounted Sheik and rode off through the woods.

Eleanor Ingram stared after Rochdale. She didn't know what had come over her either, for that matter. Her plan was a gradual, not a sudden, surrender. Oh, yes, waylaying him was her intention when she came here again, close enough to the edge of his estate without causing suspicion about her reason but with a reasonable expectation of seeing him. How else could she be sure she'd see him again after his abrupt departure the last time he came to tea? Today was her third afternoon sitting by this stream, and she was on the point of accepting failure when she heard hooves rustling leaves.

She had moved to Wiltshire a year ago for the sole purpose of meeting Richard Chadwick when he returned from the war, whenever that happened. She first saw him when he was in London three years ago. Rochdale was the answer to her needs. Wealthy. What more could a woman ask? He was also handsome. A sculptor would love to carve those perfect features in marble, like those Elgin Marbles causing such a sensation in London.

However, marriage was what Eleanor had in mind, not a *carte blanche*. She had no illusions about the way men viewed widows. They believed women became light skirts the instant they buried their husbands. Her birth did not equal his, but her lineage was acceptable to all but the highest sticklers of Society. She sighed, wondering if another opportunity like this would arrive before her situation became desperate, an impending event in the not-too-distant future.

Riding across the park, Richard berated himself. Mrs. Ingram was willing, so why had he stopped? Those blue eyes again. Only this time when they turned stormy gray, they accused him of infidelity. *Infidelity*? To whom? *She* had no claim on him, so why did he feel he was betraying her? He admitted he did, which was absurd. His questions did not have answers yet, but he would find them, come what may. On that, he was determined.

He slipped in the side door at Chadwick House, then entered his study where he paced the floor. He knew his contemporaries considered him prudish, at any rate about females. He had gotten into enough boyhood mischief to satisfy even the bullies, who called him a sissy. He had never set up a mistress, however, being content with occasional casual arrangements when he was not on the battlefield.

This situation was absurd. The unknown female's face had intervened while he was with Mrs. Ingram. Not once, but twice, she had interfered while he was with his prospective mistress. He must free himself from those blue eyes, which turned gray with anger. He must exorcise the hold she had over him.

"Ruthie, listen." Judith waved an invitation card in the air over her breakfast plate. "The Hinsons have invited us to dinner and a small dance afterward. What fun! They're entertaining a *duke*. I've never met one, but aren't they all as old as time?"

Daniel's brown eyes twinkled at her over his newspaper. "You must be thinking of royal dukes. Several younger men do hold that rank, although I've never met one. Who are we to meet?"

"The Duke of Rochdale, no other name. Do you know him?"

"From Wiltshire, I believe."

"I saw his name in the newspaper when we were in Town earlier," Ruth told them. "Something about his return from Vienna. He was with Wellington in the Peninsula too. His name is Chadwick, if I remember correctly."

"If he served with Wellington, he must at least be somewhere under the age of forty, not quite decrepit anyway."

"I'm pleased you don't consider me decrepit simply because I've reached the advanced age of five and thirty," Daniel teased her.

Judith wagged a playful finger at him but grew sober. "Oh, well, I can't dance anyway, no matter how young he is."

Ruth reminded her they had discussed this earlier. "Such a short time has passed since your father's death we must decline the invitation. They will understand."

Judith nodded and excused herself from the breakfast room. She stood a moment and then wandered out a side door, her mind a confusion of thoughts. They jumped from her father's death to his perfidy, then back to his death. She had believed she was free of him for all time. She wasn't. From beyond the grave, he still controlled her.

Susanna's voice burst into the confusion. *Time will change your circumstances. Trust me.*

My brain knows that, but my heart still rebels. I want to live the life I should have had these past years.

You were ever impatient.

Why didn't you make my life easier? Guardian angels are supposed to care for their charges. You told me so when I was four years old.

I have taken care of you and always will. I couldn't do anything about your father because he had his own angel. Now you must stop feeling sorry for yourself. Instead, get busy with your correspondence.

Judith agreed. She was still concerned about the late cargo ships. She must also contact Mr. Sizemore about the weaving industry in Arncliffe.

Wealthy. Independent. Frustrated. Those words described her life. She couldn't travel on her own to Yorkshire. She couldn't see for herself the cottage industry that was among her first investments and now showed a nice profit. She didn't need Susanna's reminder that she had Daniel to thank for this lucrative investment. He had relatives who were weavers, so at his suggestion Judith had organized them into a profitable group, all without being there. Someday, she would travel anywhere her heart dictated. For now, she would curb her impatience, accept Mr. Sizemore's reports. Someday she would travel, on that she was determined.

<> <> <> <> <>

When Judith closed the breakfast room door, Ruth lifted troubled eyes toward Daniel. "She was happy for a moment. She smiles so seldom I hate we must curb her rare enthusiasm."

"Perhaps you can invite them to tea. I should think young ladies find obeying Society's dictates confining under the best of circumstances. As things stand now, obedience would be especially difficult for Judith. Yet we can't deny her the opportunity to meet a gentleman of rank. She will meet few enough in the foreseeable future."

"I shall send Hope Hinson a note this morning explaining the matter. Perhaps we were wrong not talking about the earl's death from the beginning. I do hope things don't get awkward at this point."

Twelve

Somewhere in France

The old man cracked open his eyes. Whatever had awakened him wasn't within view, and he didn't sense anyone else in the room. Still, he looked from side to side through slitted eyes before turning his head cautiously until he could see the door.

Were those footsteps fading in the distance? The old man strained to hear. One heavy set of steps, one lighter. A man and a woman.

Memory stirred. Two people had been there when he woke earlier. He'd pretended to be asleep, but why would he do that? They had talked in French. Or did he dream the entire situation? Henri and Marie. That's what they called themselves. Why would he dream about two French-speaking people? He couldn't think of a reason, so they must have been in the room. Perhaps they'd been there again, and the closing door had awakened him. It would have been good to hear them talk. He might have learned why his thoughts were in English, but he had understood their colloquial French.

The old man raised his head, then lowered it when dizziness overwhelmed him. After the room stopped swirling around him, he willed himself to sit up and look around. Clean, uncluttered, but small as attics go. How would he know that? A chamber pot stood in one corner, and a chair minus a leg tilted in another. A large, round-top trunk was under the high window. He wished he could see outside.

Something nibbled at the edge of the old man's brain. Mud. Earlier, Henri had said something about mud. The man couldn't leave him lying in the mud. That's what he'd said. Why would he be lying in mud?

Why would he be here, in someone's attic? Most importantly, who was he?

He would think about it later, when he wasn't so tired, when his head didn't ache so badly. He lay down again and drifted into sleep.

Thirteen

Friends? Or Adversaries?

The day after Ruth's note to the Hinsons, she and Judith were entertaining the vicar's wife when the door opened. The butler announced new arrivals. "Ladies, His Grace, the Duke of Rochdale, and Mr. and Mrs. Thomas Hinson."

Judith stood in stunned silence while the others greeted the newcomers. Rochdale was Richard—the Greek god—no, the rogue who kissed her. Heat rose above the modest neckline of her bodice. Would he reveal their earlier encounter? She managed to close her mouth before the duke spotted her. Therefore, she met the startled surprise in his eyes with a cool nod.

He was the type that sent impressionable young ladies into a swoon. Judith admitted she had reacted the same way at seven years old. She was older now and knew better than to trust him. She quelled her fluttering pulse.

"I'm pleased to make your acquaintance, Miss Ainsley." He drawled in a voice that sent shivers down her spine, then bowed over her hand, speaking for her ears alone. "I've searched for you throughout Wiltshire."

The twinkle in his eyes angered Judith. She assumed a haughty air. "Your Grace, it is kind of you to say so. I understand you served with Wellington?"

"For a time. I recently met a Harold Ainsley in Town. The Earl of Monford. Is he your relation?"

She kept her face blank. "Possibly. Were you on Wellington's staff in the Peninsula? We followed his progress in the newspapers when we could."

"Yes. My sister has mentioned a Catherine Ainsley in Warminster. Is she a relation of yours?"

"You might be a spy." At his startled expression, she smiled inwardly because she had shaken his composure. "I mean for our side, Your Grace. Spies interest me. I should like to be one, I believe."

Judith babbled on, giving him little opportunity for a reply until the regulation thirty-minute visit ended.

Other visitors came, received tea, and discussed the latest parish news. The highwaymen had struck again, causing minor injuries when a man resisted them. The degree of injuries increased with each telling, yet all agreed the man still lived.

Ruth, too, had recognized the duke. "He spent the entire visit by your side. Did he tell you anything about himself?"

"Oh, no, he was much too busy quizzing me about my relations. Not that he gleaned any information."

"Have you taken him in dislike so quickly? What did he say to you?"

"I don't believe he served in the Peninsula at all. I asked him, but he turned all my questions aside. He is much too effeminate for real battle." With a wry grin, she continued. "I asked him if he was a spy."

"You asked who, what?" Daniel strolled into the room and lifted the empty teapot just before the footman came in with a fresh tray.

"The Hinsons brought the Duke of Rochdale to tea. He's the gentleman we've encountered several times recently."

Daniel assumed a bland expression. "Did you fall into his arms this time, Judith?"

He received only a disgusted glare in answer.

A puzzled frown crossed Ruth's face. "She has taken him in dislike, thinks he's effeminate. Judith, did you truly ask him if he's a spy?"

"Yes, I did. He must pluck his eyebrows to have them in such perfect shape. I can't imagine him in battle. I prattled on about spies, so he would stop questioning me about my family." She paused a moment. "He has met the new earl, and his sister knows Mama, but he doesn't know I'm related to them."

Daniel raised his eyebrows at Ruth. "Did you not tell Hope Hinson who Judith's father was?"

"If not, it was an oversight. I told her Judith's father is recently deceased." She shook her head. "Vicars are notoriously absentminded, but I can't understand why Mr. Downey hasn't spread the word about Judith's title. He must have told Mrs. Downey not to mention it, although I can't imagine why."

<> <> <> <> <>

"Who is Miss Ainsley, do you know, Tom?"

The Hinsons and their guest drove homeward after tea at the Manor, discussing their visit. "My sister knows a Catherine Ainsley, who is Lady Monford in Warminster. I recently met Harold Ainsley, the Earl of Monford. I heard of a Monford from Hampshire in my youth but nothing about his family until recently. When I asked Miss Ainsley about them, she turned my questions aside. All she would talk about was spies, even asking if I was one. For England, she assured me, else she would probably have quizzed me about Napoleon's intentions."

"A spy? Where would she get such an idea?"

Hope's startled exclamation brought a smile to Richard's face. He shrugged it off, yet the raven-haired young woman—who alternated between rudeness and naïveté—occupied his thoughts throughout the evening. Had he wandered onto Monford's estate the day he kissed her? He'd been in the saddle for several hours but didn't realize he'd crossed into Hampshire. Could Miss Ainsley be the missing daughter?

A flash of hurt had passed through her eyes when they talked this afternoon. Hurt, not embarrassment over his kiss, so why had she snubbed him? He must admit she did, which in turn irritated, amused, and piqued him. People simply don't snub a duke or a hero of Wellington's army mentioned in dispatches as often as he had been. He hid a grin at his arrogance. Perhaps he was miffed because she didn't fall into his arms this time.

Richard had arrived at East Leah at Tom's urgent request after a quick trip to London. There, he had agreed upon a buyer for his father's books and manuscripts after only two days. The sooner the better, he had told Coleman. There wasn't time to haggle over cost, if he was to keep the duns away from Chadwick Park. A conversation with his Oxford tutor assured him the figure quoted was excellent, although probably not the amount his father had paid for them.

Richard had solved the book problem and could breathe more easily about reviving Chadwick Park. Coleman apologized for being unable to locate the paintings, but purchasing them was beyond the estate's possibility anyway, at least for the foreseeable future.

Now that he'd found the bewitching Miss Ainsley, he would stay with Tom awhile. The Chadwick Park problems would wait for him. Unfortunate but true.

The following morning, while riding at a brisk canter over the countryside, Richard spotted Judith riding in the near distance. She had not seen him, so he cut toward her, reining in when their mounts came abreast.

"Good morning, Miss Ainsley. You have a beautiful mare. A Cleveland Bay, I believe."

"Thank you, Your Grace. Yes, Gypsy is a Cleveland Bay. We've been together for ten years. She's my joy." Judith ran her hand down Gypsy's black mane, then turned toward Rochdale's roan, which was somewhat smaller than one would expect to carry a large male. "I admire your mount. Such an elegant sculpted head and high-arched neck. His legs so slender I wonder they can support his body. I don't believe I know the breed."

"Sheik is a full-blooded Arabian, one of the few in England. I plan to introduce more someday. Perhaps do some breeding on my Wiltshire estate."

"Is the bluish skin around the eyes typical of Arabians? I'm familiar with several breeds but don't recall seeing that on any other horse or such height of tail carriage."

"To my knowledge, they are common only in Arabians." His enthusiasm was contagious while they discussed the relative merits of various horse breeds. All was well until he changed the subject.

"Tell me something, Miss Ainsley. Why did you get so upset when I asked about the other Ainsleys?" He instantly regretted his words. His tongue was more hindrance than help. She encouraged Gypsy into a fast gallop, putting considerable distance between them before slowing.

He watched her ride over a small hill, then wheeled Sheik in the other direction. There was a mystery here. He would learn it one way or another.

<> <> <> <> <>

After rushing away from the duke, Judith struggled with her frayed temper. She'd been excited before he waylaid her. Now as her anger cooled, the excitement returned. She urged her mount toward home. Ruth and Daniel were still at the breakfast table.

"Mrs. Blaylock has returned. I was beginning to think she would never come again."

"Wonderful," Ruth congratulated her. "We should start another book. Mr. Davison has been patient, but we should not keep him waiting longer. We can at least notify him we have begun another."

Daniel lowered his newspaper. "What inspired Mrs. Blaylock this time?"

The inspirations for the other books had come from newspaper *on dits*. Judith bubbled with enthusiasm because this one promised to be different. A mystery. Could they write mysteries? Yes, she told herself firmly, they can.

"I heard voices on my ride near our northwest border. I couldn't see anyone, you understand, just heard these disembodied voices: one speaking in English; and two, in French. They stopped suddenly before I could determine their origin. I couldn't find any trace of anyone, but guess what I did find—a cave!"

"You didn't explore on your own, did you?" Ruth fixed her horrified gaze on Judith's face. "Tell me you did not!"

Judith's laughter filled the room. "Oh, Ruthie, I know better than to deprive you of sharing the pleasure. How could you believe I would be so thoughtless?"

"Did it not occur to you that those voices could be miscreants who would harm you?"

Judith bit her lip. She had not considered that possibility. She'd thought only of apparitions.

When Ruth spoke, her voice brooked no argument. "We will all explore the cave when Daniel has the time to accompany us."

"Good! We must see the inside for descriptive purposes, but I can start the book without seeing the interior. I've already decided the voices are ghosts. Many years ago, criminals abducted a girl and held her captive there. They decided they couldn't let her live because she might betray them, so . . ."

Daniel interrupted. "Today, I must visit the outlying areas. Tomorrow, I will see the vicar about the church roof, which I expect will require all day. However, we'll visit the cave soon."

"We can see you're too busy to indulge us for a few days at least."

"You're right, Ruthie, as always," Judith conceded. "My enthusiasm is running away with me."

The following days settled into a routine. Judith still had an early morning ride around the estate, but Daniel did most of the work. She spent the rest of the morning in the small, sunny room she chose for writing. Stacks of foolscap, a jar filled with pens, and ink bottles cluttered the long writing table. The maids soon learned they must not touch anything on the table.

Being open about her writing was a luxury Judith had longed for at Ainsley Park. Here, she merely asked the servants not to discuss the matter when outsiders were around. At some point during the morning, Ruth joined her to hear the progress and offer suggestions about the ghost story. The workday ended with a light meal, and their social day began.

The unmarried neighborhood girls had welcomed Judith into their group. Envious of their easy friendship, she realized she must be more forthcoming to be at ease with them. Socializing with her peers would be more comfortable if Father had not isolated her from neighborhood girls. Perhaps there weren't any girls near Ainsley Park. However, she must not dwell on the past. Tea invitations were in order.

When she made up her mind to do something, Judith did it thoroughly. Instead of the usual drawing room tea with others present, she issued invitations to her special group for a tea party on the terrace.

Jane and Lizzie Moore were such fun-loving sisters Judith laughed often when she was with them. She was more serious with Louise Peterson who, although younger, displayed a maturity lacking in the other girls. Gertrude Haynes gave the impression she was on a higher social level than the other girls. She often mentioned "my cousin, the Honourable Sarah Finley," adding in an awe-filled tone, "Her father is a *baronet*!" Gertrude never tired of mentioning the titled people she met through her cousin. Such a reference brought up Judith's identity.

"Miss Ainsley, are you acquainted with any titled persons?" Gertrude's raised eyebrows indicated the possibility was remote.

"We're all on a first-name basis, here, Gertrude. Why do you persist in calling her 'Miss Ainsley'?"

"All right, Lizzie. Judith, are you acquainted with any titled persons?"

Judith bit her lip and wished now she had identified herself properly at the beginning. *Susanna, help me!*

You got yourself into this mess, and you can get yourself out.

Fair enough. Taking a steadying breath, Judith explained with a light laugh. "I expected either the vicar or Mrs. Downey would have said something. They both know."

"Know what?" demanded Jane.

"My father was an earl." Judith rushed on in the face of their astounded silence. "His earldom doesn't matter to me, you understand. I never think about being titled."

Louise spoke into the silence. "You are properly titled 'Lady Judith.' We've been rude. Please forgive us."

"No, no! I prefer you address me by my name. If I wanted to be addressed by my title, I would have told everybody before now."

"Not want to be addressed by your correct title? Ridiculous," Gertrude stated. "Everyone knows titled persons always demand proper obeisance. Are you sure you're not telling a Banbury story?"

"Gertrude!" Lizzie and Jane gasped, but Louise spoke sharply. "You owe Lady Judith an apology for doubting her word."

With a heated face, Gertrude muttered an apology. "You caught me by surprise, Lady Judith."

"Please call me Judith. I won't be comfortable if you use my title. I would rather be accepted for myself than for who my ancestors were."

Louise's quiet good sense ruled. "All right, Judith. We don't want you to be uncomfortable with us, do we, girls?"

"No," the Moore girls answered in unison and stared at Gertrude until she concurred.

Lizzie couldn't resist the question. "Which earl is your father, Judith? Where is he?"

"He was the Earl of Monford." At their horror-stricken faces, she added, "Please, don't be concerned about his death. He didn't want me to go into mourning for him, so I don't talk about it. I mourn him in private, of course, and we also curtail our activities to some extent. We don't dwell on the situation, however."

Please, she begged silently, don't ask about my mother.

"Are the Sherwoods family?"

"Ruth is a cousin, but she's closer than a sister could be. She's been my companion since I was fourteen. Daniel was my father's trusted agent for many years."

Louise said they had been inquisitive enough. The conversation moved on to the latest robberies. The thieves had struck again, this time stealing two horses also. Ordinary theft meant transportation to Australia, but horse stealing meant hanging on Tyburn tree, according to Lizzie's father.

The difficult moment passed. Judith's relief was silent but heartfelt.

Fourteen

Memory Interference

During the days following her discovery, Judith's thoughts often centered on the cave. As the days passed, she grew more impatient to explore. Maybe she should assume additional estate duties, giving Daniel more free time. No. Daily oversight was still beyond her. Judith admitted, but only to herself, that she didn't truly enjoy the estate work. She had enjoyed her father's attention and had wanted to please him. Just look where obedience got her, or rather didn't get her—Ainsley Park. Bitterness over the loss gnawed at her. *This* estate was truly hers. For that reason alone, she should enjoy the work.

Judith tried to suppress memories, but her father's invasion of her dreams gave her too many sleepless nights. So far, she'd managed to keep him out of her waking thoughts for the most part. Yet the shell she had erected against the hurt he caused already had tiny cracks.

Her determined avoidance of the duke also suffered a blow. She was writing steadily when a message arrived at the Manor, inviting Mr. and Mrs. Sherwood and Miss Judith Ainsley to tea with the Hinsons. After some heated discussion, she agreed to go but made it clear the visit was against her inclinations.

"The book is going so well I can't stop now. Surely you can understand, Ruthie."

Her argument didn't succeed. Did she want to offend Hope Hinson? No, so she submitted to the inevitable. "However, do not tell them my father was an earl."

During the tea, she talked animatedly to everyone there except the duke, whom she ignored.

Judith knew what to expect when they left the Hinsons. Since Judith reached adulthood, Ruth had refrained from the homilies she had given the young girl. She had corrected her even less after Judith declared her independence. Nevertheless, on this occasion, her temper burst forth the instant they entered the open carriage.

"Your behaviour was shocking! How could you be so rude to Rochdale? His manner was exemplary, which made your rudeness so noticeable no one could have missed it."

Daniel touched his wife's hand. "My dear, now is not the best time for this discussion."

She took a deep breath and nodded at her husband, who clasped her hand in his.

Judith did not answer. Arriving at the Manor, she rushed toward her sitting room, with Ruth at her heels.

"Now, young lady, tell me what's going on with you. I've never known you to be rude, yet your behaviour has been atrocious since you met Rochdale."

Judith shook her head, maintaining iron control over her emotions. She apologized for embarrassing her friends but refused to speak further.

Dinner was a subdued meal. Judith excused herself immediately afterward, pleading a headache. Not just an excuse but reality. She paced her sitting room, berating herself for letting the rogue upset her. He was a perfect example of sculptured male beauty, as if her storybook Greek god had come alive. She banished the fair hair and green eyes from her thoughts. She would not allow him space in her mind.

Judith didn't sleep well, her dreams coming close to being nightmares. Richard's face became her father's face, Sheik became Turk as they raced across an estate, which changed from the Manor to Ainsley Park. She woke with tears on her cheeks and lay there crying for her father, which she had not done since his death. She drifted back into sleep but not to peaceful dreams. Ruth's admonitions became Lady Monford's scorn.

When she woke again, Hope's hurt face clouded her mind. Judith acknowledged her many faults. Cowardice was not one. She would do what she must.

Her mirror showed dark circles under her eyes, giving witness to the difficult night she'd endured. For a change, she wore a sprigged-muslin morning gown at breakfast, rather than her usual riding habit. Pouring a cup of tea, she inquired if they needed the carriage during the morning.

"I plan to work with the roses," Ruth answered. "What about you, Daniel?"

He looked up from his newspaper. "Something is destroying the hedges near the southwest corner, so I'll be there throughout the morning. Why do you ask?"

"I owe Hope Hinson an apology. Rather than ride over, I will drive."

"Do you plan to reveal your title?" Ruth's quiet question held no inflection.

"I don't understand why they don't already know. If we were trying to keep the title a secret, everyone in the countryside would be whispering about it. We would prefer the servants not gossip, yet their tittle-tattle would be a relief if they had done so this time. Louise and the other girls know I'm titled too."

"You told them?"

"Gertrude asked me point blank if I knew any titled people. I had a choice—either tell the truth or cause a ripple later."

"How did they respond?"

"They were a little stiff at first, but soon they were just like always."

"Since you told them, why did you refuse to tell the duke?"

"It isn't his business." She left the room before Ruth could answer.

After a couple of hours at her writing table, Judith was thankful no one inquired how much she had written because not one word graced the paper. After calling for the carriage, she sat in ladylike splendor, her maid across from her, while the coachman drove toward Longview Park. She must order a chaise, perhaps the sporty two-wheel type, so she could drive herself. Her innate common sense asserted itself. She would purchase the safer, four-wheeled vehicle.

In Hope's sitting room, the children dominated the conversation until they finished their first cups of tea. "I came to apologize for my behaviour last evening, Hope. I was quite rude. Can you forgive me?"

Hope squeezed her hand. "Apologies are never necessary between us. We all have bad days."

"There's something I need to tell you. The vicar knows. We assumed he would tell everybody. We know now he hasn't. I told Lizzie and the others, thinking they would spread the word. Even the servants haven't talked, which is truly amazing."

"What don't I know?"

"Promise my confession won't make any difference between us."

"I don't believe anything could, Judith. We became instant friends, something I've never experienced."

"My father was an earl." There, her secret was out.

Hope didn't respond immediately, but then, "You're titled. I should be calling you Lady Judith, should I not? Please forgive my rudeness."

"No, Hope, no! Please don't take it that way. I don't want anyone to use my title, truly. I just want to be me, plain Judith Elizabeth Ainsley."

"You aren't plain anything but the most beautiful person I know."

"Except Richard," Judith popped her hand over her mouth. "Forget I said that, Hope, please."

"I assume you mean Rochdale. He *is* pretty, but I would never say that to his face." Hope paused for a long moment. "I don't believe he knows you're titled, otherwise he would have told us."

"He doesn't, so please don't tell him."

"I shan't, if you prefer it. However, don't you think he should know?" Receiving no answer, she persisted. "There's a problem between you. Can you tell me?"

"I took him in dislike for some reason." Judith shrugged. "Perhaps I'm jealous of his prettiness."

Hope smiled but grew sober. "Do you not think he should know you're titled?"

"I'll tell him when next we meet, even apologize for my rudeness at the same time."

Tea and confession were good for the soul, Judith decided. She returned to the Manor with a quiet heart.

Susanna agreed. *I'm proud of you. Apology requires a marked degree of maturity and an equally marked lack of cowardice.*

Thank you, Susanna. I'm easier in my mind, so perhaps there's hope for me yet.

A few mornings later, Judith draped Gypsy's reins over a convenient bush near the cave. Her promise not to explore on her own had been a mistake. She'd battled with herself over that, but in the end decided not to go against her word. She might find inspiration for the book on the outside though or hear the voices again. She lay back on the ground, staring at the sky, letting the peacefulness wash over her.

Lost in the book plot, Judith slowly became aware of a voice sounding in her ear. She turned her head and met Richard's twinkling green eyes. She sat up, straightening her bonnet.

He rolled off his hip to sit beside her with one knee clasped near his chest. "Do you realize I spoke three times before you heard me?"

She confessed to woolgathering.

"I see you've been writing letters. Do you have a wide correspondence?"

"No, I have limited correspondence. Why do you ask?"

He nodded toward her ink-stained fingers. "It didn't require much observation."

Judith watched him from the corner of her eye. Why had she not scrubbed her hands better? Would he think her a bluestocking, if she told him about Mrs. Blaylock? Somehow, she didn't want him to hold that view of her.

"The ink stains are not from writing letters. I write books. Rather, Ruth and I do." Looking him straight in the eyes, she waited for his reaction.

He stared at her, doubt flitting across his face. "Books? You ladies write books? What kind?"

"Gothic novels."

He didn't sneer, which was something at least. His incredulity turned into amazement.

"Do you hope to have them published?"

"Mr. Davison has published seven already."

"Seven! Why have I never heard your name?"

Judith didn't hide her amusement. "I don't imagine you read Gothic novels, so why should you have heard of us? Anyhow, we use a penname, Mrs. Blaylock."

"Mrs. Blaylock! My sister reads all her books and says she's all the rage. Do you tell me two young females write them, instead of an aged matron?"

Her laugh surrounded them. "I notice you don't claim to have read them yourself."

"No, not yet, but I will now that I know who Mrs. Blaylock is. I can hardly wait to tell my sister." He grinned. "Fair warning. Amelia will demand an instant introduction."

His voice became deliberate. "When something bothers me, I believe in getting to the bottom of the situation. What have I said or done which made you take me in dislike?"

She stared at him. Why had his mood changed? There had been no hard words, yet his tone demanded an answer. She shook her head.

"There must be something," he insisted. "From the moment we met at the Manor, you have shown your poor opinion of me. Is it because I stole a kiss or something you heard about me earlier, perhaps some *on dit* while you were in Town?"

All right, if he insisted, she would tell him. "You're pretty."

His green eyes turned icy. His sculptured lips thinned to a narrow line. "Others have called me pretty but not in your accusing tone. Nor have they said it more than once."

A shiver crawled up Judith's spine. She realized how far from home she was. No one knew she'd come here or even knew about this place.

A grim smile crossed Richard's face as he reached for her. When she tried to scramble away, he stared into her eyes for a moment before releasing his hold on her wrist.

She inched away from him, watching his jaw relax. He slowly gained control over his temper.

His voice steady, he talked about boys who had taunted him at school, how he'd often lost control. "They soon learned I was handy with my fists, which stopped their gibes. Many years have passed since I lost my temper over that point."

Judith murmured her sympathy.

"You looked like a terrified kitten. I haven't murdered anyone yet for calling me pretty. I won't start now, tempted though I might be."

Kitten. Judith recoiled further from him. That had been her father's name for her. She forced herself to speak despite the stab of pain. "I didn't mean to be rude. I don't know why I continue to be such a nuisance, either. Yes, I do too," she admitted. "You bring out the worst in me."

"I would much rather bring out the best in you," he murmured, smiling into her eyes. "I suppose I should apologize for kissing you, yet I can't bring myself to regret something I enjoyed so much."

She flushed and dropped her gaze. He didn't regret the kiss. Truth be told, neither did she, but she would never admit it to him.

After a moment, Judith changed the subject back to a much safer topic—Mrs. Blaylock.

They spent a pleasant hour together, discussing the book origins, the difficulties of writing.

"Now, I know why you appear lost in a dream world so often," he teased.

Could she risk teasing him? Might he become upset again? He did say he wouldn't murder her. "You see, in my dream world the females are always prettier than the males."

He stiffened.

"We gave serious consideration to including a pretty gentleman in this story. However, I don't believe pirates would be pretty. What say you?"

His shoulder muscles eased. "I don't number pirates among my acquaintances, you understand. However, I've never believed they could be pretty."

She nodded. "Besides, a pretty pirate would be unfair to my readers."

"How so?"

"It would strain their imagination too far." Ignoring his chuckle, she continued. "I could put you on display alongside the books. That would prove my point, might help with the sales too."

Their laughter faded into silence. A dog's barking carried on the light breeze. Larks chirped in the nearby beech trees. Judith was content. However, her relief at his acceptance of her teasing was short-lived.

"May I ask you something else?"

"What?" she hedged.

"Why are you touchy about those other Ainsleys?" When she didn't answer, he said, "Is wanting to know about your family unusual? It seems friendly to me."

"You haven't mentioned your family either."

"Are you interested? My father died earlier this year, my mother still lives at Chadwick Park near Amesbury, I don't have brothers but do have the sister I mentioned, Amelia, who lives in Warminster with her husband and four little girls."

"Was your father's death the reason you left the Army?"

"Yes. I had to come home, assume the estate duties. There isn't anyone else because my heir is a distant cousin, an authority on early Greek history, but knows nothing about running an estate. Neither did my father, nor did he care. He was besotted with ancient tomes. Returning Chadwick Park to prosperity will take considerable work."

"Why didn't you take an interest all along? Could you not have prevented the problem from reaching such an extreme?"

"I tried many times. My father wouldn't let me." Richard shredded another blade of grass. The silence deepened until he continued. "I was sixteen, just down from Eton when we had our first confrontation about the estate. I considered I had completed my education and wanted to tackle something more to my liking besides being my responsibility."

"He had other ideas?"

"Yes. He insisted I follow in his footsteps and read literature at Oxford. I was supposed to share his interest in rare books. I did read literature, but I went into the army for what turned out to be ten years. Over my mother's strenuous objections. She wanted me to get married. At one and twenty, mind you. Have you ever heard the like?"

She studied his face, noting the amazement that didn't quite hide the hurt. "Is marriage such an anathema?"

"At a reasonable age, no. I told her I might consider getting leg-shackled at one and thirty." He paused again. "Anyway, each time I went home, the situation was the same. The estate was deteriorating at an unbelievable pace, yet he wouldn't allow me to 'interfere.' That's his term. He almost had apoplexy the last time I mentioned it, so I didn't go home again until after his death."

Ainsley Park, the home to which she could never return, flashed into Judith's mind. Her pain was almost beyond bearing. He at least could occupy his home, no matter its condition. No one could take his rightful inheritance from him.

"So, you could say books are the reason the estate is in ruins. If they were books like those you and Mrs. Sherwood write, I could better understand— pleasurable reading—even if I didn't approve. Now, it's your turn."

Fifteen

Confession Time

Judith stared into the distance. She hadn't wanted ever again to remember what had brought her to this moment. She had resisted with her entire being, pushed away every thought—every vision—of her father as soon as it invaded but could not stop the memories no matter how she tried. Now, she took a deep breath and spoke in a monotone.

"My father died a few weeks ago. He was the Earl of Monford. My mother is the Catherine Ainsley, whom your sister mentioned. I don't have brothers or sisters. The present earl is my father's cousin and heir, Harold Ainsley."

She believed she had hidden her distress, yet a glance at Richard's face made her realize the choppy sentences had given her away. Struggling for control, her voice low, she said, "My father lied to me."

"Did he have a purpose?" Richard asked.

"Oh, yes, he had a purpose."

Facing him, Judith launched into the story. To her surprise, she found relief in the telling, after trying to bury her hurt for so long. After a moment of silence, she continued. "He planned to obtain a special license, then marry me off to an old man—his heir—on my twenty-first birthday. When I learned that, I decided to assert my independence at the same time. He died in France without knowing I had thwarted him."

"Did he travel to France often?"

"I don't know. He never discussed where he went or why."

"Without a doubt, your father's behaviour toward you was reprehensible—difficult to forgive—but don't allow his actions to make you bitter." He hesitated before continuing. "Would being closer to your mother help? You must realize I wonder why you don't live with her."

Judith shook her head. "There's no possibility. We were never close, not even during my early childhood. At my father's death, she made it clear we could not occupy the same house. She lives in her family home in Warminster."

Richard hesitated again before his next question. "Forgive my curiosity, but how do you manage to live? You said you received no inheritance, yet surely the Sherwoods would not have sufficient funds for three people."

"I outwitted my father." Gazing into the distance, she told how she accomplished such a feat.

"I inveigled a considerable amount of expensive jewelry from him: in my name, not the estate. I even cajoled furniture from him." A bleak smile crossed her face. "Father was ever generous with gifts, you see."

"The sale of those items hardly seems enough to support you for any length of time," Richard ventured.

"No," she agreed. "However, Father had always allowed me considerable leeway to learn estate matters, even encouraged me. He took my advice about sheep being a better investment than cattle. We were the first people we knew who owned a seeding machine and a thresher—both useful and less time-consuming—because of my insistence.

"I convinced him I should learn investments too. I listened to his business conferences. When I asked him for money to invest, he laughed but agreed. He even said he wouldn't interfere with me or quiz our solicitor. I repaid the original investment plus interest within six months. I was only sixteen."

After boasting, Judith studied Richard's face. Blank. No emotion. *He doesn't believe me. Typical man.*

"You see, I learned I could be devious too. It never occurred to him that I continued my investments. I deal in coal from Newcastle-on-Tyne, also Whitehaven, some cottage industries in Yorkshire, silks and tea from China, mahogany wood from the West Indies."

"Your ventures are widespread. Have you interests in our former North American colonies?"

"Not yet. I plan to trade with the rice growers in the Carolinas after our present difficulties with them are past. With Napoleon's defeat, Parliament can give undivided attention to North America and solve the problems one way or another. The shipping time will be much shorter than from the Orient."

"Have any of your investments failed?"

She grimaced. "Only one, but it was disastrous. I lost a ship when pirates from Mauritius captured one. Her sister ship escaped, returning loaded with spices and tea. I lost the ship, but worse, I lost the crew. Anytime I start thinking I'm infallible, I remind myself about pirates. I even sketched a picture of one, which I look at occasionally as a reminder."

When he didn't comment, she continued. "My wealth doesn't equal what I should have inherited, by any means. However, it enabled me to purchase the Manor where I maintain a comfortable independence."

"You own the Manor? I assumed Sherwood does."

Just like a man. Never give a female credit for any intelligence. "I own the Manor, purchased with my own funds. It's *mine.* Daniel is my agent, leaving Ainsley Park to come with me. Ruth is my cousin and has been my companion since she came to us when I was fourteen."

"I don't mean to question your veracity." He held up both hands, palms toward her. "Yet, I find it difficult to believe a female can excel in financial matters, let alone one so young."

"I did." Judith raised her chin—the chin her father had called stubborn but which she called determined. "I would have been a fool not to prepare for my independence. Devious, I admit, but a fool I'm not, nor anything like it."

"Do you advise Sherwood now?"

"Yes. The owner should always maintain control, else an unscrupulous agent could feather his own nest." To Judith's horror, she sounded just like her father. "Daniel would never steal from me, yet a wise owner maintains control. For the first weeks we were here, I stayed behind the scenes, mostly doing paperwork and tenant visits because the men couldn't, or wouldn't, accept that I knew anything about estate management."

"Your knowledge is unusual, is it not?"

"I suppose." Judith shrugged and glanced toward the sun. "I must return before Ruth gets worried."

Richard rode toward Longview Park, his thoughts in turmoil. Judith is the daughter who disappeared when her father died in France. She mentioned he passed away on one of his numerous trips. Were all of them to France? Was he a Napoleon sympathizer? Does tainted by treason account for her disappearance? But if Richard could believe her, hardly anyone even knew of her existence. He would ask people at Whitehall on his next London trip. Why did he care? Just curiosity, he assured himself.

How much had Lady Judith, which he must now remember to call her, exaggerated about her wealth and the way she amassed it? He'd heard the pain and bitterness behind her anger and had seen the way her face sharpened when she talked about her father. If she did even half what she claimed, he respected, even admired, her courage in breaking free. But could he believe her?

Richard remembered his childhood. He'd had no consolation from either parent, and Amelia had been so much older that her interests didn't include a young child. His only love had come from Nanny, who never stinted her hugs.

He cringed as he remembered his mother's showing her pretty little boy around the neighborhood. They invariably said he looked just like a little angel. Only Nanny's interference stopped her from dressing him in girls' clothing right up to school age. He, himself, had pulled the ruffles off his shirts until she finally gave up on having those made. She'd cried for two days when he sheared off his shoulder-length curls on his first holiday from school.

His thoughts returned to Lady Judith. She'd at least had her father's love and support throughout her life, even if for the wrong reason. Besides, Monford had permitted her to learn estate matters even if he did so, albeit again, for the wrong reason. She didn't realize her good fortune.

Yet, if Lady Judith is so capable and knows so much about estate management, can she also be as feminine as she obviously is? Look at his mother. She is the soul of femininity but has not a shred of business sense. How does a gentleman deal with a capable female? He would test Lady Judith within his limited knowledge, but when they next met, they were so busy laughing he forgot his intention.

With her teasing, Judith soon realized Richard's prettiness didn't matter. Truth to tell, she no longer considered him pretty. He was handsome with his sculptured features but not pretty, although she would never tell him. That would take too much fun out of her life.

"There's not a woman present who holds a candle to you, Your Grace," she informed him one evening at dinner with the Hinsons. "Are there any females in Town as pretty as you?"

He gave the matter judicious thought. "Hmmm, no I don't believe so. However, a new crop of young hopefuls invades the Marriage Mart every Season, so there's always the possibility one will challenge my supremacy."

"A remote possibility," she assured him, then turned to the gentleman on her right. She listened patiently when he launched into a recital of his prowess on the hunting field.

As she became better acquainted with the duke, Judith decided he was not even handsome. The day after teasing him about his prettiness, she experienced his scathing temper for the first time.

On an early morning ride, Judith saw a small child standing at the base of a tree, staring upwards. Dismounting, she kneeled beside him. "What's wrong, Roddy?"

He brushed away tears hovering on his eyelashes. "Missus, my kitten went up the tree. I can't climb high enough to get him."

"Ah yes, I see the mischievous creature." Yellow feline eyes gazed at her from an upper branch. "Don't fret, Roddy. I'll get the little rascal for you."

Leaning against a tree, she pulled off her riding boots and then climbed the tree, murmuring to the frightened kitten. She tucked him into the front of her jacket and descended until she almost reached the ground.

"What the devil are you doing?"

Judith lost her footing and tumbled toward the ground. Landing on her back, she struggled for air as she stared upward into Rochdale's scowling face. He was not pretty.

Judith scrambled to her feet and returned the squirming kitten to its master, who wasted no time leaving the arena to the sole use of the combatants. She tugged on her boots—bare feet having put her at a disadvantage. Then, she turned a furious frown toward Rochdale. "What do you mean, startling me like that?"

"What do you mean by climbing a tree? Young ladies do not climb trees, only hoydens. The cat would have come down in his own time."

The fact she knew he was right didn't help the situation. "That is not the point."

"No, the point is you could have broken your neck."

"My behaviour is not your concern. You have no right to shout at me. I will thank you not to interfere any further in my life." She led Gypsy to a nearby log, flung herself into the saddle, and, without adjusting her twisted skirts, rode away at a fast clip before he could reply.

Judith wished she could ride astride. She could get away much faster from the overbearing duke. Her father had never allowed that. She must always be a lady, he said. Otherwise, the estate hands might get too familiar. She reminded herself of his admonition but didn't change her actions when she slid off her mount without aid from the waiting groom. She flung the reins at him without uttering a word and stormed into the house.

Richard had made his opinion of her actions quite clear. She cringed at the memory of her words. That they had been the result of embarrassment didn't matter. She seemed to be in such a state anytime he came upon her unexpectedly. *Susanna, what can I do?*

Think before you act. Spontaneity can be good but also can be your worst enemy. At this moment, you're not angry with the duke. You're angry at yourself for having let him see you at a disadvantage.

I'm not angry at myself.

Consider your action for a moment, Judith. Helping Roddy was spontaneous without premeditation until someone you admire condemned your action. You're angry because you might have been wrong. You haven't allowed yourself to be spontaneous since you were fifteen.

I've had to think long and carefully about every single thing I've done since.

Yes, I've often been amazed at your consistent accomplishments. You've developed confidence in business affairs but not in your personal life. The lack lies at your father's door, but the remedy lies within you. Put your extraordinary mind toward controlling your tongue as a beginning. You should be confident about everything. Then you won't be as inclined to fret about others' perceptions.

Judith appreciated Susanna's advice but doubted she would ever reach that point.

After a troubled night, Judith sat in the rose garden, remembering her behaviour. Was she really a hoyden? Her father had often called her one but always with a laugh. Even if hoyden described her during childhood, she was the lady of the Manor now and should behave accordingly. Her mirror had told her she presented a ladylike appearance dressed in a pink-muslin morning gown with white bows decorating the bodice. Pink slippers peeped from the hem of her skirt, while a matching parasol shaded her from the damaging sun rays.

She glanced up at the sound of footsteps on the gravel.

"I apologize for raising my voice yesterday."

Richard lowered himself to the bench, turning sideways to face her. Taking her free hand in his, he answered, "No, no, I must apologize. You were correct. I had no right to berate you. I apologize for losing my temper. Can you forgive me?"

She nodded at the handsome apology and explained her behaviour. "I do know how to be a lady. I realize now my actions reflected poorly first on Nanny, then Mattie, which isn't fair. They taught me correct behaviour, and Ruth continued."

"Mattie. Your governess perhaps?"

"Yes, Miss Matthews. Father decreed I was too old for Nanny when I reached seven. I resented his decision but soon realized Mattie was fun too. She taught me until Ruth joined us. I was fourteen then. He found Mattie another place as a governess, so I lost track of her whereabouts. She would be horrified that I could behave so despicably."

"Let's forget that episode—pretend we didn't even meet yesterday," he suggested with a chuckle and was rewarded with an impish grin, which should have warned him.

"You do realize anyone as pretty as you should also behave in a ladylike manner. What do you have to say for yourself?"

With twitching lips, he pondered his answer, then confided in a whisper, "My parents failed in their duty. You see, I grew up without the refining guidance of a governess."

"Yes, I can see you were neglected shamefully, Your Grace," she teased. "However, it's never too late to mend your ways."

"I will strive to do better."

They talked for several more minutes before he rose to leave. She watched him ride away, a smile on her face. Their time together had been a pleasant interlude. No more quarrels with Richard, she vowed.

Her vow lasted less than a day.

The morning began pleasantly enough. Judith made good progress with the story, then spent an hour in the rose garden with Ruth, agreeing the bushes were the healthiest she'd ever seen, the blooms were the largest ever, their aroma the sweetest. After luncheon, she decided to spend the early afternoon with Hope Hinson, promising she would return for tea.

Judith never reached Longview Park.

Near the boundary, the murmur of a moving stream attracted her. Following a whim, she led Gypsy off the trail through some silver-birch trees and looped the mare's reins over a limb. The brook appeared shallow. Pulling off boots and jacket, she lifted the hem of her riding habit and stepped into the water. Cold. She soon grew accustomed to the temperature, delighting in the water sloshing around her ankles as she wiggled her toes.

Lost in her pleasure, she did not hear a horse's footsteps until a harsh voice demanded,

"What the devil are you doing now?"

Startled, she lost her footing, landing in the water. Staring upward into the duke's wrathful face, she chuckled. "I'm wading. At least I was. Now I'm sitting in the water."

"What a cork-brained thing to do! Have you been at Sherwood's brandy? No young lady would . . ."

"I knew it! I knew you would prose on about young ladies." Her chuckles turned into robust laughter.

Scowling at her, he swung down from his horse, dropped the reins, then strode to the bank's edge. "Lady Judith, get up from there this instant."

"All right." Stifling her hilarity, she attempted to rise. Unfortunately, she stepped on the hem of her riding skirt and went down, face first this time. Lifting her face above water, she lay there overcome with mirth.

"Get up, I said. *Get up.*"

Still laughing, she struggled into a sitting position.

He closed his eyes for a moment. "Take my hand."

Mischief won. She jerked his hand, causing him to land beside her.

He sat up, speechless with rage. Regaining his feet, he unceremoniously hauled her up the bank and settled her on her feet. Gripping her shoulders, he he struggled to control his anger. "Just look at yourself. You're indecent!"

Glancing downward at the clinging muslin shirt, she reached for her jacket. "It's your fault for startling me. You shouldn't have been spying on me either. I was right in the beginning—you're a spy."

"Acquit me of spying, you ninny. I heard someone laughing like a Bedlamite, so I came to investigate."

They glared at each other until Judith's sense of humor reasserted itself. She let her eyes rove from his head to his boots and back again. "I'm not the only one who is drenched, so you sit on that side of the tree while I sit on this side. I won't see your frowns while our clothing dries."

Judith sat on her chosen side, wrung out her skirt, and spread it to dry. She smothered her laughter when he muttered a word ladies shouldn't understand. She hadn't spent so much time around farmhands without learning a thing or two.

Judith would not quarrel with him or allow him to ruin her good spirits. Brandy had nothing to do with her behaviour. The day was nice, and splashing in the water pleasant. Perhaps she should be embarrassed. She wasn't.

They sat without speaking, hearing only insects buzzing, which almost lulled Judith to sleep. When the front of her riding habit was reasonably dry, she rolled over to her abdomen and spread the skirt out again. Peeping around the tree, she met his scowling gaze.

"Still in a huff, I see," she announced with a gurgle. "I will apologize to you now, Rochdale, and you don't need to apologize for startling me."

"No matter what you say, I'm convinced you *have* been at Sherwood's brandy. That's the only possible explanation for your behaviour." His lips twitched. "You truly are incorrigible."

"Am I?" she asked. "The wading was truly quite pleasant—shall we do it again?"

His laughter filled the air, leaving him prone on the ground gasping for control.

Satisfied he was no longer angry, Judith tugged on her boots, then glanced down at herself, shaking her head. "I can't visit Hope looking like this, so I'll go home now. Such a pity because I quite wanted to see her."

Gazing at him, still prone on the ground, she said, "I trust you won't come to grief over your wetting, my lord Duke."

His chuckles followed her as she rode away.

Once out of his presence, Judith tried to put him from her mind without success. She wondered what her father would think of him. He probably wouldn't approve because Richard would be much too young. She fought bitterness overwhelming her until Susanna intervened.

Judith, can you not see that your continued anger toward your father is childish? Anger accomplishes nothing but upsets you more.

I'm in turmoil too often. Why am I not more like Ruth? She's always serene. Shouldn't I have absorbed some serenity during these years with her?

You had much on your mind throughout most of those years, which excuses you to an extent, but you must think beyond yourself. Your peace comes from within, if you will only accept it."

Two days of persistent rain kept Judith indoors. She told herself it was good for the crops. She told herself being unable to ride was conducive to working on her book. What could be more interesting?

The rain numbed her brain. She needed something to stimulate her thought process. Judith considered ordering a tea tray but decided no beverage was strong enough. A quarrel with Richard would do the trick. She would welcome the opportunity to apologize again.

Upon hearing the doorknocker, Judith hurried into the drawing room, where she seated herself on a small sofa. When the butler announced the visitor, she greeted him with a smile. "Your Grace, please join me. I was this moment thinking a quarrel with you would enliven my existence beyond all recognition."

"You're getting so good at apologizing too," he murmured as he sketched a bow.

A footman bearing a tea tray followed Ruth and Daniel into the room. Ruth greeted Rochdale. "Good afternoon, Your Grace. We're pleased you ventured out on such a dismal day."

"Thank you, Mrs. Sherwood." Turning toward Daniel, he asked, "How are you bearing up being shut in the house with two females?"

Daniel's laughter drowned out the ladies' protests. "In the interest of maintaining a peaceful household, I will refrain from answering."

They spent a cheerful hour over tea, touching on estate matters.

"Rochdale, don't get Daniel started talking about sheep, I implore you!" Ruth cast a glance of pure mischief at her husband, who complained he didn't understand why females found sheep boring.

"Now it's my turn to evade answering," Rochdale said as he rose. "I leave for Wiltshire tomorrow where I must deal with estate matters—not necessarily sheep, although I will confer with my agent about the possibility of adding them and decide for myself whether they're boring. I'll call on you when I return, if I may."

With a slight curtsy, Judith hid her disappointment and pointed out, "A whole hour in your presence, Rochdale. I can hardly credit that I have no reason to apologize."

"We wouldn't want you to get out of practice, so apologize anyway." On a note of laughter, he bowed himself out of the room.

Judith excused herself and returned to the writing room, her mood better than when she'd left it. The conversation in the drawing room would have surprised her.

<> <> <> <> <>

Daniel stood in silence at the window until the duke's carriage started down the drive. "I believe Rochdale might be developing an interest in Judith. Do you agree?"

"I hope you're right. He would be an excellent match for her, unless you've learned something about him which I don't know."

"I asked Hinson a few casual questions. He's enthusiastic about Rochdale. They were schoolboys together and remained friends."

"The problem is her reaction to him. They quarrel so much."

"Sometimes that's the way love happens until a couple recognizes their true feelings," Daniel reminded her. "We were fortunate not to go through that phase."

"We were fortunate, indeed, my love. Judith isn't giving any thought to marriage though. She must first learn to trust a man enough to admit him into her life. I don't believe that will happen so soon after gaining her independence, which still enthralls her."

"She worked so long and hard to reach this point, she will think equally long and hard before relinquishing her freedom."

"Considering how the earl treated her, I shouldn't be concerned with what he might like or dislike—nonetheless, I am." Ruth had long since told Daniel of the infamous document which the earl had executed, including Judith's comments about her father's illogical thinking. "I believe, if he were thinking about Ainsley Park with a clear head, he would approve of the duke."

"I can't imagine his not doing so, although he was quite the autocrat. However, it's certainly early days to consider a match for Judith."

Ruth nodded her agreement. "In some ways she's mature far beyond her years, yet in others she's quite the opposite."

If the drawing-room conversation would have surprised Judith, Rochdale's thoughts as he rode away would have horrified Ruth and Daniel.

The rain had stopped. Richard could see blue sky through the carriage window. His thoughts dwelled on Judith. Lovely, lively, and possessing a good sense of humor, she would make an excellent mistress. He couldn't remember when he last enjoyed a woman's company as much as he enjoyed being with her. Even her ordinary conversation far surpassed any female he knew. When he was with her, no other face intruded. But set up an earl's innocent daughter as his mistress? He could put such an idea out of his head. His ancestors would spin in their graves, to say nothing about what Sherwood would do to him. He would be lucky if he didn't join his ancestors in short order. Pistols at dawn, or some such thing.

Sixteen

Somewhere in France

"*Monsieur*, you're awake at last! I must call Henri."

The old man gazed at her. She didn't look familiar, he decided, as she hurried out the door, but he'd heard her voice before. Soon, a man entered the small room. He didn't look familiar either.

"We're so happy you're awake, Monsieur. Please tell us who you are, so we can contact your family."

Beyond doubt, they were French and well-spoken, not the peasants the attic would indicate. The old man looked from one happy face toward the other and back. He'd been awake for some time, puzzling over his circumstances. Who was he? Where was he? Why was he too weak to sit up? He'd eyed the chamber pot in the corner but knew he couldn't reach it on his own. It was best he kept uncertainties to himself for a moment.

"Why am I in your attic, if you don't know me?"

Henri spoke slowly. "I found you lying unconscious in the mud near here. I didn't want to leave you for Napoleon's ragtag soldiers to find, so I brought you to our home." He hesitated. "You have the appearance of an Anglo, but I haven't known of any in this area for several years and don't know why an Anglo would be here. You speak impeccable French, so perhaps I'm wrong about your appearance."

The old man realized he must trust them, but what would happen once they knew his mental condition? He would risk their knowing—no other choice. "My brain is muddled for some reason. I don't know who I am."

They glanced at each other and then stared openmouthed at him. Henri spoke. "You had a knot on your head when I found you. Perhaps that accounts for your memory problem."

"Yes, that might account for it."

"We'll keep you here while you regain your strength. Then perhaps your brain will function again."

"Thank you," the old man murmured, then glanced at the woman. "Perhaps your lady will leave the room so you can give me some personal attention."

"Yes. Marie, please close the door behind you."

A few minutes later, the old man lay back down on the hard mattress. "I'm so tired."

He drifted into sleep, unaware when the man left the attic.

Seventeen

Judith Deals with Her Mother

"Ruthie?" Judith hadn't uttered a word since sitting down at the breakfast table. After telling Richard about her mother a few days earlier, Lady Monford had intruded into her thoughts daily, and Judith couldn't push the thoughts away no matter how hard she tried. "I want to visit Warminster. I need to see Mama. Will you go with me, please? She would certainly have something to say if I went with only Alice as chaperone, would she not?"

"She most assuredly would." After a glance at Daniel, Ruth said, "Yes, I'll go. Do you have a day in mind?"

"Is tomorrow morning too soon?" Judith turned toward Daniel. "We will be gone only a few days, I promise."

With their reassurances ringing in her ears, Judith left the room but glanced back. They were absorbed with each other. A twinge of longing surprised her. Sometimes when she saw them together, the emptiness of her own life and the need for love overwhelmed her. She blinked away tears that misted her eyes as she sought the privacy of her sitting room. There, she stared out the window for a long moment and then resolutely picked up a book of Shakespeare sonnets. Reading them didn't help.

Early the following morning, Judith entered their carriage with thoughts fluctuating between eagerness to see her mother and the fear Lady Monford would not welcome her. Throughout her life, her father had consumed Judith's time and thoughts, leaving little for her mother. Now, since so many miles separated them, she needed to see her, hear her voice. The ache to do so almost overwhelmed Judith at times, considering how little she had ever thought about her mother's attention.

When the carriage rolled into Warminster, Judith stared out the carriage window. She had been a young child on her only visit here. A village then, now it was a small town.

"I came here only once, although Mama came a few times. This was her favorite place, which I never understood. How could she prefer this to Ainsley Park?"

Ruth hesitated over her answer. "Perhaps she enjoyed the people rather than the place. Remember, this was her home, every road and lane familiar to her, which I imagine added to her pleasure. She must have found Ainsley Park intimidating after living her entire life in an ordinary-sized house."

"Yes, I can appreciate her opinion now, because the estate is huge by comparison. There were no near neighbors at Ainsley Park either. Mama would have enjoyed having ladies to visit. Still, her attitude didn't make sense when I was a child."

The coach stopped before a small brick house of no exact style, probably less than a hundred years old. The windowpanes sparkled in the sunlight. The doorknocker was bright from polishing.

The door opened, revealing a butler, who stared down his nose and inquired their business.

"I am Lady Judith Ainsley. Please inform my mother of my presence."

"Yes, my lady. Come this way, if you will." He escorted them to a small sitting room, then bowed himself from the room.

His demeanor had changed but not before Judith saw the flash of surprise in his eyes. Did he not know of her existence?

Judith hid her nervousness by gazing around the room, recognizing the furniture from the small parlor at Ainsley Park, which had been her mother's favorite room. She remembered the worn Turkey carpet from her previous visit. Her small hands had not been up to the task of holding a cup. The chocolate stain was not visible, but her mother's displeasure remained an unpleasant memory. She grimaced when she recognized the Meissen shepherdess sitting on the mantelshelf. Her mother hadn't allowed her to touch the porcelain figurine.

"What are you doing here?" Lady Monford's voice startled her daughter. It was just as well Judith had resisted the temptation to pick up the shepherdess. Without a doubt, she would have dropped it.

"Hello, Mama. I came to see how you are, whether you found everything here satisfactory after it stood empty for so many years." She took a steadying breath. "You didn't answer my letter."

"Why should I answer your letter?" Lady Monford asked. She continued standing in the open door, offering no hospitality to her only child.

Judith flinched but smoothed her features into a calmness she had faked since learning of her father's duplicity. She glanced at a chair and back to her mother's face, saying nothing.

Lady Monford had the grace to blush, but she spoke without hesitation. "I expect guests in a few moments, so I cannot offer you refreshments. How long will you be in Warminster?"

"We would like to explore the area, so perhaps a few days."

"Surely you don't expect to stay here?" Apparently seeing the affirmation in her daughter's face, she became firm. "No. Staying here is not possible. You should know without my saying that you are not welcome in my house. This *is* my house, you will recall. Mine."

Judith believed she had come to terms with the fact her mother possessed not a single maternal instinct. She was wrong. The hurt of no embraces from her mother during early childhood came back in a flood. Perhaps that was why she had adored her father, who never stinted on his affection. Memories of being tossed into the air and caught by his strong arms sustained her in this moment.

"Yes, Mama, I am aware this is your house." She took a deep breath. "I had hoped we could spend some time together. I recognize I'm much to blame for our not being close. For that, I apologize."

Something flickered in her mother's eyes, then was gone. Regret? Hope?

Accept the obvious. She isn't ready to accept a change in your relationship, yet I believe someday she will. Meanwhile, her behaviour doesn't reflect on you. Trust me.

Thankful for Susanna's support, Judith touched Ruth's arm and stepped toward the open door. Turning to her mother, she said, "Perhaps in time, we can remedy the situation between us. I would like nothing better."

Lady Monford didn't speak when the butler opened the door.

Pausing outside the coach, Judith veiled her eyes with her long lashes. "We cannot return to East Leah today. On the drive into town, we passed the Old Bell Hotel. Take us there, please."

Sitting in the coach, she struggled to subdue her emotions. Her old life was finished. Her father was dead, and her mother was out of her life by choice. She pushed away the hurt. *Susanna, will I ever stop needing Mama?*

Perhaps someday.

I'm being impatient again, aren't I?

Yes, but you're learning to curb it, which is good. Everything will work out for you someday. Trust me.

Judith heaved a silent sigh. Accepting anything she didn't want had always been difficult for her.

She had regained her composure and presented a serene face to the proprietor when they reached the hotel. A few minutes later, seated in a private sitting room, sipping tea, she managed a smile at her friend.

"I made the mistake of hoping Mama would change her attitude if we were not under the same roof."

Again, Ruth hesitated, choosing words carefully. "Lady Monford might need more time to experience her independence. She's been here only a short time after decades of submission to Lord Monford's rules. I shouldn't think she ever found that easy. I can hope for the future. However, we're here, so we might as well enjoy ourselves with whatever the area offers."

Their spirits lightened by the reviving brew, the ladies descended to the street, leaving Alice unpacking their baggage.

There was little of interest. Judith again remarked she couldn't understand why her mother wanted to live here. "I admit I'm not familiar with small towns, or towns of any size, except East Leah. Still, this is where Mama wants to live."

"This was her childhood home," Ruth reminded her. "She must have happy memories of neighborhood parties, church activities, friends her age. I imagine there was excitement when the coaches arrived at the hotel. Little girls would enjoy seeing ladies from other places and dream of someday traveling in those same coaches to exotic places."

"I suppose this is a stop on the main coach road between London and Exeter."

"You do know some geography," Ruth said with a grin. "Now let's test your architectural knowledge. Tell me about the church."

"The tower is square. From its location, I will guess William the Conqueror . . . what else did you call him?"

"William of Normandy. Go on."

". . . built the church in a cruciform design, although I don't know how people could know unless they climb the tree at its corner." Judith cast a sideways glance toward Ruth. "Or perhaps they could sprout wings and fly like a bird."

"With that bit of nonsense, I suggest we return to the hotel."

Judith's light mood didn't last. Throughout the evening, she was gay one moment, deep in depression the next.

To divert Judith's thoughts from Lady Monford, Ruth suggested they visit Bath for a few days.

Judith's uncomprehending stare was her only reply.

"Why should we not?" her companion persisted. "I know you're in mourning, but Bath is a quiet place. I understand a lot of ladies in mourning go there as an alternative to London."

"Could we go into Society?"

"We couldn't attend dances, of course, but there must be concerts."

"I'm almost sure I heard there is a theatre there too." Nodding her head, Judith continued. "We will leave first thing tomorrow."

Ruth sent a messenger to the Manor. Perhaps Daniel could join them for a few days.

The chimes of the centuries-old Abby greeted their coach when they reached Bath.

"If memory serves, my governess said Bath has been described as England's prettiest city," Judith said.

"I can well believe it."

They inched their way through town, admiring the wide avenues and crescents, and then they arranged for accommodations at the Pelican Hotel for a few days. There, they remained in their sitting room only long enough for tea before venturing forth to inspect the town.

"We must see Sydney Gardens." Ruth's excitement was palpable when they crossed the Pulteney Bridge.

Judith turned an innocent smile toward her. "Are there roses?"

Ruth made a sound suspiciously like a snort. "I imagine so, among many other interesting plants."

They spent an hour wandering in the gardens—yes, there were roses. "Oh, Judith, look at this one, the pinkish edging on the white bloom! And the pink with the deeper pink throats. I've never even seen pictures of them."

"I wonder if you can ask for cuttings here." Judith looked around for a gardener.

"I wouldn't think so, but perhaps I'll find them closer to home."

After they reluctantly left the rose gardens, they visited the grottos and managed to lose themselves in a labyrinth. They were helpless with laughter when a gentleman dressed in dull brown from beaver hat to boots approached them.

"Ladies, may I assist you?

Wiping their eyes, they assured him they could find their way out, but perhaps he would be so kind as to point the way. He guided them toward the exit, doffed his hat, and watched them leave.

A quiet evening followed dinner in their private parlor.

"The first thing tomorrow morning, we must enter our names in the books at the Assembly Rooms, Ruthie. A visit to the Pump Room is also desirable, according to my governess. Mattie said these visits were the highlight of their stay in Bath when she was a governess with another family."

Their days settled into a routine. After breakfast, they visited the Pump Room for an hour where they partook of tea rather than the improving waters, after seeing the facial expressions of people who sipped but then surreptitiously dumped the rest of the water.

Later, they strolled along Milsom Street, making a few purchases, then browsed the circulating library, although they didn't have time for reading. Late afternoon found them having tea in the Upper Assembly Rooms, after which they ate dinner in their private sitting room.

On Wednesday evening, they returned to the Upper Assembly Rooms for a concert. Ruth had hesitated over evening activities without a male escort, but they learned other ladies were unescorted by gentlemen.

Chatting over teacups in the Pump Room, Judith became aware of scrutiny. They'd met agreeable people everywhere they went, but no one had paid particular attention to them. Now glancing around, she met the somber eyes of the gentleman who had led them from the labyrinth. He averted his gaze, and she returned to her conversation. She saw him again that evening in the Assembly Rooms, then at the Pump Room on the following morning. Each time he stared at her with solemn intent.

"Ruthie, are you aware we have a shadow?"

"A shadow? No, I had not noticed. Whom do you mean?"

"The gentleman who rescued us in Sydney Gardens seems to be everywhere we go."

"Bath is a small place, after all."

They made his acquaintance the same evening at a small dinner given by some new friends, Mr. and Mrs. Simpson.

"Mrs. Sherwood, Miss Ainsley, may I present Sir Ronald Foster? Sir Ronald, these ladies are visiting from East Leah."

Sir Ronald bowed toward Mrs. Sherwood before turning his gaze on Miss Ainsley. "A pleasure to make your acquaintance. Are you in Bath long?"

"Only a few days, I believe."

With the introduction made, the ladies found they had a male escort, whether they wanted one or not. Sir Ronald was always at their disposal. He assured them he enjoyed shopping expeditions above all things. He found browsing through the shelves at the circulating library most educational. Nothing pleased him more than strolling through the various city gardens. He even had an answer to every botanical question Ruth could conjure.

Saturday afternoon, the ladies sat in their private sitting room considering their situation. The days here had eased Judith's hurt. When her mother invaded her thoughts, she shoved the image away. They had now been away from the Manor for more than a week and were giving serious consideration to a return. Sir Ronald's constant prosing had become a bore.

"I know we don't travel on the Sabbath, Ruthie, but shall we go home on Monday?"

"Aren't we promised to dinner, followed by a musical presentation with Madame Biazzi Monday evening?"

Judith grimaced. On her own accord, she would have avoided the engagement. She cared little for music but reminded herself Ruth enjoyed it, especially Italian singers. Madame Biazzi had insisted they hear her protégé, a recent arrival from Venice. "I had overlooked that, but yes, we are. Then shall we leave first thing on Tuesday morning?"

With the agreement made, they dressed for dinner with Sir Ronald and his mother, another engagement they had been unable to avoid. The evening was a disaster. Judith had a difficult time eating the poorly prepared food. A dread she might disgrace herself at the dining table invaded her thoughts. She soon decided she didn't care if she did. Giving her opinion would serve that woman right.

'That woman' was Sir Ronald's mother, who showed her hostility from the moment of introduction. "*Miss* Ainsley, is it? My son hobnobs with nobility. A mere 'Miss' is beneath his notice."

"Now, Mother," Sir Ronald admonished. "I don't believe you intend rudeness toward our guests."

"The Honourable Penelope Farnsworth has shown him marked attention."

"Now, Mother."

Distaste crossed his face. The Honourable Penelope Farnsworth poked out in front, and her feet splayed outward when she walked.

"You appear to be on the shelf already."

His frustration obviously increasing, Sir Ronald tried to change the subject to no avail because his mother ignored him.

"You're probably trying to snare a wealthy man. You should try the Cits."

"Mother, you really should not . . ."

"You don't look healthy to me, too thin by far, terrible for breeding."

"Mother!" Sir Ronald's face turned red. "You go too far!"

With a glance at Ruth after the first insult, Judith sat with clenched teeth, but enough was enough by any standards. She would give this old harridan the dressing down she deserved. Judith opened her mouth but closed it when Susanna entered her mind. *Calm yourself. Politeness will serve you better. Trust me.*

Judith changed her words. "We should leave."

She rose and started toward the door.

"Ma'am, this has been an unusual evening, to say the least." Ruth's voice left no doubt about her disgust. "Good-bye."

Sir Ronald had not moved from his chair. Fluttering his hands, he said, "No, no, ladies, please don't leave! You must understand my mother is quite elderly. She doesn't always mind her tongue."

Judith glared at him. "We are leaving now. Will you order your carriage, or shall I?"

He requested a footman to send for the carriage. He stood beside the ladies at the open front door, then helped them into the carriage, expecting to enter after them. Judith shut the door in his face.

"We don't need your escort, Sir Ronald. We will be safe with your coachman."

"But, ladies . . ."

"I don't care to be insulted further this evening." Judith knocked on the roof. "Coachman! Drive on."

She fumed all the way to the hotel, ignoring Ruth's excuses for the woman who feared losing her son.

On Monday afternoon, they visited the Assembly rooms for one last tea. They were chatting with the Simpsons when Sir Ronald joined them, a smile on his face. Judith swallowed her surprise. His audacity was beyond belief. Nevertheless, she pasted an interested expression on her face. She let her gaze wander until she encountered blazing green eyes glaring at her from the doorway. Her heart skipped a beat, then settled down to its normal rhythm.

Why was the Duke of Rochdale here? And why was he in a temper? Was he going to badger her again? Judith stiffened her spine.

Eighteen

Contretemps in Bath

"Bath? What are Lady Judith and Mrs. Sherwood doing there?"

Richard had been at Chadwick Park for several days, consulting with the Guthries—father and son. Then, avoiding his mother's machinations for his future, he returned to East Leah.

"They went to visit Lady Judith's mother in Warminster." Daniel handed him Ruth's note detailing their encounter with Lady Monford.

Scanning the few lines, Richard's mouth tightened. "I knew Lady Judith and her mother were not close, yet, surely, she could have welcomed her child. What is wrong with that woman?"

"I only know from observation and the few things my wife has told me. I believe Lady Monford has never given a reason for her antipathy toward her daughter. However, I would venture to guess jealousy is the root cause." He hesitated a moment. "Has Judith told you anything about her father?"

"She revealed his perfidy, yes. How parents could treat their child the way they treated her is beyond my understanding."

"He spent considerably more time with his daughter than his wife. Also, his various liaisons over the years were common knowledge. Lady Monford came close to being a recluse, avoiding embarrassment in the neighborhood. I doubt she could call anyone a friend. If he had offspring from any of those liaisons, at least they didn't arrive at the door with demands."

"That's a blessing in itself."

Daniel nodded. "The earl had maintained total control over Lady Judith, commanding all her time and attention, so she didn't have friends either, thereby leaving no mothers to befriend Lady Monford. I suppose that combination contributes to her attitude. You see, his peccadilloes never interfered with his attention to his daughter—only his wife, thus her jealousy."

"Yes, I can see Lady Monford might want to erase most things about her previous life, but, her *daughter*?"

"Such behaviour in a mother boggles the mind, I agree," Daniel said.

A few minutes later, Richard took his leave. He would visit Bath for a few days, then escort the ladies home. His plans came to an abrupt halt when he met the Hinsons over dinner.

"I can see you have news, so don't keep us waiting!" Tom grinned at his wife. "Own up to what you've done, whatever it is."

She flushed rosily but answered readily enough. "The evening is all set. There will be twenty-four sitting down to dinner. Isn't that marvelous? I haven't decided on any type of entertainment, but we could set out card tables if conversation seems to lag."

"When is the great occasion, my dear?"

"This Friday. I'm so excited I hardly know whether I'm on my head or my feet." She turned toward Richard. "We canceled the dinner dance we scheduled a few weeks ago because the cook came down with an ailment. I do hope everyone stays healthy for this."

"How splendid! Is this for a particular occasion, an anniversary, perhaps?"

"Oh, no, Rochdale, this is for you. I started planning the dinner when you first came to visit us. Judith could not attend a dance, since she's in mourning, but she can come to this dinner. She and Mrs. Sherwood are due back from Warminster on Thursday, so the dinner is perfect timing."

"Ah. You haven't heard they went to Bath for a few days before returning home. Sherwood doesn't know when they will arrive."

Hope turned toward her husband. "I didn't know. Tom, what shall we do?"

"You will have the dinner just as you planned, my dear. I, too, will be disappointed if they're not here, but canceling again would be the height of rudeness. You must see that."

Richard suppressed a sigh, but his innate good manners asserted themselves. "You've planned a marvelous dinner, I'm sure. I quite look forward to being here. Besides, who knows? The ladies might return by Friday."

"Perhaps they will. Even if they don't, we will have another dinner later." She cast an impish glance at her husband, who raised his eyes heavenward, drawing a laugh from their guest.

If he were honest, Richard would have to admit he enjoyed the dinner in his honour on Friday evening. There was not one giggling schoolgirl present. There were, however, several mature ladies presented for his inspection. Thinking over the evening later, he realized two things. The ladies did not appeal to his senses, and none possessed one iota of humour. They didn't have blue eyes either.

Early on Monday, he turned his phaeton toward Bath. In late afternoon, he arranged for rooms at York House and changed his attire before making his way toward the Assembly Rooms where he expected to locate the ladies.

Richard lingered in the doorway surveying the crowded room. Lady Judith sat at a table, engrossed in a man whom he could only describe as middle-aged and bordering on portly. The man dressed plainly, all in somber brown. He never burdened himself with rings or fobs or other jewelry with which some of his friends adorned themselves. Nevertheless, he always dressed the way a gentleman should, in his estimation. He prided himself on accomplishing this, despite his friends' efforts to change him. What could Lady Judith see in the nonentity leaning toward her?

Richard knew the young bucks of East Leah clustered around Judith—how could they resist her?—but Richard considered them mere pups. He could smile at their antics. This man was not a pup. Without a doubt, he was pulling the wool over the ladies' eyes. They were innocent, too inexperienced to recognize thatch-gallows. Therefore, he must protect them.

He didn't realize he was glaring when he met Judith's smiling face. He made his way in her direction, determined to extricate them without further ado. He stood staring at Sir Ronald before that gentleman became aware of his presence.

Judith's innate composure rose to the occasion. "Your Grace, it's a pleasure to see you. May I present Sir Ronald Forest and Mr. and Mrs. Simpson? Mrs. Simpson and gentlemen, may I introduce the Duke of Rochdale?"

Mrs. Simpson rushed into speech. "Your Grace, it's such a pleasure to make your acquaintance. I've heard mention of you from my cousin, whom you probably know, Mrs. Blanche Rutledge. Her husband is a businessman, and they run in the best circles." She raised her eyebrows, anticipating his answer but rushed on when he ignored her. "My cousin knows the *haute ton*. She writes me volumes, simply *volumes*, about the goings-on in High Society."

The Duke of Rochdale was a gentleman, easygoing and polite. However, at times fools drove him too far. This was one of those occasions. First, he had located the woman he had driven miles to see, only to find her absorbed with a complete cipher. Making matters worse, this gabblemonger was prattling on about someone he neither knew nor cared to know. Enough was enough.

"Madam, I have no knowledge of Mrs. Rutledge, nor do I care to have any knowledge of her. Now, if you will excuse us, I desire conversation with these ladies." He ushered his ladies from the room, basely ignoring Mr. Simpson yet directing a furious glare toward Sir Ronald.

"Ladies, how could you be so ill-advised as to be in company with toadeaters?" Not waiting for a reply, he grasped an arm of each, rushing them into the street, tightening his grip when Judith stumbled twice. "Where are you staying? I will escort you there."

"We're at the Pelican," Judith replied.

He glanced around to get his bearings, then turned and crossed the road, leaving a carriage driver shouting in his effort to control his horse.

"We don't require your escort, Rochdale," Judith informed him. "We walk that short distance daily,"

"Unescorted? Mrs. Sherwood, I expected better from you, even if not from Lady Judith." He marched them down the street in silence which persisted until they reached the Pelican. There, Judith dismissed him with a brief word of thanks.

He refused the dismissal. "Do you have a private sitting room? This conversation does not need, nor should have, an audience."

<> <> <> <> <>

Appalled at the scene developing in their sitting room, Judith sat in stunned silence while the duke reviled them for going about unescorted in Bath. Such careless, nay foolhardy, behaviour was more than he could understand. He interrupted his tirade when Ruth pointed out Sir Ronald had been escorting them.

"That's another thing. Where did you meet him? Who introduced him? Who is he? Did you inquire into his ancestry?"

Judith fumed in silence, striving to hold her temper. She'd been happy to see Richard at the Assembly Rooms. Her first thought had been she would enjoy exploring Bath with him. The trip home would be more pleasant if he escorted them. However, the idea died when he strode toward them with disapproval revealed in every line of his frame. Now this catechism passed all bounds. She would tell him so.

"What does our business have to do with you?" She rose and strode toward the door. "You're nothing to us. You have no authority over us. Daniel knows where Ruth is. If he perceived a problem with her being here without his escort, he would be here."

"But . . ."

Judith did not pause for breath. "I will have you know no one has any authority over me. I will not tolerate your ordering me about and criticizing my behaviour. This is our sitting room, not yours. Please leave." She opened the door and stood back, waiting for him to go.

He did, slamming the door behind him.

Judith paced the room, ranting about his nerve. Just who did he think he was, criticizing them, treating them so shabbily and in public too? She'd never been so humiliated as when he dragged them out of the crowded Assembly Room. It's a nine-day wonder she didn't break an ankle being hustled along the uneven roadway, nearly getting stomped on by several horses. Ordering them around, calling their intelligence into question. His arrogance knew no bounds. She rubbed her arm where he'd clasped it.

"Now do you understand why I come to cuffs with him so often? This is only a small sample of the autocratic behaviour he directs toward me almost every time we meet. This time you see it for yourself, literally placing our lives in danger."

"Yes, I can see why you are much tried with him. I admit his behaviour passed all bounds of a gentleman." Several minutes passed before Ruth calmed her into coherence. "Judith, we must dress for dinner with Madame Biazzi. We will offend her if we arrive late and in a frenzy."

"I don't believe I can bear seeing company this evening, Ruthie. Can we send our excuses?"

"Do you want the duke to control our movements?"

"Never!" Judith sat down and composed herself with deep breaths.

You gave your temper free rein again.

Judith mentally cringed at the reproof. *Will I ever learn?*

I don't see into the future, but you can learn to think before you speak. The ability to control your tongue and consider your words is part of maturity.

Why don't you remind me before I open my mouth?

That isn't my responsibility. Now get dressed for the musical evening.

Judith didn't expect to enjoy the evening and was surprised when she realized later that she had. The dinner was intimate with only a dozen people at the table, so talk was general. During the meal, a violinist played in the background, which lulled her into an acquiescent frame of mind. This lasted until the after-dinner guests arrived for the entertainment.

The first person to arrive was Sir Ronald. "Good evening, Mrs. Sherwood, Miss Ainsley." He bowed over their hands, holding Judith's a moment longer than was proper before she tugged it away.

She murmured something—she knew not what.

"Miss Ainsley, I must ask you a question. Is the Duke of Rochdale always so rude? I could not believe my own eyes when he dragged—yes, *dragged*—you ladies from the Assembly Rooms. I must tell you that everyone there stared. Does he have some authority over you?"

Judith struggled for calmness, her quiescent mood destroyed. "No, he has no authority over either of us. He is an acquaintance only."

She took a steadying breath and greeted others. She hoped he would find a seat elsewhere. She breathed more easily when Madame Biazzi led Sir Ronald across the room where she seated him with a lady who started chattering.

The musicale didn't compare with their evening at the Royal Opera House in London, nor did Judith expect it would. The music was pleasant, though, and Judith's nerves settled again.

Upon their return to the Pelican, they found Daniel waiting for them in the lobby. After a joyous greeting, he joined them in the ladies' private sitting room.

"I couldn't wait any longer to see you, my dear." He slipped an arm around his wife's shoulders. "I decided to join you here for whatever time you remain, then escort you ladies home."

Judith had been pensive during their return to the Pelican Hotel. Just think! She had begun to find the arrogant Rochdale a pleasant companion. How wrong could anyone be? Sir Ronald, on the other hand, was different. She couldn't imagine ever considering him a pleasant companion.

She couldn't stay in Bath another day. "I'm going home tomorrow. The two of you can do as you please."

With that statement, she went into her bedchamber and closed the door.

Susanna glared from her perch on the footboard of Judith's bed. The angel's task with this recalcitrant human had never been easy, like some of her other assignments. She'd learned early it wouldn't be. Still, should her job not get easier with the passage of earthly time? Perhaps God was correcting her attitude, teaching her something.

Judith slept, but not peacefully: Susanna made sure of her restlessness by invading her dreams.

You are self-centered, opinionated, and careless with other people's feelings. Did it not occur to you that your companions might not want to return home immediately? Did you even consider they would appreciate a few days away from estate work? If you don't start heeding my guidance, I'll relinquish you to a firmer hand. You need a guardian who will box your ears when you ignore her. I can't because, ridiculous though it sounds, I'm quite fond of you.

Be that as it may, I must get a few hours' rest before you embark on your next escapade.

Richard paced his room at York House, fuming at what he considered Lady Judith's insubordination. Now, if she were his subaltern, he would know how to deal with her. She wasn't. However, he had been wrong to rant at her. She had flayed him with her tongue. Rightly so. He acknowledged his guilt, even though his words arose from concern, or so he told himself. As the hours passed, the noise subsided both inside the house and out. He told himself that she was upset with him now but would think the matter through and get past it. He hoped.

There would be no point in returning to East Leah until then, so he would deal with problems at Chadwick Park. He'd resisted them too often.

His decision made, Richard tugged off his boots—why had he sent Pierce off to bed?—and stretched out on the hard mattress. Sleep didn't come, however. He lay staring at the ceiling, where stormy gray eyes stared back at him. He still didn't understand how her blue eyes could change colour, but change they did.

Nineteen

Somewhere in France

Someone else found obtaining rest difficult. An old man twisted and turned on his hard mattress. The silence, both inside and out, informed him the hour was late. Owls are night creatures. He didn't know how he knew that or why he expected to hear them, but he did. Songbirds had long since chirped their good nights to each other. He was unable to identify the various birds, but was thankful for their cheerful presence.

Marie had sat with him, patiently helping him eat the chicken broth, as she did several times a day. She'd added a few bits of bread to the bowl for his dinner. Perhaps that small amount of solid food would help him regain his strength and his memory.

Henri had come upstairs for a few minutes of conversation before seeking his bed. Now the old man was on his own until morning. He couldn't even relish memories because he had none beyond this time in a stranger's attic.

The old man finally gave up on sleep and heaved himself onto the edge of the cot, so weak he gasped for breath. He gritted his teeth and rose to his feet. This time he would get himself to the chamber pot and back onto the cot without waiting for the man below stairs. His pace was slow, but he managed the feat without landing on the floor.

He must regain his strength. Maybe then he could recall why he was in a Frenchman's attic instead of his own home, wherever that might be, and why he spoke French while his thoughts were in English. With a determined air, he vowed to pace the length of the room tomorrow and every day until he regained his strength.

For now, he would simply stand until his legs gave out. With a rueful sigh, the old man realized that took mere minutes.

He sank onto the mattress and lifted his aching legs until he stretched out on his back. As the ache eased, he drifted into sleep.

Twenty

How Could This Be?

Her Grace, the Duchess of Rochdale, stood in regal splendor three steps inside the front door when Wilson admitted Richard into the house.

"Mother, is there a problem? I didn't expect . . ."

She didn't allow him to finish. "You're the problem, Rochdale. You've been away from Chadwick Park far more than you've been here since your return from Vienna."

"My absences have been necessary, Your Grace."

His icy tone failed to deter her. "I expect your presence for more than a few days this time. Indeed, you must accept the necessity of permanent residence. Since you're so determined to return Chadwick Park to its former glory, you should stay here until you've accomplished it, which, you have stated numerous times, will be years."

The idea was enough to send Richard into a fit of doldrums.

He could already see progress in the estate. The new gardeners had scythed the lawns and pruned the shrubbery, so the immediate vicinity presented a neat appearance. He could welcome visitors without undue embarrassment, although he dreaded the idea of people interrupting his schedule.

Regardless of his wishes, he soon learned there would be plenty to welcome. At dinner on his first evening, the duchess revealed her entertainment plans. Before he could protest, she stated, "I'm aware of our mourning period. My plans do not include balls for the year you insist upon. Nevertheless, it's past time for your reintroduction to the neighborhood. Afternoon visits and dinners will serve the purpose."

During his Army years, Richard had learned the necessity of compromise. With an inward sigh, he recognized the need now.

"Mother, there is considerable estate work that will require long days in the saddle." He held up his hand to stop her interruption. "I will agree to host any dinners you give for our *immediate* neighbors. You will not issue invitations further than the *immediate* neighborhood. In any event, you must excuse me from your morning and afternoon plans."

The Duchess showed she, too, had learned the art of compromise. "Very well, Richard, I will arrange dinners only. However, you must agree to accept return dinner invitations." She did not drop her gaze from his until he capitulated.

Thus began a new, and unwelcome, regimen in Richard's life. Mornings, he breakfasted early, then rode out on estate work. He soon learned, despite his injunction, if he returned to the house at midday, the duchess would insist on his presence to greet visitors. The evenings were bad enough. Therefore, each morning he filled his pockets with apples which he munched when hunger pangs came, returning home in late afternoon.

Paperwork, much of which was still an enigma to him, filled the afternoon. He found satisfaction in learning estate functions, even realizing he could enjoy the work, in time. His youthful desire to learn estate management had arisen from a sense of responsibility. Now, he recognized his subconscious had known the truth. He enjoyed estate management.

Evenings were not quite the torment Richard had visualized. Mrs. Ingram was never present, nor did he expect to see her. She no longer interested him. However, he had to suppress considerable irritation when faced with the giggling Odom chits. They were older than little Gretchen in Vienna—therefore, they should know giggling is repulsive to gentlemen. At the Odom residence for dinner one evening, he learned they were not the only gigglers in the vicinity. There were the Blair twins, alike as two peas in a pod, who blushed, stammered, or giggled when he addressed them on any conceivable topic that might interest schoolgirls.

There was also the pampered only daughter of Colonel and Mrs. Lancaster. The colonel had retired from the army after an undistinguished career, which did not stop him from discussing the military at length. Mrs. Lancaster was loud in her praise of dog breeding and regaled her audience with details Richard doubted anyone wanted to hear. Their daughter, Georgina, sat in elegant solitude, her nose tilted upward, her gaze fixed at some distant point. She ignored everyone who attempted conversation with her. Richard relaxed only when the butler announced the Lancaster carriage. He immediately called for his own.

On the morning after the Odom dinner, Richard returned from an early ride to find his mother seated at the breakfast table. "What are you doing out of your rooms so early? I've never known you to partake of breakfast downstairs."

"I want to discuss our recent dinner engagements, Rochdale, and this is the only time I'm sure to find you alone."

"Need I remind you, it is you who issues and accepts evening engagements?"

"Don't be preposterous, Rochdale," she scolded. "What did you think of the Blair twins? Delightful creatures, are they not?"

"Delightful? I would use a different word to describe them. Can you discern any difference between them and the Odom chits?"

She stared at him. "You must be addled, Rochdale. The Odom girls are fair-haired with blue eyes. The twins have auburn hair and brown eyes."

"Mother, I do not refer to their colouring, although I would call the twins' hair carroty, at best. I meant their demeanor, their maturity level."

"Rochdale, I am losing patience. All these girls are either seventeen or soon will be. Naturally, they are much alike. What else can you expect from girls just out of the schoolroom?"

"My point exactly, Ma'am. Schoolroom chits don't interest me. Is that clear?"

She ignored his question. "What about Georgina Lancaster? She's past eighteen. She didn't giggle even once."

"No, indeed. I'm convinced her face would have cracked if she had so much as smiled. She wouldn't even look at me when I tried to converse with her, which I consider the height of rudeness in young ladies."

"Rochdale, I despair of you." She narrowed her eyes. "Have you never heard of an Attitude?"

"Yes, I have. Some are pleasant, others arrogant. Her attitude was the latter."

"No, no, no. You don't understand. I refer to the current penchant for striking a pose reminiscent of a character from a play."

"My Oxford tutors failed in their responsibility because such a thing is beyond my scope of knowledge. What character was she supposed to be?"

"I'm sure I don't know." The duchess rose from the table, shaking out her skirts before turning toward the door. "You're making things difficult for me. You must settle down . . ."

"Your Grace, we discussed this before. I don't care to continue repeating myself, yet I will. This is not the time for marriage discussion, nor will it be anytime soon. Years, probably. Furthermore, I will choose my bride when I decide to marry. Hear this. My bride most assuredly will not be a chit just out of the schoolroom."

Raven hair and blue eyes flashed across his mental vision, then disappeared before he could react. "I told you before I purchased my army commission that I'll consider getting leg-shackled when I am one and thirty, not before. I still have a few years of freedom yet."

Her only answer was the firm closing of the door.

Richard finished his coffee. Acquaintance with Lady Judith had eased his barrier against respectable females, but these last days threatened to harden his heart again.

Mid-afternoon found him searching the one room he had avoided since his return—the late duke's bedchamber. Master or not, Richard insisted upon occupying the chamber he used following his nursery days. He consigned his father's clothing to the housekeeper with instructions to deal with everything as she saw fit. Next, he searched the armoire shelves. Wadded up neckcloths? Even stray shoes. Something in the shadows caught his attention. Pulling out a flat metal box with rusty hinges, he sneezed when the dust flew.

The contents puzzled him. Three conveyance deeds dating back more than two hundred years of Rochdale ownership. Why were they here, rather than in the study with the Chadwick Park deed? He hadn't even known the duchy owned other property. He cringed. Were these locations in the same shape as Chadwick Park? He picked up the third document, and his jaw dropped. The Manor at East Leah? How could it be entailed to the Rochdale duchy?

Box in hand, he rushed down the stairs, calling for Wilson to find Guthrie.

"So, you know nothing about these properties?" Richard stared at his estate agent across the cluttered desk.

"I never heard them mentioned, Your Grace."

"Considering the dusty box, they'd been in the armoire for a great many years. Could even Father have known? The ledgers did not reveal any income from them over the past ten years, which is all I studied. I didn't see any reason to go farther back, but now I suppose I must."

Richard pushed his hands through his hair. "I have my work cut out for me, going through the older ledgers. All right, Guthrie, go on about your business. I'll take care of this, no matter how long it requires."

Rochdale sat through dinner, his eyes burning with strain, his brain in turmoil. The vicar was in a talkative mood, requiring his attention on parish affairs. All he wanted to do was sort through duchy affairs.

Two days later, Richard closed the last ledger. There had been no entries regarding the Yorkshire property since 1780 and none for the Cornwall property since 1785. The East Leah records stopped in 1790. Before those years, the ledgers showed regular rental receipts. All three properties had been prosperous and no problems recorded. What had happened thereafter?

Perhaps Coleman could enlighten him.

He couldn't, Richard learned after a hurried trip to London. Coleman, too, hadn't known the duchy owned any property other than Chadwick Park. Rochdale had handed the property conveyances to his solicitor, then sat back waiting for information. Beyond agreeing Lady Judith couldn't own the Manor at East Leigh, Coleman could offer no further information.

With instructions to look into the matter, Richard settled into his townhouse waiting for the results.

Coleman quickly found the deed copies in his father's old documents. It took longer to chase down the transactions on the three properties. The late duke had sold them off, piece by piece.

"He sold *entailed* property? He couldn't, not without my signature, which I certainly never gave!"

"I agree with the legality of what you say, Your Grace. Nevertheless, he did sell the property."

"How could you possibly allow the sale?" Richard stared at the older man, who straightened in his chair. "The ledgers contained no indication that he sold them. All references to them simply stopped. You've been our family solicitor for years. Your father before you, is that not right? How can you explain these sales?"

"I took over my father's business in 1800 and kept at hand only those boxes in current use. His older records are in a back room." Coleman aligned papers on his table before he continued, his voice carefully controlled. "Your father hired another solicitor to handle the sales. I found him, not one of the better-known businessmen. He vows complete innocence. After all, his new client was a duke, no less, who certainly knew what he could and could not do about his property."

"What about the money from the sales?" Richard answered himself. "Paid to him. Then he paid to anyone who would sell him a book. What can we do? Worse still, if possible, how many more illegal sales might we find?"

"To answer your last question first, we've checked all our deed boxes and don't find evidence the duchy ever owned other property. What we can do about these three parcels is another matter."

They spent the following hours deciding how to deal with the late duke's illegal transactions. It went without discussion that the duchy didn't have the funds to return the purchase prices, even with the book sales coupled with Rochdale's personal funds. Much of the windfall from the successful trade ship had gone toward refurbishing and resupplying her for another voyage. The remainder had paid some long overdue bills.

Yet, he couldn't ignore the sales, legal or not. Richard couldn't be certain no one would ever search the records, thereby learning the truth. The knowledge that one of his descendants would condemn him for not correcting the situation was not pleasant. In the end, he decided they could do only one thing, and that was approach the supposed current property owners. He and Coleman, accompanied by the other solicitor, would visit the new landowners to sound them out about considering what they had paid as lease payments rather than purchase. The supposed owners could continue to lease for whatever time they chose at an agreed-upon figure.

Coleman stared Rochdale in the eyes. "I warn you, though, you're facing a forlorn hope. People buy property because they want the pride of ownership. We can expect lawsuits, which will bring the notoriety you want to avoid."

Lady Judith's pride of ownership popped into Richard's mind. This one he must handle by himself. He'd rather face the entire Peninsula war again. Through no fault of her own, she would lose something she valued, something she had earned by her own efforts. This might do what Monford had not—break her spirit.

After leaving Coleman's office, Richard walked in silence, weaving through the crowd, paying no attention to the drivers who yelled at him while they fought to control their horses. His insides coiled anew, memory taking him back to several confrontations with Judith. Her face became a frozen mask just before her temper erupted. She always confronted him with her shoulders squared, tension obvious in her stance, eyes blazing. He admired her for not backing down, even while he wished she would, which was quixotic of him, to be sure.

His thoughts returned to the present when hands jerked him to a standstill. He spun around, fists raised, then relaxed when he recognized an old friend. "Pardon me, Sanderson. I didn't see you."

"That was obvious. Your mind was miles away." He stopped suddenly. "Oh, I forgot. I heard you came into your title shortly after Waterloo, so I should call you Rochdale."

"I would rather you stick with Richard." He and Charles Sanderson had ridden side by side through the Peninsula battles: enduring the elements, scavenging for food, and dodging bullets. He knew of Sanderson's betrothed who eloped with a man with deeper pockets.

Sandy was the only person on earth who knew Richard dreamed about a schoolgirl with eyes the colour of water on a sunny day. He also knew the problems at Chadwick Park, just as Richard knew his lack of an estate.

Richard could depend on Sanderson now in the same way he had at Salamanca, when Sandy hauled Richard up behind him after the French shot his mount from under him. They had shared many bottles of cheap Spanish wine. Richard could offer something better now.

"Let's go to Chadwick House and broach a bottle of brandy. I need it even if you don't."

Drink in hand, his legs stretched toward an empty fireplace, Richard told the complete incredible story.

"Facing Napoleon didn't require the fortitude I must have to face Lady Judith, telling her she doesn't own the Manor. I've never known anyone who valued property ownership to the extent she does. The estate is the sign of her success attained by her own efforts, and it's *hers*."

"Tough. There's no possibility of a mistake?"

"None. Coleman found the recorded papers and confronted the solicitor who drew them."

By the time they had finished mulling over the possibilities, they'd done more than broach the bottle—they'd emptied it. Richard would have a terrible headache later in the morning, not helped by real-estate nightmares.

Twenty-One

Judith Faces Her Future

Judith hadn't admitted, even to herself, how much she missed Richard. She'd been so angry with him in Bath that she hadn't expected he would enter her thoughts, not only daily but multiple times each day. When her characters refused to cooperate with her storyline, she often rode to the place where she and Richard seemed most comfortable together—near the cave. During her many hours there, the book occupied her mind, preparing for the next day's session. Today, she was neither thinking of Richard nor seeking inspiration for her ghost story.

A short distance from the cave, Judith had looped the reins over a shade-tree limb. Smoothing Gypsy's mane, she'd murmured, "I intend to explore the cave. Yes, I know Ruth wants to be with me, but she stays too busy, and I need to know how large the cave is and how far it goes back into the hillside. So, I can't wait any longer."

At the cave entrance, Judith stopped when coarse voices reached her: one English, two French. She inched forward around the blooming shrub, which almost hid the entrance. She stepped into the cave, straining to hear the muffled words, then moved still further inside. The voices became clearer.

"That's quite a haul. When do we start moving the stuff?"

Another rough voice answered the eager query. "When we're told, not before."

A scream died in Judith's throat. Ghosts? Speaking French? Don't be a ninny. She remembered her promise to Ruth but, after a moment, set her qualms aside and entered the cave, ignoring the little voice urging caution. Susanna was trying to control her again.

Her heartbeat surged when she heard footsteps. The voices drew closer.

Judith rushed toward a narrow opening on one side of the entrance. When she stepped inside, her foot skidded on a small stone, kicking it away. The noise reverberated. The voices stopped. She held her breath when footsteps moved toward her.

"What was that?" The harsh masculine voice speaking French ricocheted around the cave.

"Probably just a dog," the Englishman answered. "There are plenty around here."

Judith strained back against the rock wall as the footsteps came closer.

"Come on," the second French voice said. "You can see there's no place for anyone to hide in here. We should look around outside, though, and make sure nobody is about."

Judith clapped a hand over her mouth stifling a gasp. Gypsy! *Susanna, help! They might find Gypsy. I deserve whatever harm they might have in mind for an intruder because I chose to be here, but she's innocent of wrongdoing.*

Judith took one step forward when the men's voices grew faint. Should she find a place outside to hide? Before she reached a decision, the men's voices became louder again.

The English voice said, "There's nobody here. Let's go, we have miles to put behind us before nightfall."

The footsteps receded. Judith soon heard horses moving away in the opposite direction from where Gypsy waited. She released her pent-up breath, then slipped back through the slit. Almost on tiptoes, she crossed the cave's small open area and peeked around the curve in the cave wall. It was too dark to see beyond a few feet. A faint oil odor indicated the men had used a lantern. Frustrated, she stepped out of the cave. She'd heard the voices again and had seen a small part of the cave, so she had enough to go on with, but, still, she needed to explore the cave.

After a quick look around, she retraced her steps to Gypsy, who whinnied a welcome. Judith hugged the mare. *Thank you, Susanna.* It's a good thing there wasn't a shade tree closer to the cave. Otherwise, without a doubt, those men would have found Gypsy. Herself, too, she acknowledged but didn't dwell on possible results.

On the ride home, Judith pondered the situation. Should she share this adventure with Ruth? No, she was busy with her new life—didn't care about writing anymore, although she hadn't said as much. Ruth probably had always participated in their endeavours just to keep Judith occupied. She missed the closeness they'd shared for so long.

She could tell Richard. The thought surprised her. Why would she want to tell him? He would condemn her, and they would quarrel again.

Judith made her decision. She wouldn't mention this adventure. She would bring candles tomorrow to explore the cave. She would tell Ruth if there was anything of interest. Perhaps. Perhaps not. Would it not be more fun to write this escapade into the book, letting her learn about the adventure that way? The idea put Judith in amazingly good humor the rest of the day.

At the breakfast table on the day after Judith visited the cave, Ruth reminded her she needed to accept household responsibilities. This didn't sit well with Judith, so she objected.

"Ruthie, you know I'm far from adept at household tasks. Mending is beyond my ability—remember, I got blood on some pillowcases. I take care of tenants' needs. I do more estate work since the hands accepted me. Over the past few days, I dealt with two ailing sheep and checked the barley fields. We expect a large crop, although not the amount we had at ho—Ainsley Park, but just as healthy."

"I understand, but . . ."

"Those chores require a considerable amount of time away from my desk. I won't have writing time if I spend time counting sheets or whatever you have in mind. You do remember Mr. Davison sent us an urgent appeal for a book just a few days ago?"

"Mr. Davison's letter didn't sound urgent to me. I know you do outside estate work. The fact remains, you must give attention to household tasks also. Yes, I remember the bloody pillowcases, also the table napkins that became dusters. For that reason, we won't even consider putting a needle in your hands. However, look at it this way. We can discuss the book while we sort through the attics. Who knows?" she added with a mock shiver, "there might be a ghost up there."

Judith grinned at the dramatics but bowed to the inevitable. Later, she admitted spending time with Ruth had been pleasant, almost like years gone by. They didn't find any ghosts but did find a trunk filled with hats, which sent them into whoops. Did ladies of the previous century truly wear them? Judith sank onto the floor with her skirt bunched around her knees. Her gaze sharpened when she peered under a low cupboard. Leaning forward, she pulled out a metal box the size of the cashbox in the study.

"Ruthie, look what I found." She tugged at the rusted clasp, breaking two fingernails before she lifted the lid. Inside, she found a pair of knitted baby slippers with a matching bonnet. "How tiny they are. I suppose the baby died."

"Why would you think so?"

"We haven't found other baby clothing." When she smoothed a wrinkle, something crackled under the bonnet. The paper, yellowed with age, revealed a faded black square shape with a gold and black shield surrounded by gold leaves, the whole topped with a lion. "Looks like a family crest. No one has mentioned nobility's owning this place."

Ruth reached for the paper, bringing it closer to her eyes. "The words have dimmed too much to read. I believe I'm right, though, when I say commoners can have crests, not only nobles."

Judith repacked the box and shoved it back under the cupboard. "We'll leave the box there. We might be able to use the contents in a future book. Right now, though, I must concentrate on the one we have in progress."

"I agree. One book at a time is enough."

"Then, if we're finished here, I believe I will sit in the garden and think."

"Yes, we've done enough for one day. I wouldn't want to try your patience too far."

Their laughter followed them as they descended the stairs.

Judith strolled out the side door toward the rose garden and relaxed on a wrought-iron bench.

She needed to hear the cave voices again, renew their cadence, or perhaps hear some new words to fuel her imagination. That was impossible until she could absorb the atmosphere inside the cave. Ignoring her promise to Ruth, Judith decided to visit the cave on her own.

Judith put her plan into practice the next day.

After checking on the two sheep, she reviewed the estate books with Daniel. "So, we agree. We'll sow a winter-wheat crop, rather than oats this year, on the southeast acres now lying fallow?"

Daniel nodded. "There's one more thing. I believe we should expand the kitchen garden to include winter salad greens, followed by asparagus and onions in early spring. Some tenants assured me asparagus grows well in this soil."

"That's good to know. My favorite green vegetable. I believe we've covered everything and at the right moment."

Ruth opened the door to ask if they were ready for lunch.

"We are," Judith answered for both, then stated she would be from home the rest of the day. "I want—nay, I need—a long ride."

"Do you not expect visitors this afternoon?"

"I don't believe we have plans for this afternoon, do we, Ruth?"

"No, but if anyone stops in, I'll visit with them. You go ahead and get some air.

With candles and a tinderbox in the reticule hanging from the saddle horn, Judith headed toward the northwest corner of the estate. No matter what the angel said, this was her opportunity to explore the cave, and she would this afternoon.

After tethering Gypsy under the usual shade tree, Judith cautiously approached the cave. Remaining within the forested edge, she walked around the area, alert for horses. After deciding she was alone, Judith hurried across the open space and entered the cave.

No oil odor assailed her nostrils. She nodded her satisfaction. After lighting a candle, she stepped into the interior. Holding the candle high, she gave a quick look around before examining the cave bit by bit. It was so small her head almost reached the roof, which she learned when cobwebs swept across her face. Near the front, she didn't see anything to explain the presence of the men. Toward the back, however, she saw large burlap bags filled with something that gave them a knobby appearance.

Pacifying her curiosity, she opened one and saw silver candelabras and small silver dishes. The next one contained silver plates. The glitter in the third bag almost blinded her.

Stunned, Judith sat back on her heels. The robberies! She counted the bags. Ten. She must tell Daniel. Would the authorities hold her accountable because the thieves used her property to hide their ill-gotten gains? She had not anticipated this problem when she contemplated owning an estate.

Blowing out the candle, she stood in the cave entrance until her eyes adjusted to the brightness before crossing the open area. She stepped into the trees seconds before the sound of horses coming from the other side reached her. Her eyes wide with fear, remembering the candle smoke, Judith hurried to Gypsy. Gathering the reins in one hand, she mounted and wheeled the mare toward home.

Hearing a shout behind her, she knew the men had discovered her presence in the cave. What would they have done if they'd come earlier and found her inside? She might find herself living her book instead of writing it. Bending low over the mare's neck, Judith urged Gypsy into a gallop. She heard something whistle past her head followed by a sharp pain in her left shoulder. They were shooting at her! She clung to the reins, but the mare stumbled, sending her passenger flying. Terrified, Gypsy raced to her stable, leaving Judith with her head lying against a rock.

Her last thought before blackness descended was, *this is hoydenish behaviour, indeed. Even worse than climbing trees and splashing in the brook. Susanna, where are you?*

Twenty-Two

The Aftermath

After he'd consulted Coleman in London, Richard had gone to Chadwick Park where he confronted both his mother and his agent.

The Duchess had shrugged off the previous duke's activities as unimportant, refusing to understand the implication of selling entailed property. She stated the late duke owned the property. He should be able to do what he chose. Richard wasn't surprised because he hadn't expected her to know about the sales since she confined her interests to the usual feminine pursuits of clothing, visits, and tittle-tattle.

However, he'd hoped for some information from Martin Guthrie, something that perhaps had slipped his mind when they previously discussed the property deeds. Richard soon learned otherwise.

Neither Martin nor Anthony could enlighten him, although both understood the ramifications. As they had said before, neither knew about those properties, didn't know the duchy had ever owned other property, and they had never heard the second solicitor's name.

Richard hadn't expected them to know of his father's deviousness in acquiring funds for his rare books. They could have done nothing about it if they had known because nothing stopped the late duke from satisfying his obsession with ancient books.

Now Richard had come to tell Lady Judith— probably break her heart, he acknowledged, because, again, a man's deviousness had destroyed her dreams. He'd called on his military training to ready himself for what he believed would be the worst ordeal of his life—far surpassing anything Napoleon's army had thrown at him.

After greeting the Sherwoods, he had turned toward the opening door. Disappointment vied with relief when a footman entered with a tea tray. Accepting a cup, he inquired for Judith. "Is she occupied with Mrs. Blaylock this afternoon?"

"No, she gave herself the afternoon off from both the book and estate work."

"Estate work?" This was Richard's opportunity to learn the limits of her active participation. "She did mention she'd had some training, but I believed she meant dealing with the tenants and their needs. Perhaps teaching children to read."

"Oh, no," Ruth assured him. "She can manage an estate larger than this one. The earl gave her thorough training in all aspects of property management. She was in charge whenever he had to be elsewhere."

Rochdale hid his surprise. The idea of a female having even academic knowledge of animal husbandry appalled him. Maybe she only oversaw the crops, no matter what Mrs. Sherwood said to the contrary.

Judith's absence might be a blessing in disguise. He could tell the Sherwoods about the land problem, perhaps gain an insight into how best to tell Judith. With that in mind, he told them of the duchy predicament.

"So that's the way it is. The Manor is my property, not Lady Judith's."

Richard forced himself to meet the Sherwoods' horrified gazes. His heart threatened to jump from his chest, while anxiety gripped his mind. He had ridden into battle with more composure. "Neither my solicitor nor I found a way to remedy my father's behaviour, even though we spent these past days trying."

"Why have you not mentioned this before now?"

He couldn't avoid Mrs. Sherwood's accusing eyes or demanding voice. Before he could answer, she continued.

"We've talked with you many times, so you had plenty of opportunity. Or did you just cozen up to us so Judith wouldn't push the matter?"

"Easy, my dear," Daniel cautioned. "Let's hear his explanation before condemning him."

"Oh, I dare say he has quite a tale for us, all thought out, cut and dried."

Richard appreciated Sherwood's forbearance, but he could not expect the same from Mrs. Sherwood. She'd been Lady Judith's companion for many years, her close confidante during the years they plotted their future. He excused her sarcasm—could he do otherwise? Yet, he must try to make her understand.

"The thing is I never knew there was family-owned property anywhere except Chadwick Park. My father cared nothing for the estate, so he didn't discuss it."

He gave them a brief explanation of the late duke's passion for ancient books and manuscripts.

"Obsession with rare books perhaps clarifies why he sold entailed property," Daniel said. "However, his passion doesn't excuse his Machiavellian brain."

"Nothing can," Richard agreed. "I can't begin to explain how distressing this is."

"Have you even considered how Judith will react?" Ruth shot him a vicious frown before turning toward Daniel. "How are we to tell her? She'll be devastated."

Daniel grasped her hand. "There can be no mistake, I suppose."

"None. Both my solicitor and I checked the records going back two hundred years when my ancestor received the original grant for Chadwick Park. There's no question the Manor is an entailed part of the Rochdale duchy. I believe we can verify that here to your satisfaction."

Ruth and Daniel exchanged glances. "How?"

"Chadwick Park and the other two estates . . ."

"Are you saying this is not the only estate the late duke sold without legal authority?" Daniel's disbelief hung in the air.

"He sold two other parcels which, with Chadwick Park, all have the family crest near the entrance door. If there's one here, I believe the heraldry will satisfy you of duchy ownership."

"Crest?" Ruth turned widened eyes toward him. "Describe it."

"A black square shape with a gold and black shield surrounded by gold leaves, topped with a lion. You appear to recognize the description."

"Let's look at the door," she replied.

Outside, Daniel tugged intertwined vines from the left side of the door. No crest. However, tugging vines aside on the right side revealed the etched crest. He turned to his wife. "You recognized the description."

She explained the afternoon she and Judith had searched the trunks. "We left the box where we found it."

"Another mystery," Richard said. "I know nothing about a baby. I don't suppose there's any reason I should."

"How could even a duke sell entailed property? That's what I don't understand," Ruth said. "I'm not by any means an authority on estate law, but do know the meaning of entailed property."

Rochdale closed his eyes in despair. "My father was an obsessed man. He couldn't resist ancient books. He did anything necessary, by fair means or foul, to own them. He hid his deviousness very well, even hiring a different solicitor for his dirty—well illegal— work."

After heaving a sigh, Ruth said, "Poor Judith. Losing another home. This will be more devastating than losing Ainsley Park. Should I break the news to her? I might soothe her until she can deal with losing this estate."

No matter how much he'd like to accept her offer, Richard knew it would mark him a coward—one thing never ascribed to him except in the face of his mother's tears when he was a child, which was excusable. But never again.

"I appreciate your willingness, Mrs. Sherwood, but telling Lady Judith is my responsibility. The knowledge has me quaking in my boots, I can tell you, because I do have some understanding of the pain I'll cause." Rising, he said, "If she's rewarding her diligence with a ride, I believe I know where she is. I'll ride out to meet her."

Riding in a northwesterly direction, Richard heard pounding hooves coming toward him and stared with dismay when Gypsy galloped past him. What could have happened to Judith? He urged his own horse into a gallop, calling her name.

"Lady Judith? Judith! Can you hear me? It's Richard Chadwick. Answer me!" Frantically searching both sides of the trail, he rounded a curve barely controlling his mount when Judith raised, then lowered, her head from a spot in front of Sheik, causing him to rear, almost unseating his rider.

Richard slid from the saddle, dropping the reins. "Stand." Tapping Judith on the arm, he appealed for her to open her eyes. "Judith, talk to me."

She blinked at him before her head fell back to the ground.

"Where do you hurt? Can you stand?" He ran his hands along her limbs, then turned her onto her back. Judith screamed. When he turned her to her side, a horrified groan escaped his lips. There was blood on her jacket. He opened it enough to see a small round hole in her shoulder. "You've been shot! I must take you home, but how I can manage without hurting you is more than I know."

He welcomed the sound of pounding hooves and stood, waving his arms.

The stable hand jumped from the saddle. "You found her! When Gypsy came home without her, I knew she'd been thrown."

"Here, help me with her." Richard mounted and reached for Judith. The stable hand lifted her into Richard's arms.

"I'll ride on ahead with the news you found her, Your Grace."

Judith opened her eyes. Smiling, she patted Richard's cheek. "You're pretty. You look like a Greek god from my storybook."

"I wonder if you'll remember saying that," he said with a chuckle, urging Sheik into a gentle stride.

<> <> <> <> <>

Opening her eyes, Judith frowned at the faces surrounding her. Ruth and Daniel were there as well as several servants. And Richard. Why was he in her bedchamber? He was supposed to be on his estate, not hers. Anxious expressions covered their faces. Trying to sit up, she let out a yelp and grabbed her shoulder, then collapsed back against the pillows.

"You must lie still, my dear. The doctor is on his way." Ruth's quiet voice soothed her.

With Ruthie here, nothing could be too bad. Judith smiled at her.

"Not Gypsy's fault. She stumbled when we were galloping." Judith frowned. "Galloping? Why would we be in such a hurry?"

"Don't worry about that now, Judith. You can tell us later."

Daniel's voice reminded her she must tell him something. Her eyelids popped open.

"The robberies! I found the stolen goods we've heard about. The thieves shot at me when I was coming home to tell you."

"Take it easy, my dear." Ruth clasped her hand. "Don't upset yourself."

"You must go inside the cave, Daniel." Judith's voice faded but became strong again. "There are bags filled with stuff I expect came from the robberies. I counted ten bags. Hurry before the thieves move them."

Daniel and Richard stared at each other. The latter spoke, "Lady Judith, is the cave near where we talked the day you told me about Mrs. Blaylock?"

"Yes, left of the shrubs with the white flowers."

"I've never been inside, but I know where the cave is," Richard told Daniel.

"That's more than I can say. I promised her we would explore it together after I completed some things I needed to do. I must say the cave slipped my mind. I suppose she decided not to wait." Turning toward his wife, Daniel said, "We should check this out now. Also, I must send for the village constable. On the way out, Rochdale will give Taylor the particulars on how the constable can find us."

When the men left the room, Ruth pulled a chair closer to the bedside, worrying while Judith passed into and out of consciousness. The doctor bustled into the room almost an hour later.

"I understand the young lady has a bullet in her shoulder. Now, why would anyone shoot a beautiful girl like her? Such goings-on are beyond me." He leaned over the bed touching the wound with a gentle finger. "The bullet is still in there. I'll need hot water. Bring brandy too."

"Brandy?" Ruth stared at the doctor. Heat rushed up her face when he chuckled.

"For the patient, Mrs. Sherwood, for the patient."

With Ruth's holding the glass, Judith gulped a large mouthful of brandy relishing the fire going down her throat even as it numbed the shoulder pain. She gritted her teeth yet passed out when the doctor probed for the bullet.

Moments later, he held up the small object, allowing blood to drip on the sheets. "There. It wasn't very deep and didn't hit anything vital."

Judith moaned.

"I'm sorry, Lady Judith, but I must pack this tightly to stop the bleeding." He busied himself with lint and sticking plaster, humming an indistinct tune.

"Did you get the bullet out?" Judith whispered.

"Yes. Do you want to keep it? Entertain guests with your tale?" he asked. Not waiting for an answer, he handed Ruth a bottle of laudanum. "A couple drops in water should ensure Lady Judith a night's rest. I'll come back tomorrow morning and change the bandage. She should be over the worst within a few days, unless she develops a fever. However, we will deal with that if we must."

Nodding goodbye, he hurried out the door.

At the mention of fever, a shiver passed through Ruth's body. Fever had killed her mother. Straightening her shoulders, she rang for the maid. "Alice, please sit beside Lady Judith's bed until I return."

"Yes, Mrs. Sherwood."

Ruth hurried to the kitchen. "Cook, the doctor said Lady Judith might develop a fever. Do we have a sufficient supply of lemons and barley?"

The cook reassured her. "We can prepare whatever she needs."

They didn't contend with a fever but something much worse. Judith didn't wake up the next day or the next.

For forty-eight hours, Ruth sat beside the invalid's bed, praying. She took nourishment only when Daniel held a cup to her lips, forcing her to swallow broth. She left her post only when he picked her up on the second morning and carried her to their chamber. There he stretched out on the bed, cradling her in his arms.

"Daniel, I must be with her. I *must*," she repeated. "Can you not understand? She has no one else. *No one*. Only me."

"My love, I see you're fatigued to the point you're not thinking. You can't go on this way, neither eating nor sleeping. Can you not see you'll be worthless to her when she wakes if you don't take care of yourself now?"

"When she wakes. Oh, Daniel, do you truly believe she will?"

"Yes, I'm sure she will," he declared. "She's a strong young woman. This long sleep helps her recovery."

Ruth collapsed into tears, drenching his lapels. Soon the wrenching sobs dwindled into sniffles. She slept around the clock and woke refreshed. Daniel insisted she have tea and toast before allowing her out of their bedchamber.

Hurrying to Judith's bedside, Ruth found Alice standing at the window. Rochdale stood immobile beside the bed, staring into the pale, set face on the pillows. He'd spent most of his waking hours at the Manor since he carried Judith home. He returned to the Hinsons' late at night, only to return at first light. Ruth wondered what thoughts passed through his mind while he gazed at the unconscious girl.

His expression was bleak. "She moves, and she opened her eyes for a moment. I talked to her, but I don't know if she heard me."

"Your Grace, I believe she heard you," Alice told him. "She grew quiet."

Rochdale nodded but didn't answer. The maid slipped out the door and closed it behind her, leaving them to their vigilance.

Ruth sat in a chair at Judith's side and motioned the duke toward another chair. However, he moved to the foot of the bed and pushed aside the brocade curtains.

Thus, when Judith opened her eyes, she saw his haunted features.

"Judith!" Ruth leaned over the bed. "You're awake. Oh, thank you, God. You answered my prayers."

"I dreamed Father is alive."

Ruth and Rochdale exchanged startled glances. Then Ruth laid her hand against Judith's forehead. "She isn't feverish."

Rochdale's voice was steady when he asked why she believed her father was alive.

"Only a dream. Susanna would have told me if he is."

"Susanna? I don't know who she is."

"My guardian angel."

Daniel tapped on the door before stepping inside. "Any change?"

"Judith is awake, but she's having delusions, I'm afraid," Ruth whispered. "I'm not sure she even knows us."

Judith turned puzzled eyes toward her companion. "Why would I not recognize you, Ruthie? And, why is Rochdale in my bedchamber?"

"It appears she knows us," Rochdale commented. "She has rejoined us, so I'll take my leave and call later today if I may."

"By all means, Rochdale," Daniel replied. "I'll let you find your way out while I try to determine what's happening here. Will you ask Taylor to send for the doctor?"

With a nod, the duke left the room. Daniel turned back toward Judith. "You've had us on tenterhooks."

"A little sore, Daniel, but what's this about two days?" She raised her head from the pillows, promptly lying down again with a groan. "I remember. I'm not so well after all. My head aches, my shoulder aches."

Ruth reached for the bell to summon Alice and turned to Daniel. "Judith dreamed her father is alive."

"I don't believe he is, though" Judith repeated. "The authorities sent his signet ring home, remember, Ruthie? He once told me he would never remove the ring from his finger until he passed it to the next generation, so he must be dead. Besides, Susanna wouldn't hide anything so important from me."

"Who is Susanna?"

Judith grimaced. This was the first time since her early childhood she had allowed that name to cross her lips and now twice within minutes. She regretted her lapse but knew she must answer Daniel. "My guardian angel."

"If so, she didn't do a very good job this time, and I'll tell her so if she dares show herself around here, angel or not." Ruth's voice brooked no contradiction, nor did her ferocious frown.

"This is my fault, Ruthie. I knew I wasn't supposed to go inside the cave. Susanna has warned me about my behaviour on regular occasions."

Daniel quieted his wife by touching her shoulder. "Judith, tell us about Susanna."

"I first became aware of her when I was four years old." Judith recounted her dash toward the lily pond and then related other incidences.

"You've seen the angel?"

"No, Ruthie, I've only heard her. She talks to me often but only in my mind. Nurse told me people would think I'm loony if I talk aloud when there's no one near."

The others exchanged startled glances but dropped the subject.

"Alice should have answered the bell before now. I'll go down to obtain tea for Judith."

When Ruth opened the door, she understood why Alice hadn't answered the bell. The entire staff crowded around, hopeful expressions on their faces.

"Mrs. Sherwood, His Grace told us Lady Judith is awake." Taylor's voice trembled.

"Yes, I'm thankful to say, she's awake and hungry, which is a good sign. Cook, will you send up some tea and toast, please?"

"Make it cinnamon toast, Cookie. Lots of it," Judith called weakly. "I want some coddled eggs too."

"After the doctor has seen you, we will discuss additional food, Judith. For the moment, plain toast and tea are all you get."

Judith frowned at Ruth's words.

With Judith on the mend, the household returned to normal. She listened with disbelief when Ruth told her how long she'd slept.

Judith knew she must explain her behaviour, yet she avoided the issue until Ruth insisted. On the third day after Judith woke, Ruth opened the subject the moment Judith finished her morning cup of chocolate.

"Are you ready to explain yourself? I'm very angry with you."

"I know I deserve a thorough scolding, not only for breaking my promise but also for scaring you."

"Yes, you do."

However, before the scold could begin, Judith hurried into speech. "Did they find the cave? Did the thieves get away with the stolen things?"

"I will consider answering your questions after you answer mine." Her pent-up emotions exploded. "Judith, how could you do such a thing? How could you go into a cave by yourself? Even if there hadn't been robbers in the area, there could have been wild animals. You must have realized the danger."

"Yes, Judith, it's time for an explanation."

The carpet had muffled Daniel's footsteps, so his voice startled Judith into hasty words. "You never had the time, so I decided to explore the cave on my own." Defiance tinged her voice. She described hiding in the cave some days before, then going back with candles to explore the interior on the day the men shot her.

They listened without interruption, albeit with grim faces. Ruth burst into speech when Judith described the pain that ripped through her shoulder.

"You could have been killed. Did you even consider that? The bullet could have entered your heart. You would be d-d-dead!" She erupted into tears.

Ruth's tears were too much for Judith. She had avoided thinking about such a possibility. She wiggled into a sitting position and reached her healthy arm toward Ruth. Together they cried themselves into exhaustion. Judith lay back on her pillows, prepared to sleep some more. Daniel sent Ruth to her own bed. He would consult further with the constable, who would have to wait longer before interrogating Judith.

Judith didn't mention her father or her guardian angel again until one morning when Ruth sat with her.

"Has your guardian angel said anything about your father?"

"No. You don't believe Susanna exists, do you?"

"You do, which is the important point. Perhaps your wishful thinking took control of your dreams. Deep down, do you wish he were still alive?"

When Judith didn't answer, Ruth persisted with another question. "Would you welcome him if he did return home?"

Judith stared into the distance for a long moment. "No."

"No, what? You don't hope he is alive, or you would not welcome him?"

"No, I wouldn't welcome him back." She challenged Ruth with fire in her voice. "Why should I? His being alive wouldn't change what he did to me."

"Do you truly wish difficulties for your father, or is your hurt talking?"

Judith clenched her hands until the knuckles turned white. "He had every opportunity over a six-year period to change his behaviour. He didn't. Why should I not wish him to suffer?"

"I know little—essentially nothing—about guardian angels, the powers they have, but they surely have the task of instilling moral values into their humans. What does yours say about your unforgiving attitude?"

Judith shrugged, unwilling to admit how often Susanna condemned her attitude and how equally often she ignored Susanna's admonitions.

"Your lack of an answer tells me this is an ongoing rebellion." Ruth rose and walked away, leaving Judith to ponder her words.

Twenty-Three

And then What Happened?

Relief had flooded Richard when Judith woke. He hadn't been able to stay away from the Manor until that moment. He'd wondered why Sherwood or Mrs. Sherwood hadn't demanded a reason for haunting the Manor. Richard could only have answered that he had to be there.

Now, with fear for her behind him, he decided to see the cave for himself. Candle and tinderbox in hand, he stepped inside. Dark and empty. He lit the candle and explored to the back. Nothing to be seen except loose stones, so he rode away, his fear for her renewed but also his temper. How could she have been so foolhardy as to endanger herself? He allowed Sheik to lead the way, heedless of direction, his thoughts in turmoil.

Richard flung Sheik's reins over a limb, leaving him to graze, then settled his back against the oak tree, long legs stretched toward the stream. He didn't know what had led him to this place where Judith had displayed a spurt of temper midst her mischievous fun in the stream. Typical Judith, as he had come to know her.

His lips twitched at the memory of her teasing him out of his temper. If he admitted the truth, anger had been his only defense against the temptation caused by her wet, clinging shirt. Her innocence was beyond belief for a female her age, even one secluded on a rural estate.

Innocent. Mischievous. Intelligent. Temperamental. Stubborn. Haughty. Incorrigible. Thoughtless. All those things wrapped up in one wonderful, beautiful package.

And I love her.

The thought exploded into Richard's brain.

Preposterous! How could he possibly love such a female? He did not intend to love any female, he reminded himself. Especially one who couldn't keep a civil tongue in her head, one who courted danger the way Judith had done at the cave. As for climbing trees, she could have fallen and broken her beautiful neck. Richard pushed away that vision. He had his future planned, and his plans did not include love, whatever that might be. If such a thing existed, which Richard doubted. Love was simply a figment of somebody's imagination—someone who lacked mental sharpness. Nothing more.

Further thought on such a ridiculous notion was preposterous to the point of imbecility. He was concerned for her safety, yes. He was concerned about the head injury even though she brought it on herself. But love her? No. Besides, his eventual duchess must be dependent on him. Lady Judith Elizabeth Ainsley had shown her independence to an alarming degree. Imagine her, a mere chit, disobeying her father and striking out on her own.

Her situation reminded him of the mess his father had created by selling the entailed property. He must tell Judith but couldn't bring himself to upset her at this moment. He ignored his relief at postponing the inevitable.

Astride Sheik, Richard gave one last glance toward the stream where Judith had waded with such glee. As then, he could see the bottom: only this time water burbled over small, smooth stones, not bare toes.

The furor over Judith's accident lasted only a few days, but they were harrowing ones for her. She had to answer the constable's questions and suffer the horrified words of afternoon visitors. The horrified words came from the adults. The younger people were in alt, begging to take part in her next adventure. Judith quivered at the idea.

"Never again," she vowed. "Mark my words. From this day forward, the most exciting thing in my life will be afternoon tea."

Answering the constable's questions was a different matter altogether. He was polite, yet firm.

"Lady Judith, I want you to tell me everything you can about those three men. Every little detail, do you understand me?"

He made her feel about six years old. However, she answered in a confident voice designed to hide her apprehension. "I didn't see them, sir. I only heard their voices."

"What can you tell me?" His sharp eyes demanded the truth.

"One spoke common English. The other two spoke French, also common."

"What do you mean by common?"

"They didn't have the refined accents of the upper classes."

"Did they say anything that indicated where they came from or were going?"

"The Englishman said something about plenty of dogs being around the area, so he must know the area well to have located the cave. Perhaps a former tenant who decided robbery was easier than working. The entrance is not easily visible behind shrubs. I had ridden in that area several times without realizing its existence."

"Hmmm. Anything else?"

A frown marred her brow as she struggled to remember. "One Frenchman said they had a lot of miles to put behind them before nightfall. I don't remember anything else about their voices."

"When they shot at you, were they close enough you could see them? Could they recognize you?"

Her eyes grew wide with horror. "I did look back, but I don't believe they were close enough to distinguish my features. Do you think they might come after me?"

The constable's harsh features softened. "Probably not, my lady. Still, the possibility exists if they were able to recognize you or your horse."

"They might recognize Gypsy."

"There's one more thing. Are you sure there were ten bags?"

"Rochdale asked me the same question. Yes, I'm sure I counted ten, although I only opened the three closest bags." She described the contents of each.

"You're certain one contained jewelry?"

"Yes, I'm certain. Was it missing? Why would they take only one? Oh, they carried the jewelry away in their pockets."

The constable nodded. He paused, a thoughtful look on his face. "They would need a wagon to carry the rest away. We removed the bags before they could obtain one. There was another bag there, an empty one. I thought the thieves meant to fill it later, but they emptied it instead."

Apparently satisfied she had told him all she could, he bowed himself from the room.

A subdued Judith reclined on a sofa in front of open French windows the following morning. The warm breeze moved the sheer drapes, allowing her to see the sculpted boxwoods beyond the terrace. Alice moved to a chair across the room when Taylor showed Richard into the room.

He stared at Judith's face a moment before bowing over her hand with an inquiry about her health.

"My shoulder aches a little, Your Grace. Otherwise, I'm all right."

He pulled a chair closer. "Would you care to tell me about your adventure?"

Judith searched his face for condemnation, but seeing only interest, she nodded.

"The whole thing started when I rode in that area. It's my favorite part of the Manor grounds. On that day, I heard masculine voices near what I know now is the cave. I couldn't distinguish words, you understand, just voices. Ghosts entered my mind first, then a full-blown scenario about an abduction. That's when the idea for Mrs. Blaylock's next book was born. I hurried home to tell Ruthie about the idea because we had been unable to think of one."

"You didn't investigate the voices?"

"No, I didn't dismount. I saw the cave entrance, but people being in there never occurred to me. Daniel said we would explore the cave together when he could find the time. He stays quite busy because I haven't helped with the estate work the way I should have." She searched Richard's face, wondering if he understood. Given his attitude toward her independent nature, he might not.

"So, you agreed to wait."

She shifted her arm against the supporting pillow. "At first, I didn't mind waiting because I was in a hurry to start writing the story. Investigating the cave could come later."

"I've talked with you there several times. Why did you not mention the cave?"

"Telling you never occurred to me. I didn't give the inside of the cave much attention, although I often rode that way hoping for further inspiration for the story. Perhaps hear the voices again, but more clearly, or new words."

"Why did you decide on exploration this time?"

"Ignoring my promise to Ruth and Daniel, I rode out one morning intending to explore the cave," she confessed. "I heard the voices again and decided to see if they were ghosts. Inside the cave, the voices grew louder, followed by footsteps. Ghosts don't walk, do they? These were real people, and they were coming toward me." She relived her fright as she told the rest of the story.

He calmed her nervous hands with his own until she clasped hers in her lap.

"You could have been killed." His face hardened but then softened when he saw her stricken face. "The day I found you there and we talked about Mrs. Blaylock, your thoughts were so far away you didn't know anyone was near. What if the thieves had found you before I did?"

A sudden gasp for breath was her only response.

He ran his hands through his once immaculate hair. "I'm sure you've heard all this from the Sherwoods, so you don't need to hear it from me. I'll resist my real inclination—to rake you over the coals. Instead, I'll appease my curiosity about something you said when you roused from your long sleep. Will you tell me about Susanna?"

Judith eyed him a long moment. Would he believe her? Would he discount the presence of an angel? She couldn't walk away from his question, so she would risk his ridicule. After a deep breath, she said, "Susanna is my guardian angel."

"Yes, you told us when you awoke. Tell me more. How do you know you have a guardian angel?"

"Everyone has a special angel." Judith met his gaze with a serene face, although she was fluttering inside.

"If I have one, I'm not aware of it. What does yours look like?"

"I've never seen her, but she's taken care of me since I was four years old."

"She failed in her responsibility toward you this time."

"Ruth said the same thing. I'll tell you what I told her. My injury is my responsibility because I didn't always listen to Susanna," Judith confessed. "I must admit there have been too many times when I listened but then ignored her."

He smiled. "I've seen your strong will, so I can sympathize with anyone, including an angel, who tries to control your behaviour."

Judith joined his light laughter. Then they sat in silence for a moment. "Will you tell me what happened about the robberies? Daniel and Ruth won't talk about it. Did the constable capture the thieves?"

"No, they have not yet been apprehended, perhaps never will be—the two Frenchmen anyway. When the constable reached the cave, the only evidence they'd been there was where they'd tethered their horses. The constable took nine bags of stolen goods in charge so the robbery victims will get back their possessions."

"There were ten bags, so the thieves got away with one."

"You are quite sure there were ten?"

"Yes. I counted them." She stared at him with wide eyes. "Do you think the thieves will return to the cave? They might look for the other bag, you see. Perhaps the constable should put a watch on the place."

"There isn't anyone except himself, so a watch isn't feasible. I imagine the culprits already have returned and found the bags missing. I don't suppose they'll come again." He took a deep, steadying breath. "The entire area owes you a debt of gratitude for finding their possessions, but you're lucky Daniel Sherwood didn't strangle you for upsetting his wife."

"I didn't mean to cause all this distress. Truly, I didn't. When Susanna decides to talk to me again, she'll rake me over the coals too." Judith closed her lips to stop the trembles until she could speak again. "I fear she might have given up on me this time. I couldn't bear that!"

"Easy, Judith, we realize you meant no harm," he soothed her. To lighten her forlorn expression, he changed the subject. "I've never seen any ghosts, have you?"

"No. I'm not sure I believe in ghosts or apparitions or spirits remaining after the person is dead, but Mrs. Blaylock does. Otherwise, she couldn't write about them."

"You see her as a different person?"

"Yes, I do. Lady Judith Elizabeth Ainsley, devious and independent though she is, could never write what Mrs. Blaylock does yet still be acceptable to Society, which I intend to be someday. I don't intend to confine myself to my estate."

"And you shouldn't. Do you believe female authors are a breed apart, people who must hide their true selves?"

"Only novelists, Ri—uh—Rochdale. Serious writers might be called bluestockings, but they're admitted into most levels of Society, which a novelist could never be." Perhaps he didn't notice she almost called him by name.

"You could write serious books, if you chose."

"I suppose I could now," Judith agreed. "However, when I started writing I had neither the knowledge nor the inclination. I've continued doing what was successful."

"That makes sense." He rose to take his leave and stared into her eyes for a long moment. Picking up her hand, palm upward, he kissed it lightly, then closed her fingers. He hurried from the room before Judith could react.

Judith stared at her hand, slowly uncurling her fingers. Her palm didn't look different, so why did it tingle? Why was her pulse racing? She nestled that hand in the other. For safekeeping.

On Richard's ensuing morning visits, they sat beneath a shade tree within full view of gardeners, so Ruth left them alone. Judith wondered if he would kiss her palm again—she still didn't understand the tingle. He was his usual amiable self, so she was able to relax in his presence. He didn't mention her recent behaviour either. Instead, he asked about her estate work.

"Mrs. Sherwood said you give Sherwood extensive help on the estate."

"I must admit I have become a real help to him only recently. During our first weeks, I dealt primarily with the families because the men didn't believe a female knew anything about estate management."

"Does that ability not seem unusual to you?"

"Not if your father is obsessed the way mine was." Judith changed the subject. "One of my favorite things in our early days here was reading fables to Susie, a darling little girl with fiery curls."

"She's learning to read too, I wager, as a result."

"Yes. I almost regret she is because I'll miss our time together."

"You'll find another needy child," he assured her.

Judith smiled her acknowledgment. "I also read our Mrs. Blaylock books to a bedridden woman on the estate. She didn't hesitate to voice her opinions on what she called our namby-pamby heroines. She entertained me at least as much as I did her. I asked some estate women to take my place when I got busy writing another book. I miss her pithy comments and would like to hear her thoughts on the current story, but I can't read my book without revealing the author's identity."

They sat for a few minutes, each lost in thought, until Richard roused himself to leave, saying he would see her on the morrow.

<> <> <> <> <>

Morning brought bright sunshine after a night filled with nightmares of Ainsley Park deteriorating before her eyes. Judith sat in the garden wondering if the duke would visit her. Would he mention her father again? She'd given some attention to what he said, but she was not ready for more of his opinions on her attitude. Therefore, when he arrived, she greeted him coolly. "Good morning, Your Grace, is it not a beautiful day?"

"Yes, Lady Judith, a beautiful day indeed."

She glanced at him. She didn't remember when he last addressed her by her title when they were alone, so why this time? "Why did you use my title? I would rather you did not."

"You used mine."

"That's altogether different." She started to say he didn't have reason to hate his title but remembered his difficulties with his father about their estate. She said instead, "You're a duke."

"Thank you for telling me."

Noting the twinkle in his eyes, she relaxed against the garden bench, and her mouth curved into a teasing smile. "Besides, a man as pretty as you are must be addressed with due reverence by ordinary mortals."

"Yes, we must not forget my prettiness, must we? I have it on good authority I look like a Greek god."

Diverted, she inquired, "Truly? Whose authority?"

"Yours." He lounged against the wrought-iron bench, folded his arms across his chest, laughing down at her.

"Mine? I confess I've thought that several times, but I don't recall telling you. Is mind-reading one of your accomplishments?"

"I won't admit to clairvoyance, but I will remind you when you told me, if you will agree to call me Richard."

Calling him by his name was not difficult since she had called him Richard in her thoughts since she was seven years old. She would not be missish about that or anything else, she assured herself. Independent females don't simper like a ninny.

"I have long thought you resemble a Greek god— Richard—but I can't believe I had the audacity to reveal it. Now, tell me."

His face became serious, yet he answered readily enough. "When I found you on the trail and carried you home."

Her mouth gaped. "I have no recollection of how I arrived at home and hadn't thought to question it. Did I say anything else?"

Bursting into laughter, he shook his head. "No, those were your only words. Naturally, after being compared favorably with a Greek god, I didn't need to be told anything else."

Their lighthearted banter continued until he realized the time. "I must be going, Judith, before I overstay my welcome."

"Oh, you couldn't do that, Richard. After all, any man as pretty as you can do anything he chooses."

"There are none who match my prettiness, so how can you compare me with others?"

Judith gurgled deep in her throat in an effort not to laugh at his audacity.

He rose to his feet. "How do you produce the little gurgle? Do you have an extra vocal cord, perhaps?"

Without waiting for her reply, he flicked her cheek with one finger and left the garden, leaving her without time for an answer—the only way she would allow him to have the last word.

Judith's nightmares of Ainsley Park's deterioration had faded while Richard was with her. She could only hope they would not return.

Twenty-Four

Somewhere in France

Faceless people, not real-estate nightmares, disturbed the old man in his attic hiding place. Those people chattered in English, but nothing they said made sense. Papers. Something about papers was mixed with something about sheep. Crops and thatched cottages intermingled with military uniforms and horses. Was he a farmer? A soldier? He ran his fingers over his palms. No calluses, so not a farmer. Surely soldiers had rough hands too, so he ruled out that occupation.

Henri had mentioned Napoleon. That name, at least, had become clear in his mind. But what did he, an Englishman, have to do with the self-declared French emperor?

And who was the child who danced around the perimeter of the nightmares? Sometimes she cuddled a kitten. Everything would become clear if only he could bring her face into focus. He didn't know why he was so sure of that, but he was. The child with the raven curls was at the center of his life, one way or another.

As usual, he woke early, anxious for the broth and toast, which Marie supplied throughout the days since he woke. She'd had to spoon-feed him the first few meals, but, now, he could at least feed himself, although he needed both hands to clasp a cup. He could probably eat two slices of toast this morning, which would rebuild his strength faster.

He hadn't left the attic but hadn't heard a key turn in a lock when Henri or Marie came, so he wasn't a prisoner. His brain remained so fuzzy that he was beginning to despair he would ever know his identity. What would he do if he never remembered who he was? He couldn't live in this attic forever, dependent on Henri and Marie, but he wouldn't know where to go.

Who were those faceless people?

Twenty-Five

Unplanned Journey

Judith missed being on horseback. Shoulder pain prohibited holding the reins, yet her need to be outside in the early morning had not diminished. A walk around the grounds would have to suffice.

Twittering sparrows had waken her at dawn. Rather than ring for her maid, Judith had eased herself into an old riding habit with a loose jacket and slipped outside as the sun peeped over the treetops. Breathing the fresh scent of roses, she walked across dew-sparkled grass toward the home wood. Strolling under the canopy of leaves high above her head, she listened to chaffinches greet the new day.

Judith eyed the low branch of a spreading oak but knew she shouldn't swing herself onto it. Instead, she sat sideways at its base, her wounded shoulder touching only air. Peacefulness surrounded her until, unbidden, thoughts of Richard penetrated the stillness.

He paid her considerable attention, although there was nothing lover-like in his manner. With a small smile, she remembered her seven-year-old self shouting her vow to marry him even though he was prettier than she was. Judith had dreamed about the young Richard for eight years, but she vowed to forget him when he didn't recognize her at the theatre. She learned of the earl's perfidy the same year. Together, they convinced her she couldn't trust any man.

That was then. This was now. She knew Daniel was trustworthy, but he didn't exercise any control over her. A husband would, the way her father had attempted to do. No, she had nothing against matrimony for others. For her, independence was too precious to lose. She would not trust her future to any man.

She brushed herself off and started back to the house. After taking only a few steps, she heard footsteps rustling in the leaves. Two men wearing shabby clothing hurried toward her.

"What are you doing on my property?" Judith glared at two shabby men. Her haughtiest voice demanded an explanation.

"Ah, so we find you alone at last, Mademoiselle. We knew if we watched the house long enough, we would catch you on your own."

Judith stifled a gasp. The robbers had seen her face! *Susanna, where are you?* She understood their French, common though it was, and made the instant decision to pretend ignorance.

"If you have something to say, speak English. I cannot understand your heathen tongue."

"That's all the better, Mademoiselle," said one in heavily accented English. He grabbed her right arm. When she struggled, he hit her on the side of the head with his fist. She collapsed against him.

Judith revived to find herself slung across her captor's shoulder. Her head throbbed, her arms hung straight down his back. The strain on her wounded shoulder was almost more than she could bear, but she stifled her nausea and listened to their talk.

"She should have been mounted, Jacques. I wanted her mare."

"I agree the mare would be some compensation for what she did to us, but we'll get our money another way, Philippe. Payment might take longer, but we can wait."

Jacques and Philippe. She must remember those names. Jacques appeared to be in charge.

"You've never said what you intended to do once we got our hands on her. Are you going to demand ransom?"

"No. We would get our money quicker, true, but we would also have the English gendarmes after us. This filly will pay in a different way. I will sell her to Madame Duvalier in Paris. She always wants fresh merchandise for her bordello, especially English. How does my plan strike you?"

Philippe snickered. "It's a long way to Paris. Perhaps we should sample the goods along the way."

Her eyes widened with horror until she heard the first man's reply.

"No!" Jacques ordered. "Madame has warned me she won't pay for damaged goods. When she pays us for this package, we can find all the women we want. Meanwhile, you watch how you treat this one. I don't want a mark on her, do you understand me?"

"You hit her."

"I hit her on the head where her hair will hide any bruises. Now stow it in case anyone is around."

Judith breathed a sigh of relief. It was a long way to Paris, as the man named Jacques said. She would contrive her escape in some way before they reached there.

"Here are the horses at last. She's heavy. You mount. I'll hand her to you."

She forced herself to limpness until her feet touched the ground. Then she shoved her captor and took off in a run.

Shouting words Judith had never heard but could guess, they gave chase, catching her when she stumbled over a tree root. She screamed with pain when they dragged her upright by her left arm. The shriek earned another fist against her head.

Susanna, where are you?

When Judith again revived, she sat in front of one man, leaning into his chest while their mount found its way around trees. The stench of his filthy clothes almost overpowered her. Fortunately, her right shoulder pressed against him. She listened to them while trying to ignore the throbbing pain assaulting her left shoulder.

"Philippe, are you sure you can find the carriage you hid?"

"It's in a copse this side of Bishop's Waltham. Our only problem will be getting around Southampton without anybody seeing us."

"We're not going anywhere near Southampton. Our route lies through Midhurst."

"Midhurst? We must leave England immediately. Southampton harbor is closer."

"With so many people around, we couldn't escape notice," Jacques reminded. "We're going farther east."

"Dover? How can we keep her quiet such a long way? We'll be discovered long before we get there."

"We can't risk any main ports." Jacques' voice was impatient. "We'll leave from Dungeness and put in at Sangatte, which means we'll avoid Calais too."

Judith's heart sank. Even if Ruth or Daniel thought she might be on her way to France, they would naturally go toward Dover. She imagined they would look toward London anyway. What would Richard do? A pang of regret she might never see him again spread through her.

Philippe interrupted her thoughts. "What about Carter? He'll be angry when we don't give him his share."

"Let him."

"You're not thinking, Jacques. He might go to the authorities."

"He won't risk prison or deportation, if not hanging for horse theft. We'll be in France. There's no reason for us to come back here. We'll be safe when we've crossed the channel."

"Shouldn't she be waking up?"

"I hit her hard enough to keep her quiet for a while."

Judith remained silent, allowing her body to move with the sway of the horse, but her mind was busy. Maybe she could escape from the carriage, unless they rode inside. Still, they must change horses, so they would stop at least twice before Dungeness. She would be ready.

At length, a leg cramp forced Judith to shift her position, thereby drawing her captors' attention. She kept her voice groggy when she demanded where they were taking her.

"Paris, Mademoiselle. Is that not every female's dream?"

"Paris!" She forced shock into the single word. "Why?"

"You shouldn't have stuck your nose into our affairs." Judith recognized his voice as Philippe. "You cheated us out of a lot of money. You're going to pay for it."

"Shut up, you numbskull. As for you, Mademoiselle, unless you want my fist against your head again, you'll keep your mouth shut."

She glared at him but subsided. Her head couldn't take much more battering. After what seemed hours, they reached the carriage.

"You will be much more comfortable the rest of the way."

Judith looked around. Where were the other horses? Where was the driver?

When Philippe dismounted, Jacques pushed Judith off the horse into his grasp and swung himself to the ground. Opening the carriage door, he shoved her inside, climbing in after her. He pulled a flask from beneath the bench and squeezed her jaw until her mouth popped open.

She choked when the foul-tasting liquid slid down her throat. Sputtering, she moved as far from him as the seat allowed.

Susanna, where are you?

"There, that should keep you quiet until we reach Dungeness. Philippe, hitch up the horses, so we can be on our way. We'll reach the boat well after dark, but we don't want to tarry between here and there. You drive first. I'll ride inside. We'll swap every hour or so."

Judith didn't know what drug they gave her, but her eyelids drooped. Then she slumped sideways. She awoke disoriented, finding herself stretched along the seat with a rug over her. Sensing someone's presence nearby, she remained quiet while jumbled thoughts fought for supremacy. The robbers had abducted her and were going to Paris. The carriage hit a bad bump rolling her into the floor. Judith couldn't pretend to sleep any longer, so she pulled herself up and glared at the man sitting opposite.

"What was the vile stuff you poured down my throat? I have a monstrous headache. My stomach is heaving too. Unless you want me to cast up my accounts all over you, you'll stop this carriage on the instant."

"Considering you haven't eaten all day, I doubt I'm in danger, but in the event you do, I'll leave you alone." He hammered on the roof, then clamored out when the carriage stopped. "You can't escape, so don't waste your efforts, Mademoiselle."

No, she couldn't escape because Jacques tied the door shut on the outside. At least she was alone with her thoughts.

Soon the carriage stopped deep inside a stand of trees, and then one of her captors fumbled with the door.

"Come on."

She wouldn't make abduction easy for them. She didn't budge.

Reaching inside, he jerked her left arm causing her to scream in pain.

"No need for screaming, Mademoiselle, no one can hear you. Still, perhaps you'd better have another swallow of this nice brandy I bought for you."

He forced her mouth open, but this time she managed to hold most in her mouth. She let it dribble out the side as Jacques lowered her toward the ground and stood over her while Philippe released the horses from their harness.

Jacques took the reins and turned away. "I'm going to sell these nags. You stay here and make sure you don't touch her. If I find you've harmed her, I'll put a bullet between your eyes."

"Oh, go on. I won't touch her. She's already asleep, so she won't be any trouble. Don't forget to bring us something to eat."

Her shoulder was hurting so badly sleep was impossible, but she didn't see how she could escape because the man stood with his foot on her skirt.

It seemed hours before Jacques returned.

"Did you get a good price for the horses?"

"Yes, considering how far we drove them without much rest. How is she?"

"Sound asleep."

"I didn't see anybody near the boat, so you can sling her across your shoulder. That's the easiest way to carry her on board."

"Why do I have to carry her? You're bigger than I am."

"I carried her before. Just do what you're told, or I'll leave you here."

Again, Judith lay across a man's shoulder for what seemed an eternity. She bit her tongue to keep from moaning when he stumbled along. There was no one around when they reached the waterfront, so her escape hopes dwindled.

Susanna, where are you?

In despair, Judith lay on the hard floor of the boat, thinking about Ruth and Daniel. They must be frantic.

Twenty-Six

Searching

"Is Judith still asleep?" Daniel glanced up from a letter in his hand.

Ruth refilled her teacup before answering. "I imagine so. She sleeps more now than before her accident. Did you need her for a particular reason?"

"This letter is from a Mr. Parker, who asks if we want to join his endeavors in starting a horse farm. Judith might be interested, but it can wait until she comes downstairs for breakfast."

"She might indeed be interested, considering her love for horses."

Daniel stacked his letters. "There are a couple of other letters needing her attention too. I'll put them on her desk before riding out to the Nelsons' place. She can read them, then tell me at lunch whether she's interested in working with Parker on a horse farm. You're right about her love for horses, so maybe she will approve this idea for an investment."

"I'll tell her." Ruth lifted her face for a kiss, then returned to her own correspondence. She'd notified relatives of her marriage and new direction, thereby causing a nine-day wonder in the family because they'd considered her on the shelf.

Reading between the lines, Ruth realized they'd expected her to return home and make herself useful after Judith reached maturity. They would want her to go from one family member after another depending on the need at a particular time, staying as long as that family needed her, and never knowing where she would go next. She would never have a place she could call home. She had escaped the life they planned for her, thanks to the Monfords' bringing her to Ainsley Park and treating her like close family, followed by Judith's financial acumen, and finally her marriage to Daniel. Any one of those gave her a future she hadn't expected. Altogether, they were astounding.

An hour passed. Ruth sat at her desk in the morning room going over household accounts when Judith's maid tapped on the door. "What is it, Alice?"

"Ma'am, have you seen Lady Judith this morning?"

"No, I haven't. Is she not still asleep?"

"I waited for her to ring for chocolate, and when she didn't, I looked in on her. She isn't there."

"I imagine she went for a walk," Ruth soothed the perturbed maid. "You know how she is about being outside during the morning hours."

"Yes, Ma'am, if you say so." With a curtsy, Alice left the room.

Another hour passed. Ruth wiped the pen's nib on a soft cloth and returned them to the desk drawer. After closing the ledger, she flexed her fingers. Judith should do the household accounts. Despite all the writing exercises she had been assigned through the years, by first her governess and later Ruth, Judith's hand was near illegibility. Ruth frowned as she stood. Stepping into the hall, she inquired whether Taylor had seen Lady Judith.

"No, Mrs. Sherwood. I haven't seen her at all this morning."

Her frown deepening, Ruth hurried up the stairs to Judith's bedchamber where Alice was hanging clothing in the cupboard.

"Has Lady Judith returned, Alice?"

"No, Ma'am, and I'm getting worried."

"I'll send a message to Mr. Sherwood. He'll begin a search of the grounds. She might have fallen and re-injured her shoulder." Ruth chewed her inner lip. An injury possibility should have occurred to her sooner, the minute Alice approached her.

Daniel asked the estate workers for help. Together, they began the search. Another hour passed.

When he returned, Ruth met him at the door, her eyes huge with fear. "What do we do now, Daniel? Is it possible the robbers found her outside and abducted her?"

"I fear so. I sent word to the constable. Perhaps we should now contact the neighbors, although Judith won't appreciate the attention if she returns safely after losing track of time."

As one, they turned toward the study to wait for the constable. When the door opened, however, Rochdale entered.

One glance at their faces told him something was wrong. "Is Lady Judith ill again?"

"Perhaps worse than recurring illness," Daniel answered him. "We haven't seen her this morning. No one has."

"Have you searched the estate?"

Daniel nodded. "The constable should be here soon. We fear the robbers found her when she went for a walk."

Ruth gripped her hands together in her lap. Her thoughts were a jumble: some beseeching God to take care of the headstrong girl, others berating herself for not taking immediate action when Alice inquired about Judith.

What was that guardian angel's name? Susanna, that's it. She'd better be on the job and protect Judith better than she did the last time.

They sat in grim silence until Taylor opened the door admitting the constable, red-faced and winded. Ruth guessed he had come at a fast clip if not an actual run.

"What's this about Lady Judith missing?"

"We've searched the estate. There's no sign of her," Daniel told him.

The constable settled himself into an oversized leather chair and proceeded to question them. When had they last seen her? Late the evening before, Ruth replied. Had anyone seen her that morning: the servants, perhaps? No. Did she normally go out in the early morning? Yes, invariably while she could ride, but since her accident, no.

"I must know how she was dressed if I am to question people outside the immediate neighborhood."

Ruth rang the bell for Alice, then sat clasping her hands, trying to ease her fears.

"You sent for me, Ma'am?"

"Yes, Alice. Please see if you can determine what Lady Judith wore this morning."

"I can tell you now, Ma'am. I've been clearing out her cupboard. The only thing missing is her old, dark blue riding habit and jean half boots. She didn't even take a hat."

"Thank you, Alice."

As the maid left the room, Taylor ushered in one of the estate farmers who held a lad by the hand. "Mr. Morrison has some information about Lady Judith."

"Oh, thank God," Ruth declared. "Please tell us what you know."

Mr. Morrison dipped a bow, then pulled the small boy forward. His voice was harsh. "Roddy, here, told us he saw her ladyship this morning. Tell them what you told us."

His eyes dark with fear, the child hung back, muttering something unintelligible.

Rochdale held out a hand toward him. "It's all right, lad. No one is angry with you. Come over here and tell me where you saw Lady Judith."

The others remained quiet while Rochdale questioned the boy.

Glancing at his father, the boy moved closer to the duke before he whispered, "I wusn't s'posed to be there."

"Your father will forgive you this time if you tell us where you saw Lady Judith. What you tell us is important because you can help us find her."

"She wus in the home wood. I heard 'em talkin', and one hit 'er. He slung 'er acrost his shoulder. I follered 'em a little way 'til they come to the horses."

"Did you see what happened next?"

"She ran from the men, but they caught 'er. One of 'em hit 'er on the head again, and they took 'er away on a horse."

Ruth's gasp fell into the silence. She might never see Judith again. Her charge had given her some difficult times through the years, but she would accept whatever problems the future held if only Judith would come home. *Susanna, you'd better be doing your job. I can talk to God, you know.*

"Can you tell us the time?"

"Early. The sun wus just coming up."

Rochdale grimaced but kept his voice matter-of-fact. "Why didn't you tell Mr. Sherwood?"

"Cos I found a badger," he whispered. His eyes flooded with tears. "A big 'un, and I follered him."

"I would have done the same thing at your age," the duke assured him. "What can you tell us about the men? How many were there? What did they say?"

"Two. They didn't talk like us. They didn't call 'er Lady Judith neither, like they ought. It's only perlite, my ma said so."

"What did they call her?"

He frowned in thought. "Madazel. Something like that anyways."

"Would they have said Mademoiselle?"

"Yes sir. That's what they called Lady Judith."

"You need to tell us where in the home wood you saw her."

Roddy hung his head and slanted a glance toward his father who stood scowling at him. "At the other side," he whispered.

"Which direction did they go?"

This time, Roddy's face showed bewilderment.

"Did they go toward the road?"

"No, they went over toward where Susie lives."

Rochdale raised his eyebrow to Daniel. "Do you know where he means?"

"East. There's a lot of wooded area before they reach a road."

The constable cleared his throat. "What did the lad mean when he said they talked differently from us?"

"Mademoiselle is the French word for 'Miss', Constable. I fear Lady Judith has fallen into the hands of the robbers."

"Do you think they will take her to France?" Ruth twisted her hands together and gazed at Daniel with a pleading expression. She might never see Judith again if they crossed the channel.

"Possible," he answered. "We would have heard from them by this time, if they wanted ransom."

"Southampton is the closest port," the constable said. "I'll start in that direction."

"No, they wouldn't leave from Southampton. For one thing, there's too much activity going on there. For another, it would mean too much time at sea with the risk of revenue cutters," the duke told him. "They more likely would go toward Dover."

"So far on horseback?" Ruth stared at him in consternation. "It's much too far for her to travel with the shoulder wound. Just being on a horse with an unsteady gait and at probable fast speed could reopen the wound."

Rochdale said, "I imagine they have obtained a carriage someplace. They wouldn't risk being seen traveling any distance with a female riding double with one of them."

The constable rose. "I'll ask in the village about anybody wanting a wagon."

With thanks for his help, Ruth sat in frozen silence, leaving everything to Daniel, who addressed Mr. Morrison. "Your lad has been a big help. I hope you won't be too harsh with him for disobeying you. If he had not been where he was, we wouldn't have any information about Lady Judith."

After they left, Rochdale asked, "What do you suggest, Sherwood?"

"Let's ride in the direction the lad mentioned and see what we can find." He cupped Ruth's face with his hand. "Try not to worry too much, my dear. Judith is resilient."

"Come back immediately when you know something," Ruth urged.

In the home wood, Richard spotted where Judith had crushed the leaves while she sat under the tree. Riding further, they found spilled oats and decided this was where the miscreants had tethered their horses. "Where would we come out if we continued through this wood?"

Daniel mulled over the question. "Assuming they are headed toward Dover, they would continue east through Bishop's Waltham, then across Sussex."

"We will continue in this direction at least to Bishop's Waltham."

They wove their way through the trees until Richard spied the deep ruts where a carriage had stood.

"It appears they came this way, but something puzzles me. Only one pair of horses left tracks, and they were pulling the carriage. What happened to the ones the men were riding?"

"I imagine they hitched them to the carriage, which means they didn't hire a carriage and driver," Daniel replied. "They're driving themselves, so they must travel slowly because they won't have horses stabled along the way. I'll go back for my carriage, then go after them."

"No, you leave it to me. I can travel faster by horseback." When Daniel protested, Richard continued, "We might be wrong in our calculations, Sherwood. You go back to East Leah and look toward London. I'll find some way to send word."

Daniel reluctantly agreed.

Richard asked a few questions in Bishop's Waltham but could get no information without the carriage description. He continued east without help through Midhurst, then Billingshurst. There, he stabled Sheik and rejoiced to hire another fast mount. Exhausted, he stopped for the night.

Over a late meal of indifferent food and worse wine, Richard relived the day from the time Sherwood told him Judith was missing. Was this the right direction to find her? What would he do if he never again saw her heart-stopping smile, her eyes the colour of water on a sunny day? He stifled a groan as he found his way up the stairs to his assigned bedchamber. The room was musty, and the single window probably had not been opened in decades. The sheets were unaired, but he was so deep in his misery that discomfort didn't matter.

After a night filled with restless tossing on a mattress, which he vowed contained rocks instead of feathers, Richard swallowed a quick cup of bitter coffee with some bread and cheese, then was on his way east again. So sure was he that he would find his quarry in Dover, he cut across country to Tenterden. There, he still didn't find answers but hired another mount for what he hoped was the final leg of his journey.

Arriving at Dover, exhausted and filthy with dust, he headed first for the harbor. No one had seen two Frenchmen with a raven-haired female. The best he could do was obtain useful information about tides.

Richard rode to the Dover Arms and asked for a room and meal. He brushed himself off before going to the private parlor, where he paced the floor, waiting for food. On the long ride from East Leah, he'd struggled with the possibility he might never see Judith again. Never see those bewitching blue eyes turn stormy gray again, never hear her tiny gurgle again. He must find her because living without her was impossible.

She was independent and hot-tempered—unable to keep a civil tongue in her head—so how could he possibly love her? There was no denying his love now. Preposterous that the Duke of Rochdale, who could have any female he wanted, had fallen in love with one far removed from his oft-stated expectations, yet he acknowledged it.

"I love her."

"Beg pardon, sir?" The maid placed a tray on a small table.

"Never mind. I was just thinking out loud."

"Yes, sir."

Eating roasted mutton and potatoes, Richard continued his thoughts. Had he been wrong? Did the kidnappers leave England's shores from a smaller harbor? Folkstone, perhaps, or even Hythe? If so, he was wasting his time in Dover. Yet he had to be certain he wouldn't find Judith here.

He would watch the harbor tonight until he could be sure the captors didn't get past him, then find his own way across the channel. If only he could find her safe, unharmed, he promised himself not to strangle her if—when—he found her.

Rochdale laughed at himself for such a ridiculous promise, as if she would stand still for him to manhandle her in any way. With a wounded shoulder, her physical toughness could not match her mental toughness, but he'd wager her abductors were not having an easy time carrying out their plans.

Twenty-Seven

Journey's End

Her stomach heaved.

Judith struggled to her feet and leaned over the side, retching but producing no results. She couldn't remember when she last ate a meal, yet hunger pangs didn't assail her, only a terrible emptiness. She had no idea of the time, although the moon had passed its zenith, so dawn must be approaching.

"Here, Mademoiselle, eat some bread. We can't have you collapsing on us before we reach Paris, can we?"

Judith glared at Jacques but was too anxious to maintain what little strength she had to quibble. She ate slowly, hoping the food would quiet her roiling stomach, and then she lay down on the floor again. Lying flat eased the pain in her shoulder, although it didn't help her throbbing head.

Susanna, where are you?

Moments later, the boat scraped the sides of the landing. Her captors whispered but not softly enough to keep her from hearing, so she knew they'd reached Sangatte. Judith regretted her knowledge of geography was so limited. Was Sangatte anywhere near Paris? Probably not, because the outlying areas would be crowded with people. Nevertheless, there would be people about. Fishermen, at least. Mending nets, or whatever it was they do in the early morning. Without warning, Jacques grabbed Judith's head, stuffed a smelly handkerchief into her mouth, and hauled her to her feet, hurrying her off the boat.

Judith deliberately stumbled on cobblestones risking a broken ankle but slowing their progress while she looked around, hoping someone was close. The small harbor was empty. She didn't know which was worse, the smelly handkerchief in her mouth or the stench of dead fish that assailed her nostrils.

The men pulled her around the village into a wooded area beyond, all without uttering a word. When they were several yards deep within the trees, Jacques pushed her to the ground and tied her hands with his neck scarf.

"Philippe, give me your scarf, so I can bind her feet."

"I don't have one."

"Tear a strip off your shirt tail, then." Exasperation coloured his voice. "Use what little brains you have. I have to tie her feet, numbskull, else she will escape while we get horses."

Jacques stood, hands fisted on his hips, and spoke in deplorable English. "Ruined Philippe's shirt, but it will keep you from running away for an hour or so. We might bring you some breakfast just to show you how considerate we are."

When their laughter faded in the distance, Judith started straining her wrists in their binding. They didn't loosen. She bit back tears, then tried again.

Susanna, where are you? You followed me around all my life, telling me what I must do—and not do—so why aren't you with me here? I've never needed you more, and you aren't with me. You probably found someone you like better than me.

Richard's image bore into Judith's brain. She tried to push the image away, tried not to think about what he would say about her behaviour this time. Her current situation was far beyond anything he knew about her thus far.

Judith continued her struggle with the bindings. Slowly the scarf loosened, then fell from her hands. Pulling the filthy handkerchief from her mouth made her retch, bringing up the stale bread she'd eaten. She waited until her stomach stopped heaving before untying her ankles.

Which way should she go? She stood still, listening, but heard only birds as she flexed her sore shoulder. It was a nine-day wonder the wound didn't open when they jerked her around. She wondered if Madame Duvalier would have considered a wounded shoulder "damaged goods." Judith didn't intend to find out, so she'd better leave this place.

While she stood, debating directions, two male voices approaching from behind her made the decision obvious. They didn't sound like her abductors' voices. Galvanized into action, she hurried at an angle away from both the voices and the village until she found a tree with a low branch. Could she climb the tree, especially wearing half boots? No alternative solution presented itself. She grasped the limb, then in sheer agony hoisted herself upward. She climbed higher until leaves hid her from view. Perhaps the moisture on her left shoulder was perspiration, but she feared not. Clasping the trunk with her right arm, she forced herself to breathe evenly.

The men stopped a few feet from her hiding place, so she understood their common French.

"André, what makes you think anyone will come this way?"

"This is the usual route that smugglers use from Sangatte to Calais. They'll have full pockets, Louis, you wait and see."

They settled down to wait.

Judith also waited. She heard horses' hooves before the men did. She held her breath when the men below her rustled dead leaves, getting to their feet.

"Quiet," one of them said.

"Where is she?" Jacques' shout sounded loud in the quietness.

"Maybe this is the wrong place," Philippe offered. "But the trees look the same."

"No, numbskull, there's my scarf."

"You didn't tie her very well, did you?"

"Raise your hands!"

"Who're you?" Jacques and Philippe demanded in unison.

"Doesn't matter. Get off the horses and empty your pockets."

"We'd better do what he says, Philippe, else they'll shoot us. Stop waving those guns around," Jacques shouted at the strangers.

Judith heard the scuffling and wished she could see but didn't dare move. She cringed when two shots rang out followed by horses' hooves galloping away.

"Why did you kill them, Louis? I never bargained for murder."

"I didn't mean to, André. The guns just went off."

"No, they didn't. You shot them on purpose. We could've used those horses, but we'll never catch them now."

"Their pockets are nearly empty too. All we get for this morning's work is a few francs and stale bread. Let's go back to Calais before somebody investigates those horses."

"What about the bodies?"

"Ignore them."

Judith held her breath as their footsteps faded, leaving birds to their conversation. Probably thankful those humans were gone. Judith smiled at her ridiculous thought, then sobered. Was it safe to leave the tree? She had moved down one limb when she heard horses coming and became still again.

"There they are, dead by all appearances," an unfamiliar voice said. "I knew something was wrong when their horses came back without them."

"They're dead," another unfamiliar voice said. "Shot through the head. What do we do with the bodies?"

"Let somebody else find them. Let's go."

Again, Judith listened to horses trotting away and waited until the only sounds were chirping birds. She climbed down from the tree, protecting her throbbing left shoulder the best she could until she reached the ground.

"Which way should I go," she murmured. "I must get away from here before anyone else comes. Should I go into the village? Surely, from there I can find my way home. No. Coming from this direction, those men might think I shot my abductors."

Judith forced herself to look toward her captors' bodies. Much to her surprise, she saw a dark-haired woman hovering above them. Hovering above the bodies, not standing on the ground beside them. Judith gasped and went still. Was she truly seeing her guardian angel? *Are you Susanna?*

Yes.

In my storybooks, angels had fair hair. Maybe there's hope for me yet. I've gotten myself into a mess this time, have I not?

You have, but you've done well rescuing yourself. I commend you.

Even though I can see you, I suppose you still can't talk like a human being.

Only humans talk like humans.

This situation is just too much. Where have you been? Why did you allow it? Allow those horrible men to abduct me? Drag me around? Force drugs down my throat? You're supposed to take care of me. You've told me so many times. I know much that's happened is my fault, but you could have stopped me.

I can only protect you up to a certain point when you're determined on some course of action. However,

God won't allow anyone to harm you beyond what you can endure.

Many of the times Judith had been obstinate flitted through her memory bringing a new humility. *I've often resented you, Susanna, for what I considered your interference, but I've never been so glad to see anyone. Will you help me again? Take me home? Can you make me invisible and whisk me back to East Leah in the blink of an eye? I'm sure Ruth and Daniel are worried out of their skulls.*

No, Judith, I can't do what you ask, but yes, I can and will help you. Trust me. Susanna floated past her and turned her face toward Judith before starting forward again.

Judith's mood lightened. She wasn't alone. *I guess you want me to follow you. All right, I will. I can only hope you know where we're going.*

They moved in silence through the woods until Judith's quick temper erupted. *Susanna, don't float so fast. I'm stumbling over roots, which hurts my shoulder. Why don't you lift me and let me float with you?*

Humans aren't meant to float, only walk.

After what seemed like hours, they came to a clearing where, in the distance, Judith could see a small, frame farmhouse with smoke rising from its chimney.

"Are you taking me there? Wait, don't leave!" Judith watched the angel float back into the trees. She took a deep breath, then, in a determined stride, made her way through a field of clover toward the farmhouse. Honeybees buzzed around her feet but couldn't sting through her half boots. They gave a pleasant sound, though, in the otherwise quiet field.

"All right, Judith Elizabeth Ainsley, you're on your own again. No," she reminded herself, "Susanna is here too. I just can't see her. She promised.

Susanna, if you're listening, I don't understand why you can't go with me to the house. You could explain matters better than I can. You know the reason for this debacle, and I don't."

Judith listened in vain for an answer.

Moments later, she walked across the yard midst chickens clucking around her feet and tapped on the whitewashed door of the weathered gray house. Checked gingham curtains billowed out the windows on each side of the door, which swung open, revealing a plump woman who glanced past her into the distance, then back into Judith's face.

"*Bonjour,* Madame." Judith spoke in fluent French. "My name is Judith Ainsley. I've lost my way. Can you help me?" She supported her left arm in her right hand, which eased the strain somewhat.

"I don't understand how you came to lose your way, but come inside, Mademoiselle. I'm Marie Beauregard, and this is my husband, Henri."

Stepping into a small room, Judith curtsied to the tall wiry man who bowed. "Good day to you, Monsieur. I come seeking aid."

"Marie, perhaps you will make tea for us." The man's appearance proclaimed him a peasant, yet his manners were impeccable. His language, although not precisely upper class, was by no means common.

Sipping the hot brew, Judith began an edited version of her story. "Two men abducted me in England and brought me over here. They left me tied in the woods near Sangatte while they went for horses. I managed to work my way loose and escape. Then more men came."

Judith recounted the murders.

"Murders?" Henri and Marie exchanged glances. "We haven't heard of any strangers in the area, have we, Henri?"

"No, and we didn't hear any gunshots, but I doubt we would from deep in the forest. Tell us more."

Noting Marie's eager expression, she continued. "Perhaps this part will sound ridiculous, but I assure you it's the truth. An angel led me here, at least to the edge of the woods."

"An angel?" Henri exchanged a glance with his wife. "You don't sound all about in your head, but why would an angel lead you here?"

"I don't know, Monsieur." Judith settled her cup into its saucer. She had learned early in childhood she couldn't understand Susanna's actions, so she had stopped trying. "Do you perhaps have means to return me to England?"

"No, Mademoiselle, we do not." Henri shook his head. "An angel brought you. This is truly a puzzle. I've heard that angels leave heaven when God directs them, but I've never encountered one. Nevertheless, you must rest here and have a meal while we consider the matter further."

Holding her injured arm near her body, Judith said, "I fear my shoulder wound has opened. Do you have a bandage I could use?"

"Come into the kitchen," Marie directed.

Judith winced, biting back a yelp when Marie pulled the blood-soaked bandage away from the puckered wound. The wound had been healing so well, but now mending must start over again.

Marie placed strips of sticking plaster across the new bandage, gently patted it into place, and sat back to admire her handiwork. "There, Mademoiselle. That should hold."

Judith hid a yawn behind her hand. "Thank you, Madame. I apologize for my rudeness. I hurt too much to sleep last night. The fresh bandage eased the ache, so I believe I could rest now."

"That's a sound idea, Mademoiselle. Our sofa is quite comfortable. Henri and I will stay in the kitchen, so we won't disturb you." Marie bustled about finding an extra pillow to support Judith's wounded shoulder.

Judith lay with her back against the sofa with her injured arm propped on a cushion embroidered with deep red roses on a tan background. Perhaps Ruth could stitch some like them. With that drowsy thought, she drifted into the deep sleep she'd experienced soon after her accident.

A few hours later when she awoke, Judith lay still, frowning. Where was she? It was a nice room, furnished with an eye to comfort with colorful cushions nestled on wooden chairs. Needlework of some sort graced a couple of small tables. Not opulent like her rooms at home but more than adequate with a sizeable fireplace. She had never seen a mantelshelf devoid of clutter.

A twinge in her shoulder brought the circumstances back to her—abduction, escape, rescue. She swung her limbs off the sofa and straightened the skirts of her dirty habit before making her way toward voices.

Henri stood when she entered the kitchen, while Marie bustled around with a tea kettle.

Judith inhaled the scent of cinnamon-flavored sweet biscuits and hoped the others didn't hear her stomach rumble. "I feel better after sleeping."

"You must have tea with us," Marie told her, putting a plate of sweet biscuits on the scrubbed wooden table, followed by a Brown Betty teapot, like the one in the Ainsley Park kitchen. As a very young child, Judith had found her way there when she was hungry between meals. Cook always had sweet biscuits for her.

"Yes, I will, thank you."

After they finished their tea, Judith and Marie talked while Henri killed and plucked a chicken for their supper. She admitted cooking was beyond her capabilities but would try to do whatever her hosts suggested. Her laughter rang out as she shelled garden peas, which flew around the kitchen. Her mirth subsided when the door opened from the parlor. She hadn't known anyone else was here but now saw a gaunt old man clinging to the doorframe.

"I heard familiar laughter."

Twenty-Eight

Surprise!

"You're dead!"

When the room stopped spinning, Judith stared into blue eyes so like her own and slowly released her grip on the table edge. "You can't be here. You're dead,"

She buried her face in her hands and burst into wracking sobs. Henri almost carried the frail man to a chair beside the table. "Monsieur, you should be on your bed."

The feeble man slumped against the table. He didn't speak but continued to stare at Judith.

Her sobs turned into hiccups, then sniffles. She mopped her tears with a towel Marie pressed into her hands. "Father? Is it really you? I dreamed you were still alive, but I didn't believe it."

Marie gasped, then was still when Henri shook his head at her.

"I suppose my guardian angel knew, but she didn't tell me." *Susanna, how could you do this? Why did you allow me to believe he was dead? Why did you allow me to suffer this shock? I can hardly think!*

Judith scarcely recognized her father so emaciated was he. She saw only puzzlement in his eyes. "Father, don't you know me?"

"He doesn't even know who he is, Mademoiselle," Henri told her.

"Doesn't know who he is? I can identify him. He's Alexander Elliott Ainsley, the seventh Earl of Monford, from Hampshire, England."

"Ainsley. You called yourself by that name. You say he's your father?"

"Yes, but authorities notified us several weeks ago that footpads murdered him."

The earl didn't react upon hearing his name or title but asked in a feeble voice, which barely reached Judith only a few feet away, "What did you say about an angel?"

"Two men abducted me in England and brought me to Sangatte and left me in the woods. An angel led me here today." Explaining Susanna was beyond her at this point. Someday, she would remind him she had tried to tell him about her guardian angel long ago, but he had ridiculed the idea.

"This is all too much for me. I'll think about it later. I'm quite tired, Henri. Will you help me back up the stairs?"

Henri helped him to his feet before turning toward Judith. "I'll get him back to his bed, and then we can talk about this."

Judith nodded at his crisp words and sat in motionless silence until he returned. Her thoughts were in a whirl. Father is alive. He can't be, but he is. Has he been here all the time we thought he was dead? Why doesn't he know who he is?

When he entered the kitchen, Marie voiced her one thought. "Their eyes are alike."

"I noticed," her husband replied.

"I have so many questions I don't know where to begin. Tell me how my father came to be here," Judith urged.

He raised his hand, signaling his wife to silence, then recounted finding the old man lying in the muddy lane. "I couldn't leave him there at the mercy of Napoleon's soldiers, so I brought him here. He has Anglo colouring. The possibility he might be a spy occurred to us."

"That's why we kept him in the attic." Marie turned toward Judith. "The small space isn't very comfortable, but we couldn't risk anyone's knowing he was here."

Judith calmed Marie's fluttering hands with her own. "No, you couldn't. I'm sure he was thankful to be inside out of the weather."

Henri took up the story again. "He was in a stupor for a while. Unfortunately, when he awoke, his mind was a blank. His strength is returning slowly, but I admit it puzzles me to know what we should do if his memory never returns. Marie and I talked some while you were asleep. We don't know whether you're really his daughter or if you mean him some harm. We don't know who injured him, you see."

"I appreciate your concern." Judith's voice grew crisper as she straightened her shoulders. There was something constructive she could do instead of sitting here asking questions. "We were quite close, so it might help if you would permit me to stay for a few days. Perhaps being around me, hearing my voice, will aid his memory."

"If not?"

"I will find a way back to England. I can bring many people who know him, including our businessman who has known my father most of his life. A portrait even, if necessary."

Henri and Marie exchanged glances. He said, "All right, Mademoiselle, we agree to that."

Marie rose. "If you stay here a few days you must allow me to clean your habit. You can wear one of my gowns."

Judith glanced at her stained habit with disgust. "I appreciate your offer, Madame. However, between the carriage filth and the fish odor on the boat, I doubt you can get my clothing clean."

"Oh, the dirt will wash out easily enough," Marie assured her. "We can depend on the breeze to remove the fish smell. My gowns are much too large for you, but we'll contrive."

She bustled from the room, returning with a faded blue gown large enough to accommodate Judith twice over. A yellow sash bunched the fabric around her narrow waist, pulling the gown above her ankles. Judith rolled up the sleeves four turns and swallowed a laugh at what the ever-exquisite Lady Monford might say if she could see her daughter now.

While Marie undertook cleaning the riding habit, Judith strode back and forth across the yard, holding her wounded shoulder close to her body. Memories bounced around in her head, memories of the healthy man who'd left Ainsley Park. Those memories, in turn, reminded her of his perfidy. *Susanna, are you here?*

I've told you before, I'm always with you.

You should have answered me earlier when I asked why you let me believe Father was dead.

You were not coherent, Judith, and wouldn't have understood then.

The shock of finding him alive overset me, but I'm coherent now, so tell me. Judith stomped her foot. Enough was enough. *Tell me!*

You needed to know what your life would be without him.

My life is what I choose. It has nothing to do with Father.

You willfully refuse to recognize your life connects with him, whether he's dead or alive.

I still believe you were wrong when you shocked me with his sudden appearance.

Shock is sometimes necessary to force humans into a realization they may not truly want what they believe they do. You must spend some time thinking about the future.

Susanna was right. Father's reappearance didn't affect only his daughter but also Ruth and Daniel. Would they return to Ainsley Park? How would she find an agent for the Manor? Perhaps Daniel would know someone she could trust.

You told Ruth you don't need an agent.

Judith gripped a rose and gasped when a thorn dug into her finger

I've changed my mind. I don't want to be bothered with the day-to-day farm functions. I'm only interested in the financial side of the business, which includes traveling. Yorkshire, for example, and anywhere else I might expand the weaving operations. Scotland comes to mind. Even I recognize that traveling to far-flung places like China and the Indies is impossible for a female, no matter how independent. Seeing some of the world outside England would be wonderful.

Keep an open mind, Judith. There is much about your future you don't know.

Then tell me.

I cannot. Trust me. God has plans for you, plans that will help you, never harm you. Until He reveals His plans, I recommend that you pay attention to your reaction concerning your father's return.

Ruth asked me if I would welcome Father back if he were, indeed, alive.

You said no when you believed he was dead. Now that you know he's alive, what is your answer?

Still the same. No, I will not welcome him back. He is nothing to me now.

Yet you said you'd return home, if necessary, and find people who can identify him, so you can't be completely heartless about your father.

No, I suppose not. Judith acknowledged Susanna's words. *However, the moment he regains his memory, I'll shut him out of my life. I've proven I don't need him.*

Don't judge him too harshly. He's only a man.

Where were you when he told me falsehoods? Judith demanded. *Why didn't you make him tell the*

truth? Why didn't you stop him from signing that horrible document?

I told you before. I'm your angel. He has his own. I was always with you even though you were not aware. You've given me a hard time. Angels suffer from stress too, and your determination to hate your father does not help. Must you persist in believing you hate him, or will you finally realize you love him?

Judith ignored her question. *After I help him get his memory back, I will let him know just how much I hate him for the way he treated me. He won't understand how I outwitted him otherwise. Telling him will give me tremendous pleasure.*

To reach that satisfaction, Judith decided to talk about her childhood.

<> <> <> <> <>

Meanwhile, in the attic, the old man lay on his bed. A tiny girl perched on a pony invaded his dreams. The little girl who had been on the edges of his dreams. Sun glinted off her raven curls, and exhilaration brought a gleam into her wide blue eyes. Now he could see her face, but knowing didn't clear fuzziness from his brain.

"Father, look at me! I'm riding Pepper all by myself!"

His eyelids were heavy with exhaustion, but he couldn't rest. He sat up with effort. The little girl—could she be the young lady below stairs? Could she truly be his daughter? It would be nice to have a daughter capable of such joyous laughter. No curls, but raven hair. Why can't I remember? I *must* remember!

He had told himself that many times since his brain worked its way through a dense fog. Why was he sitting on a bed in someone's attic? The only window was open enough to allow fresh air inside. Sounds of roosters and cows indicated he was on a farm. He knew the farm was in France because he conversed with Henri and Marie in French. Although he was comfortable speaking French, his thoughts were in English. The young lady downstairs had solved one puzzle when she identified him, although his being an English earl didn't tell him why he was in France.

He made his way to the door and called for Henri.

When the old man again sat at the round kitchen table, his eyes sought the young lady with the raven hair and blue eyes.

"Do you have a pony named Pepper?" He clasped his hands together and listened to her voice.

She smiled, remembering her first pony. "You gave him to me when I was four years old."

"I dreamed about you."

He stayed awake long enough to sip some broth and eat a slice of dry toast, then requested Henri's help getting upstairs.

<> <> <> <> <>

Each day, Henri helped the gaunt old man down the stairs. Either he or Marie sat with their visitors and listened as they talked.

"You remembered Pepper, but do you remember my kitten, Snowball? The day you gave him to me is one of my best memories."

"Tell me about the kitten," he urged, his gaze resting on her face.

"I was five years old when I persuaded you to take me to visit a farm on the far side of Ainsley Park. The distance was so far that you admitted you didn't think I would get up early enough, but I surprised you. At the Emerson farm, I drank warm milk and munched sweet biscuits while you discussed crops with the tenant. The biscuits were gingery and filled with currants." Judith smiled with delight. "Ginger biscuits have never again tasted so good."

"How does Snowball come into it?"

"There was a basket filled with kittens near the hearth. While I examined them, the only white one squirmed his way out of the basket and into my lap." She smiled into her father's intense face. "You indulged me. I named the kitten Snowball. Mama objected to a cat in the house. Nevertheless, Snowball's home was a basket in my bedchamber for more than ten years."

The room grew quiet allowing him to drift into sleep where he lay stretched on the sofa.

Judith stared at him for a few minutes, then told Henri she would stroll around outside for a while. The windstorm the night before had left behind a clean scent she savored while she rambled around the yard, her thoughts in a whirl with memories. Her heart softened when she acknowledged he had loved her. No, he hadn't, she reminded herself, her heart hardening again. His love was all a sham, part of his devious nature.

When she returned to the small parlor, her father was sitting upright. "Did you have any other pets?"

"Oh, yes. There was Floppy, a puppy I rescued from a large dog which seemed intent on devouring him."

"Did your Mama also object to a dog in the house?"

Judith grinned. "I'm afraid she did. You overruled her, though. Floppy had a basket in my bedchamber too. He and Snowball became best friends. He was bereft when the cat died, but he lived a couple more years. I was fortunate to have him so long."

Judith didn't know if her presence helped, but her father improved steadily. His appetite increased, and he could walk without grasping a support every few feet. However, when supper was over, he was ready for his bed.

A change occurred on the third morning of Judith's stay at the farm.

<> <> <> <> <>

In the attic, the old man awoke and lay staring at the ceiling. One could not call it a ceiling, just a sloping roof with bare beams, blackened with age. Where was he? Why was he here? He raised his head, scanning the small area. An attic containing the cot on which he lay, a covered chamber pot in one corner, a three-legged chair tilted in another corner, and a round-topped trunk sat under the window. He'd never seen an attic so empty, or such a small attic. At home, the attics rambled throughout the top floor, which was sizable. This place was not Ainsley Park.

His brow furrowed. Why would he, the Earl of Monford, be lying in somebody's attic? His tenants' attics were about this size, but he wouldn't be lying on a bed in their attics. He shifted, trying to get comfortable on the hard cot and even harder pillow. If this were what his tenants had, he must correct the situation before they deserted Ainsley Park for better accommodations. Heavy footsteps penetrated his thoughts. He turned toward the wall and closed his eyes, willing his breathing to be even. He heard the door open and steps approach his bed.

"Are you awake?"

Turning, the earl stared up at the tall wiry man bending over him. He didn't speak, waiting to see what happened next.

"Do you need any help before I go to the fields? Marie will serve you breakfast when you're ready to come downstairs."

The earl nodded and watched the man leave. Left alone, Monford relieved himself in the chamber pot, then sat on the bed, giving his situation some thought. French. He understood the man. Monford had spent so much time in France, both when a young man on tour and during his more recent government work, he was comfortable with the language. Why could he not remember seeing him before? Who was this stranger? How long had he, England's Earl of Monford—who should be at Ainsley Park in Hampshire—been occupying a French attic? Considering the man's words, several days. He seemed friendly enough.

Weak as a baby, the earl stood upright and walked the few steps to the door. The handle turned, so he was not a prisoner. He paced the attic a few times, before sinking onto the hard cot and drifting into a light sleep.

Waking again, he picked up his thoughts. A few spotty memories returned. He remembered why he was in France. He recalled he had delivered the papers into the right hands, then started home. The war was still raging when he left Paris, making his slow way toward the coast, too often in a downpour of rain.

Could the war be over? There had been times during which he doubted there would ever again be permanent peace, not like the temporary truce in 1802. If the war was, indeed, over, Napoleon had lost. The British earl refused to believe any other outcome.

His weakness puzzled him. He prided himself on his ability to work alongside field hands at Ainsley Park when he chose. He'd never allowed himself the luxury of over-imbibing either food or drink. Now, he grasped the railing and walked down the stairs like an old man. The scent of baked sweet biscuits tickled his nose. His stomach rumbled as he stepped through the kitchen doorway, where he stood in amazement.

"Judith? What are you doing here?"

"Father! Your memory has returned at last. Here, sit in this chair, and eat your breakfast."

Bewilderment settled on his face. "Before I eat, perhaps you will explain why you are here. Why both of us are here."

"After you eat, we will have a long talk," Judith told him.

The beaming Marie set a plate of coddled eggs before him. "Monsieur, you must regain your strength."

He chewed each bite slowly and sipped his coffee, clasping the large cup in both hands. With the plate empty, he pushed his chair back from the table. "Now, tell me."

She did, with help from Marie and Henri who had come from the fields in answer to his wife's call.

"Have I been unconscious all this time?"

"Not all the time, Monsieur," Henri assured him. "You were unconscious for an appreciable period with a high fever several days, but you've been alert since, just without memory."

Monford stared at them in disbelief. "I must have been a tremendous burden on you. I apologize and will recompense you at the earliest possible moment."

They demurred, but the earl was adamant. Alexander Elliott Ainsley would not be beholden to anyone for longer than necessary. He could see they were not destitute, but the food was simple and the furniture sparse. Marie didn't even have an enclosed stove. He surely had been a burden.

"What about the war? Napoleon?"

She briefly explained Wellington had demolished the French troops at a place called Waterloo.

Judith's voice trailed into silence, which lasted several moments. The only sound was the low bubble of water heating on the hob. The quiet ended when they heard a pounding on the outside door, followed by its slamming against the wall.

"Hello! Is anyone here?"

Before anyone could answer, heavy footsteps crossed the floor and a large unkempt man strode into the kitchen. His hurried gaze jumped from face to face before settling on Judith. In one stride, he grasped her shoulders and pulled her away from the table.

"You're hurting me!" She clasped her shoulder when he released his grip.

They stared at him in openmouthed surprise. Monford was the first to recover his powers of speech. "Fiend seize it, who are you?"

Twenty-Nine

Revenge Is Sweet . . .

Judith stared at him in stunned silence.

"Did you shoot those men in the forest?" The newcomer demanded. "Answer me!"

"How dare you burst into my home this way?" Henri demanded as he stepped toward the miscreant, fists raised.

"Shoot people? I've never in my life heard anything so preposterous." Marie grabbed the fireplace poker and started toward the intruder.

The earl spoke over their shouted words. "Unhand my daughter this instant and identify yourself!"

The intruder clasped Judith in his arms and rested his head against hers.

"I apologize, Judith. I've been half out of my mind worrying about you. The *gendarmes* are practically at my heels. Tell me. Did you shoot those two men?"

She relaxed against his broad shoulder and slid her arms around him. Safety. And, Richard would help get her father home.

"How did you get here, Richard? How did you find me?"

He shook his head at her. "I came on a collection of bones pretending to be a horse. I met a female in the forest who sent me here."

"A female? Must be Susanna because no one else knows I'm here. She brought me to my father. That's him." Proper grammar went by the wayside in her surprise at seeing Richard. Susanna had warned her there might be more shocks. She hoped they all would be this welcome.

"You seem to know this man, Judith, so perhaps you will introduce him," her father commented.

"I apologize. This gentleman is Richard Chadwick, the Duke of Rochdale from Wiltshire. Your Grace, may I introduce my father, the Earl of Monford? These wonderful people are Monsieur Henri Beauregard and his wife, Marie, who have given us much-needed shelter."

Rochdale nodded toward the Beauregards. Turning, he clasped the earl's hand. "Monford, it is a genuine pleasure to meet you, and I look forward to hearing your story. However, I first must ask your daughter about the dead men in the forest."

"I believe we will be more comfortable in the parlor," Henri interjected and led the way.

"No, Richard, I didn't shoot them," Judith assured him. "What makes you think I did?"

"A fishwife in Sangatte saw them come ashore in the early hours the other morning with a female."

"I didn't think anyone saw us," Judith interrupted.

"She did and described you. I had inquired for you along the coast from Calais to Sangatte, so the gendarmes followed me."

A loud banging on the door interrupted him. Henri opened it, revealing a burly man who identified himself as a gendarme.

"You found her." He stepped into the small room closing the door behind him.

"As you see," the duke answered.

"Who are all these people?"

"The gentleman sitting on the sofa is the Earl of Monford from Hampshire, England. This is his daughter, Lady Judith Ainsley also from Hampshire. These people are Henri and Marie Beauregard, who welcomed us into their home. I am Richard Chadwick, the Duke of Rochdale from Wiltshire, England."

The gendarme appeared bemused with all the titles but persevered. "I must question the young lady."

Monford spoke for the first time. His voice was not strong yet carried the authority of several generations of earldom. "Why should you question my daughter?"

"With all due respect, Monsieur," the gendarme bowed slightly, "a person we believe is this woman arrived by boat in Sangatte with two men since found dead in the forest. We must question her."

"I didn't kill Jacques or Philippe." She met his skeptical eyes without flinching, her voice steady.

"Jacques and Philippe?"

"I don't know their other names." She told the story of her abduction. "I had thwarted the recovery of their ill-gotten possessions, so they retaliated."

"I gather they didn't hold you for ransom, so what were their intentions toward you?"

"Sell me to Madame Duvalier in Paris."

Gasps greeted her statement. They recognized the name of Paris's leading brothel owner, Judith mused, but didn't ask.

"That's reason enough to kill them."

"Yes," she agreed. "I didn't, although I freely admit I would have, had it been possible. They left me bound and gagged in the woods, while they went into the village to obtain mounts. I freed myself and moved deeper into the woods when two other men came. They lay in wait, expecting smugglers with deep pockets to use that route. When Jacques and Philippe returned, they all scuffled, ending with two shots."

"Did you see the two newcomers?"

"No, but they called each other André and Louis. I must say only one shot the two men. Louis did, but he said it was an accident. The other one, André, said Louis shot them on purpose. They complained about getting only bread and a few francs for their trouble before they left. I don't know anything else about them."

"Where were you while the shooting took place?"

"In a tree."

"In a tree! You must do better than that. Ladies don't climb trees."

"I did."

The gendarme studied her face. "I might believe it if I see you climb a tree with my own eyes."

Judith glared. "Then, I must show you, Monsieur."

"No, Mademoiselle! You might open the wound again." Marie turned toward Lord Monford. "Please, my lord, stop her."

"If I must climb a tree to prove my innocence, I will," Judith declared and stalked out the door.

"She was ever a determined female," the earl said, pride filling his voice. He leaned on Henri's arm until they reached a tree stump where he lowered himself.

Judith glanced about until she found a tree with a low branch. Then, gasping from pain, she clasped the limb with both hands and pulled herself upward until she reached higher limbs. Pain almost overwhelmed her, but she climbed until leaves surrounded her. Chaffinches squawked their displeasure and flew in widespread directions.

"All right, Mademoiselle, you can come down now," the gendarme called. "You've convinced me."

Judith descended to the lowest limb, then jumped the rest of the way. She shook her head in disgust when Richard sprang forward and caught her.

"You ninny, haven't you done your shoulder enough damage?" he growled as he set her on her feet. "Just look! Blood is seeping through your jacket."

"Oh, Mademoiselle Judith, please come back into the house so I can replace the bandage."

"In a moment, Marie. I must hear the outcome."

Monford broke the silence. "Perhaps either André or Louis attacked me some weeks ago. Someone did, and left me for dead."

"I don't believe so, Father. Authorities found your signet ring on a dead man who they believed was you."

"Did they return the ring?"

"Yes, also your saddlebags and your mount, which is how we learned of your death."

"The ring is important. Someday, it will pass to your son."

Before she could answer, Henri spoke for the first time since opening the door to the gendarme. "I heard Louis Gastón has his cousin visiting from Paris."

That drew the gendarme's attention. "I've had difficulties before with Gastón. Perhaps I should pay him a visit."

With a bow, he took his leave. The others turned toward the house.

Richard began scolding Judith the moment they were inside and continued in the kitchen.

"My lord duke, you will please be quiet until I bandage Mademoiselle's shoulder," Marie scolded.

"Yes, Richard, hush." Judith grimaced when Marie pressed against the open wound.

"You brought all this on yourself, my girl. Don't you forget it!" Rochdale ignored their words while he vented his temper. "If you had stayed away from the cave, you wouldn't have been shot and those men would never have seen you. If they hadn't seen you, they wouldn't have abducted you. If they had not abducted you, I wouldn't have made the terrible trip across Sussex searching for you."

"Stop shouting," Judith ordered. "I didn't ask you to find me. I got myself into this mess, and I can get myself out. Go home. Leave me alone. I never want to see you again. I never want to hear more lectures from you either."

Monford cleared his throat. "Rochdale, I believe you should leave for a while. I need to talk with my daughter. I prefer her in a reasonably tranquil frame of mind when I do."

"You expect Lady Judith Elizabeth Ainsley to be in a *tranquil* frame of mind? Such calmness is a rare occurrence, based on my experience since the day we met. She's independent to a fault, infuriating, and shrewish as a fishwife."

Before Judith could open her mouth, the earl spoke in icy tones. "That's enough, Rochdale. I will not tolerate even a duke criticizing my daughter."

After a muttered apology, the duke said he would ride into Sangatte and send a message to England.

"I must rest for a short while, Marie. Meanwhile, I suspect my daughter needs a restoring cup of tea." Turning toward Judith, Monford said, "We need to have a talk. There are several things I don't understand."

Judith gazed at him, then nodded her head before turning away.

<> <> <> <> <>

An hour later, Judith sat on the couch in the parlor with her hands clasped in her lap. Henri was about his duties on the small farm. Marie tended the kitchen garden. Richard had not returned, nor did she expect to see him again after her latest outburst of venom. She told herself he deserved her words. The house was quiet when her father came down the stairs.

Judith watched him shuffle toward a chair across from her. He had questions for her, did he? Didn't understand something? She doubted he wanted to hear anything she would tell him. First, though, she had a question of her own.

"Why did you come to France? All those other times you were away from Ainsley Park, were you in France then too?"

He hesitated. "I came on government business."

"Government business? You? At your age? You were forever going off without saying where. Now you say you were on government work. You couldn't have said so at some point over the past years?"

"My work was confidential. I couldn't risk anyone's knowing my destination."

"Which government?" She scooted far back on the chintz-covered chair, dreading his answer.

He lifted his startled face to meet her gaze. "How can you possibly ask such a thing? English, of course."

"There's no 'of course' about it: Napoleon had friends in England."

"I was not one of them."

She ignored his words. "I once accused Rochdale of being a spy. Now it turns out my father was one."

"Courier is a more accurate word." He waited for a response, but Judith only shrugged. "If you're satisfied with my answer, I have a question. Where is Harold?"

"Harold who?" she inquired with surprise.

"Your husband, Judith."

"I don't have a husband." She gritted her teeth, her fists clenched. "How could you do that to me, Father, after your promise when I was thirteen years old?"

"What promise?"

Judith leaned toward him. "Are you saying you don't remember? I shall refresh your memory. You promised to find me a husband of my generation when Sybil's father forced her into marriage with an old man. You told me a lie. You never intended to honour your promise, did you?"

"Ah," he answered. "I remember the occasion well. I didn't make you the promise you think I did. I said you needed a husband at least ten years older."

He held up his hand for silence. "Yes, I know I deceived you, not only about your husband but also about your being my heir. I apologize for both. However, Ainsley Park needed you. You wanted Ainsley Park so much I was secure in the knowledge you would make sure the next generation would care for the estate. Constant attention from one generation to another is the only way any estate remains solvent over time. Sometimes a father must be devious to bring about the best outcome for everybody."

"Your lies were not the best for people, only the estate. Certainly not for your daughter."

"Nevertheless, explain why you disobeyed me. Why did you not marry Harold Ainsley as my will instructed? Which brings my next question. Why are you here instead of Ainsley Park?"

"Because I outwitted you," she said. "I overheard you and Mama talk about my future when I was fifteen. You were confident of your control over me. My anger fueled my determination to show you differently. I decided on the instant that no one would control me. I spent the next six years becoming financially independent so I could leave Ainsley Park rather than marry an old man. So how do you like hearing that?"

He stared at her in stunned surprise. "It isn't like you to tell me falsehoods, Judith. I realize there are still blank spots in my memory, yet I don't see how you could be financially independent. You couldn't have obtained funds without my knowledge."

"I could and did." She spoke with smug satisfaction. "You might remember loaning me five hundred pounds to invest, which I paid back with interest. I suppose you believed I stopped my investments. You were wrong. It hasn't been necessary to sell any jewelry you gave me, but I will if necessary. In your arrogance, you didn't even question why I insisted you record all your gifts in a ledger as mine, not part of the estate. I can live quite comfortably without you or Ainsley Park."

"I taught you to be independent from childhood, yet it never occurred to me that you might use my training to thwart me. I never thought you would go against my wishes."

She smiled at his muttered words. "Mr. Sizemore believes I inherited your head for business. However, I have another legacy from you."

"I can't imagine what that could be. I do have a clear recollection of my will."

"Oh, nothing tangible, I assure you." She gave him a mocking smile. "I inherited your deviousness."

"So you did." He ran his hand across his thinning hair. "I expect Sherwood can keep the estate operating until I can take over again."

"You're wrong there too. Daniel married Ruth. They're with me on an estate I purchased in East Leah. I have no idea what has happened at Ainsley Park. Your heir told me he would leave only a skeleton staff."

"Harold left a skeleton staff to run Ainsley Park?" His voice rose in disbelief. "His decision is outrageous to the point of absurdity. He should know an estate the size of Ainsley Park needs a full staff, unlike his smaller Kent estate."

"He also said he might lease the estate, perhaps to a wealthy Cit," she told him. "Now if you will excuse me, I need some fresh air."

"You despise me, don't you? I suppose I can't fault you for that."

"Despise you? I have ample reason, but no. I'm quite grateful because you taught me two things."

"I don't know what you mean."

"First, you taught me I could never trust any man. Second, you taught me I can get along quite well without you."

Hurt, then sadness settled on his face. With his head bowed and his shoulders slumped, the seventh

Earl of Monford rose to his feet and trudged toward the kitchen.

Smug satisfaction radiated through his daughter as she turned toward the outside door.

Thirty

. . . Or Is It?

When Richard returned from Sangatte, he went to the woods near the farmhouse. There, he paced among the trees berating himself for being a fool. How could he have yelled at Judith? Worrying about her didn't excuse his boorish behaviour. He should have been sympathetic toward her plight. After all, those men had abducted, drugged, and treated her in ways no one should treat a female. She could have faced years in a Paris brothel, enough to daunt even the strongest female, which Judith was not with a bullet hole in her shoulder. He feared he'd lost her this time. Heaviness settled around his heart.

Footsteps rustling dead leaves sent him behind a large tree. Had those footpads ventured this far from Sangatte? Peering around the tree, he saw Judith enter the woods. He wanted to call her but stopped himself. The triumph in her face puzzled him. He mulled over the situation when her grin broadened into a smile. She supported her left arm with her right hand. She appeared to relive a conversation.

His curiosity roused, yet knowing she wouldn't appreciate his company, he stepped away from the tree.

She whirled around, then recognizing him, an expression of deep satisfaction settled on her face. "I'm happy as a singing lark, Your Grace."

"You look like the cat that got into the cream pitcher. Care to tell me why?"

"I just told my father how I outwitted him. You can't know how much pleasure I had seeing the chagrin on his face. He knows I'm independent of him. I can do what I please regardless of his intentions." Her laughter rang out. "He couldn't believe I'm out from under his control, that I own an estate."

Her callous words brought Richard up short. Anger at the way she treated a sick old man, mixed with revulsion for her gloating, caused him to blurt the news he had concealed from her.

"You would do well to ingratiate yourself with your father. He might accept you back at Ainsley Park despite your disobedience."

"Accept me back? He'll never have the opportunity. I'm finished with him and Ainsley Park. The Manor is my home now."

"You don't own the Manor."

"Oh, yes, I do," Judith's voice rang out with supreme confidence. "I purchased the estate with my own funds. It's mine!"

Richard already regretted his outburst, but couldn't stop now. This would be a battle to the finish. He knew obstinate resistance would be Lady Judith's response. Waterloo was nothing compared to what he knew was coming. Gathering his wits, he explained.

Judith stood shocked into silence, her mind in turmoil. An eternity seemed to pass during which thoughts bounced off the walls of her brain, but at length one fact rose to the surface. One man had already taken property rightfully hers. Now here was another one trying to do the same. He would not succeed. On that, she was determined. She told him so, her sharp tongue lashing out at him.

Rochdale's face was set in rigid lines. "It's obvious you didn't understand my words. I will repeat them. The Manor in East Leah is not your property. It's mine."

"I have a proper conveyance," she declared. "I paid my own money for it."

"The conveyance deed may well be properly prepared. I'm confident your solicitor made sure of that, but the document still isn't legal," he explained in a strained voice. "My father had no legal authority to sell entailed property."

She took a hasty step forward, fists balled. "I didn't purchase the Manor from your father. I had never heard of the Duke of Rochdale or any other name he might have called himself. I purchased the Manor from Mr. Woodall's estate. It's mine, I tell you, *mine*."

The duke shook his head.

"You're wrong." Judith kept her voice steady, denying the turmoil roiling inside. "You misread the deed or something. After all these years, the print would be too faded to decipher."

"Even if that were true, you'll find our crest on the wall beside the front entrance. The same crest is on all the property the duchy owns. Recall how heavy, intertwined ivy surrounds much of the Manor's portico."

Crest! Judith caught her breath, remembering the crest she'd found in the attic. "I haven't seen a crest anywhere on the house. Describe it."

"A black square with a gold and black shield surrounded by gold leaves, the whole topped with a lion. The words are Latin, but the translation is *The Lion Shall Reign*. My ancestors supported Richard the Lionheart."

Judith held her voice steady. She recognized the crest, yet refused to admit Rochdale owned the Manor. "I'll consult my solicitor immediately upon my return to England. He'll convince you the property is mine. You can't take the Manor from me."

Judith whirled on her heel, leaving him standing in the woods.

<> <> <> <> <>

Richard waited until Judith was inside the door before following her across the road. Her icy voice hadn't hidden her anguish, her knowledge she would lose the one thing that meant most to her in the world: property ownership—her symbol of independence. His anger faded as a deep compassion for her invaded his heart. Judith had already endured more than any female should face and would undoubtedly endure much more before regaining the independence she'd had—and which he was taking away from her. She would strive for that independence, though.

However, Judith must first accept his ownership of the Manor. She was too intelligent to believe otherwise, once she calmed enough to analyze the situation. Still, that would not, could not, happen on the instant because Judith was too stubborn to give in easily. In the end, though, she would accept the situation and go forward to wherever that might lead her.

His duchy had regained a badly needed profitable property, but in the process he had lost the only woman who had ever meant anything to him beyond a casual relationship. That unwelcome thought pounded his brain as he entered the kitchen where the others gathered for supper.

Richard took his place at the table, casting a smile of thanks toward Marie when she handed him a full plate. They ate their way through the meal with few words spoken. Later in the parlor, silence still reigned over last cups of tea. He roused himself when the hour grew late.

"I must seek lodgings somewhere for the night, Henri. Can you advise me?"

"There's no need to go elsewhere, Your Grace, if you don't mind a pallet on the floor of his lordship's room. We don't have a bed frame," he apologized. "We do have a comfortable mattress, which you're welcome to use."

"A pallet will do nicely, thank you. A mattress is a welcome change from the ground I slept on during my army career." Turning toward Lady Judith, he inquired, "Where do you sleep?"

She ignored him.

"Lady Judith sleeps on the sofa where she can support her shoulder on the extra cushion," Marie said.

"Henri, I'm ready to go upstairs now." Monford roused himself, then glanced toward his daughter, who sat in stony silence. "Good night, my dear."

She didn't answer, nor did she lift her gaze from her hands clasped in her lap.

"Your manners leave a great deal to be desired, Judith. For the first time in your life, you shame me." He leaned on Henri climbing the stairs.

The former Army major, with all the authority of his recent command, reached a hand toward Judith and gripped her chin, forcing her to look at him. His voice was thinly disguised steel. "While you're a guest here, you could at least fake maturity."

Ignoring her blazing smoky eyes, he turned away before she could speak. Moments later, he entered the small attic. There, he folded his long legs and sank with a thump onto the mattress.

Monford sat on the bed, his head cradled in his hands. "I fear I've lost my daughter, Rochdale."

Richard tugged off his boots while he considered how to answer. "Monford, you did hurt her. Perhaps not intentionally. Nevertheless, you hurt the one person who adored you, who existed throughout childhood with the sole intention of pleasing you. Still, I believe she'll forgive you someday. I only wish I could believe she will forgive me."

"You appear to care for her."

"I love her. Admitting that love, even to myself, took me a long time. Now I fear I've lost her."

"You say you love her, yet you used some quite harsh words to describe her earlier today."

"That was frustration, Monford, deep frustration."

Judith lay awake long into the night, staring into the darkness. Father had always been proud of her, never ashamed. Yet why should she care how he regarded her behaviour after the way he'd treated her? This entire situation was her father's fault. If he had been honest with her, none of this would have happened. She was right and had every reason to hate him.

Why, then, did she suffer this guilt? Why had the hurt in his face pierced her heart? She had not experienced the expected satisfaction after telling him about outwitting him. Her gloating to Rochdale had been a sham. Why? There were so many questions but no answers. Judith was frustrated at the turmoil churning deep inside, the twists and turns of guilt mixed with justification, the uncertainty of her feelings. It was almost dawn before she slept but then not easily.

"Father, look at me! I'm riding all by myself." Judith turned Pepper eagerly toward the big man galloping down the curving drive. Before her horrified eyes, the horse bolted past her. Her father's face dissolved into the face of a stranger. He wasn't a stranger, she realized when his mount threw him, and she was no longer a four-year-old on a pony. She drifted through the air, reaching out her hands to the fallen man. Kneeling beside him, Judith implored, "No, no, Richard, you can't die! I won't have anybody to love if you do. Open your eyes. Look at me. You can't die. I *need* you."

The dream faded, tears wetting her cheeks and sliding toward her ears. She knew it told her something important, something she didn't want to face. Refused to face. At length, she dozed off again.

Birds chirping in the otherwise quietness of dawn woke her. She knew what she must do. Never a coward, Judith entered the kitchen.

"Marie, Henri, I apologize for my rudeness last evening. You've both been considerate in allowing me to remain here. I should not have allowed my personal feelings to lead me into bad manners."

"Don't fret yourself, Lady Judith," Marie soothed her. "Everyone has bad days. We'll put it behind us, shall we?"

Judith smiled her gratitude, then settled herself before the fire, a platter containing thickly sliced bread beside her. She took the last piece off the toasting fork as her father entered the kitchen with Rochdale on his heels. Taking a deep breath, she rose and faced them.

"Father, Rochdale, I apologize for my behaviour last evening. My boorishness was inexcusable. I shall mind my manners in the future." She glanced from one to the other while she apologized. Their faces softened into smiles.

"That's my Judith." Monford eased himself into a chair at the table.

Rochdale paused beside her long enough to murmur, "Staying in practice, I see."

She ignored him. She'd apologized, but, her dream notwithstanding, she clung to her anger with both men. Without it, she would collapse.

<> <> <> <> <>

Over the next few days, while the earl regained his strength, Judith helped about the house in whatever way she could. Without a doubt, Ruth would sigh over her efforts to dust furniture.

"Marie, I fear I am more hindrance than help."

"Oh, no, Mademoiselle. Your company gives me much pleasure because, as you have probably guessed, we don't have near neighbors. Being here must be boring for you."

With breakfast finished, Judith strolled outside and enjoyed the quietness surrounding the small farm. The only sound was the clucking of chickens mixed with the lowing of cattle and chaffinches twittering in the trees above her. She gazed toward the cloudless sky. How could it be so blue when storm clouds filled her life?

She leaned upright against a broad tree trunk, thinking over the past several days—her abduction, finding her father, her terrible behaviour. However, Rochdale overshadowed everything. He had sent a message to Ruth, so that worry was off her mind. He'd given her another one, though, a worse one. She didn't see how she could get around it. The Manor at East Leah. Rightfully *her* estate, yet he claimed ownership. Part of his duchy, he said. Judith fought tears because she knew she couldn't fight Richard over this.

"I apologize for being so abrupt in telling you about the Manor." Rochdale stood before her, head bowed.

Lost in thought, Judith hadn't heard his footsteps rustle leaves. He must have read her mind. Common sense told her he wouldn't have mentioned his ownership unless he was sure, but, oh, how it hurt. Another man had outwitted her. Not just any man but another one she cared for. She admitted it. She had begun to trust the duke. Look where that got her. Tears receded when bitterness took their place. She lifted her chin.

"Apology accepted. My solicitor will handle the reversal. I'll purchase another estate with that money.

Far from Hampshire and Wiltshire, you can be sure," she added in a clipped voice.

The duke shuffled his feet in the dead leaves, releasing an earthy scent. "Would you consider the purchase price as lease payments until such time the amount is used? You can then renew the lease on a long-term basis."

"You can't be serious." He wouldn't meet her eyes. She straightened and took a step toward him, ready for battle. "I should be your tenant on an estate rightfully mine? Answer to *you*? Be subject to your whims? I repeat, you cannot be serious."

"The thing is, the Rochdale estate doesn't have sufficient funds to repay you or the two other people who believe they own their estates."

She ignored his embarrassment. Her words dripped ice. "You'll find the money somewhere, Your Grace. I'll see you bankrupt, if necessary. Do you understand me?"

She watched him stalk away, his head down, his shoulders slumped, without answering.

Taking a deep breath, Judith let her anger seep away when he disappeared deeper into the forest. He'd begun to care for her, but no more. Not with the Manor between them, by rights *her* Manor. However, Ainsley Park was hers by right too, yet another man claimed it. She must leave East Leah, the friends she'd made there and start all over again. Her legs crumbled until she sat on the ground, her body racked with sobs. When they stopped, she wiped her face with her skirt.

You'll feel better after you forgive them. Trust me.

At Susanna's words, Judith's temper erupted. *You taught me to trust you, which I did. You told me to buy the Manor, which I did. I wouldn't have purchased the estate otherwise. Admit your fault! We'd arranged to see another estate, but you said to buy the Manor.*

Yes, I know, and I understand your reaction, but you must accept reality. Your happiness does not depend on property ownership or on independence but on loving and being loved.

Love!

Yes. Two excellent men love you. You love them too, if only you would consider the possibility with an open mind and admit it.

Love men who took what was mine, who insist I bow to their will? Don't be absurd.

Before Susanna could answer, Judith's mental words turned from sarcasm to accusation. *You knew father's deviousness. You knew the Manor's true ownership. Yet you not only allowed me to go forward with the purchase, you told me to buy it. Why?*

Consider the sequence of events, my dear, then you'll understand.

Judith sensed emptiness around her. Susanna was gone.

Love two men? Judith Elizabeth Ainsley love *any* man? The idea was laughable, except she wasn't laughing. The only person she loved was Ruth, and she needed her now, needed the serenity only her friend could provide. Ruth reminded her of the water in the ornamental pond at the foot of the lawn on a calm day. Not a ripple. She, herself, was more like a stream plummeting over rocks after a hard rain.

She left the quietness of trees and returned to the farmhouse. There she found the duke in conversation with her father.

"Rochdale has explained the situation, Judith. He has my sympathy over his father's behaviour. You will return to Ainsley Park with me. He'll repay you when his funds permit. You do not need the money."

"So, you've worked out my future between you. Autocrats, both of you, ignoring my opinion." Her bitterness hung in the air. "I don't care for your solution. I have other funds and will make my own arrangements when I return to England."

"You will do nothing of the kind, Judith." Monford's voice would have cut steel. "You will live at Ainsley Park."

"So you can marry me off to Harold Ainsley, I suppose."

Monford shook his head at her sneer. "No, I realize my mistake in that regard. I apologize for my thoughtless actions. However, there's no need for all this upheaval. We can't change the past, Kitten, only our future. Both of us must put mistakes and hurts behind us. We must look ahead. We'll reach a compromise when we return home. Right now, I need to rest."

Rochdale helped him up the stairs and returned to find Judith, blank-faced, shoulders slumped.

<> <> <> <> <>

Richard sat beside Judith on the short sofa. Despair radiated from her tense body. He wanted to gather her close but didn't dare. He contented himself with taking her limp hands into his. Pity overwhelmed him. All those years of work, striving for independence—all for naught. His independence was an accident of birth. He'd never had to work for it, never feared losing it. Even if he lost Chadwick Park, he would still have enough wealth to live where and how he chose. No one could forbid him. He wouldn't be a female for anything on earth.

"Judith, your father is right." Richard resisted taking her into his arms. "There's no need for this upheaval. You can stay on at the Manor until you're ready to leave. There's only one thing. I don't know where you'll go if not Ainsley Park. You haven't mentioned any other friends. You see, since I learned about my ownership of the Manor, I've thought I would ask Sherwood to stay on as my agent. Monford's return, however, makes Sherwood's staying at the Manor a remote possibility. He might prefer to return as agent at Ainsley Park. Regardless of Sherwood's choice, though, you'll be alone."

She roused at his words. "Do you tell me they know about this and didn't tell me? That *Ruth* knew?"

"I had just told them when I rode out to find you the day those miscreants shot you. We agreed not to tell you until you had recovered."

Judith jerked her hand away. "Did you tell them the financial situation?"

He nodded.

"Oh, they'll stay on at the Manor, even leap at the opportunity. Daniel knows I can't purchase another such estate. Although his time at the Manor is admittedly limited, I believe he will choose the relative independence he's had there, rather than return to Ainsley Park's more limited scope."

Her bitterness cut him like a knife. She would lose the only support she'd believed was certain. Richard ran his hands through his hair. Admitting his impecunious state was embarrassing.

"I would return the full purchase price if I could, Judith. I've wished my father in purgatory over this, except for one situation. I would never have met you if he hadn't sold the property. Even after this short time, it hurts to think I might never have known you. I care quite deeply for you."

Judith jumped to her feet. "You're just trying to beguile me, so I won't raise a fuss about the Manor. It won't work. Do you hear me? It will not work."

He walked out on her tirade.

<> <> <> <> <>

Judith buried her face in her hands. He didn't really care about her. He'd found the perfect excuse to distance himself from their friendship. Yet why should she care? His behaviour showed she couldn't trust men. He had already made his opinion of her clear. She was infuriating, a hoyden, a shrew. He had said so and in such tones that she couldn't doubt he meant every word. He couldn't possibly want an infuriating, shrewish hoyden for his duchess, no matter what he said.

She'd had a deep lessening of worry when he burst into the farmhouse, and when he held her close to his broad chest, Judith had wanted to stay in his arms forever, her safe haven. Now, she couldn't even hope for anything forever with him. Not even banter over his prettiness. Especially not that.

It wasn't that she loved him. How could she love him when she didn't even like him? Judith admitted she did like him a little, even though he was arrogant, overbearing, high-handed, temperamental . . . she could go on and on but never anything good. Never? Judith fought, but honesty won. His humor matched hers. Her writing novels hadn't bothered him, not once mocking her. He hadn't ridiculed her belief in guardian angels. He wasn't terribly disbelieving about her intelligence. He carried her when she was injured and came to France to rescue her.

Judith clasped her arms around her body. Rocking back and forth, she considered her life without him and muttered, "I don't see how we can even be friends. She would miss that the most.

<> <> <> <> <>

A shrew. Without a doubt, Lady Judith Elizabeth Ainsley was a shrew.

Richard paced from tree to tree, dodging low-hanging branches. He hadn't spent this much time in the woods since childhood. Those days with Anthony had been fun, but not now, not when he was in turmoil brought about by others. First his father's illegal actions, now Judith's refusal to accept his offered compromise. He'd considered going for a ride, which would rid himself of his temper, but one look at the hired nag changed his mind. Riding that bag of bones would throw him into a rage like none since his school days when the boys had ragged him about his pretty face.

Why couldn't Judith understand his circumstances? Did she sympathize with his predicament? No. She screamed like a fishwife and rejected his solution to the Manor ownership situation. She'd rejected him, he acknowledged. His pace slowed when one fact forced itself through his temper.

Lady Judith had reason to be upset. She'd suffered her parents' treatment—her father's deviousness, her mother's indifference. She'd gained independence through her own efforts. Now, she suffered again because she was losing the one thing she prized most, the symbol of her independence: ownership of the Manor.

Rochdale admitted he'd gone about this whole thing the wrong way. He must make her understand he truly cared for her. She would get over her temper. They could reach an agreement on the property. He depended on that, perhaps more than the possibility they could not.

Something nibbled at the edges of his mind, turning into sharp little bites. He stopped in his tracks when the truth slammed into his brain. If he convinced Judith that he truly cared about her, she would expect an offer in due form. An offer of marriage.

Rochdale's emotions screamed no, even while his brain answered yes. Pro and con battled for supremacy in his mind. He didn't want a wife, only a mistress. However, she couldn't be an earl's virtuous daughter. He was too young for marriage with anyone, especially an independent female who didn't know her proper place. She might marry someone else. Wouldn't he prefer a lively intelligent wife to the giggles of a chit just out of the schoolroom? If he didn't act fast, no one even remotely comparable to Lady Judith Ainsley would be available. As far as he knew, there wasn't one even now.

The last thought stopped him in his tracks. Thinking about his friends' wives, he realized there wasn't even one he'd choose over Judith. She was temperamental, true, yet never boring. She was a hoyden but ladylike when necessary. She infuriated him as no other female ever had, yet she could always turn his anger into laughter.

He loved her. Either of them marry someone else? Impossible. Over time, Richard had come to realize life was better when he acknowledged his feelings, even if they didn't coincide with what he had maintained over the years. Forget remaining a bachelor until he reached one and thirty. Eight and twenty was a good age for marriage.

Richard had noted Judith's flush when the earl mentioned his signet ring going to the next generation. Was her blush from anger or from the idea of having a son? He didn't know the answer but did know his mother would be ecstatic he'd finally accepted his family responsibility, even though she might need some persuasion to accept someone she had not chosen. He smiled. There was no question about one thing. Lady Judith Elizabeth Ainsley would not succumb to tears in the face of his mother's demands. There was only one solution. If Judith refused . . . no, he wouldn't even consider a possible refusal. Determined steps carried Richard Chadwick, Duke of Rochdale, back to the farmhouse.

Thirty-One

Two Shall Be One

"I love you."

Richard found Judith still in the parlor, tearstains marring her face, which rested on a cushion she hugged against her chest. His heart went out to her in her unhappiness, much of which lay at his door. What would he lose by admitting his love? Seating himself beside her, he repeated himself.

"I love you."

This time Judith raised her head.

Her eyes changed from bleak to the blue of water on a sunny day but then turned stormy gray.

"You just want my property," she accused. "You're getting the Manor, so you don't have to pretend."

He shook his head at her stubbornness. "You're wrong. I'm not pretending. I do love you."

She stared him straight in the face. "You can't love me. You don't even like me. All we do is quarrel."

A soft laugh escaped Richard's lips. They had been at odds from the moment they met. He could count on a like future. Truth be told, he even looked forward to it. He asked why she thought they annoyed each other.

Judith answered with a question. "Because you're arrogant and overbearing?"

"You're not? Now be honest!"

"Maybe a tiny bit," she admitted with a sidelong glance.

"Or perhaps you're jealous." He loved watching her outbursts, provided they didn't last long. She didn't fail him.

"Jealous!" She whipped around to face him, her smoky eyes flashing. "Preposterous. Why would I be?"

He raised an eyebrow.

"Oh, yes. Because you're prettier. I brought that on myself, did I not?"

He joined her laughter, but sobered the next instant. "I do love you."

"No."

Richard continued in a conversational tone. "I first saw you at the theatre when you were a child. Later at the Academy, you fell into my arms again. I couldn't recall ever holding a child in my arms, yet you felt familiar. I realize now you were older than you appeared, but, at the time, I believed you were still a schoolgirl."

"Father preferred for me to look childish."

"Your vision would appear in the heat of battle, reminding me why I wanted to live. Even on the cloudiest day, I would remember your shining blue eyes, and my fatigue would ease. I must have been the only soldier in the Peninsula who dreamed about a schoolgirl, a stranger, one whose name I didn't even know. I knew you were no longer a schoolgirl when I kissed you at the apple tree."

"You used me abominably that day, Your Grace."

Richard grinned at her accusation but didn't deny the truth. She was listening. He must not push, or he might lose her. "You slipped in and out of my life. I puzzled over your familiarity at Grillon's Hotel and later at East Leah. I could hardly take my eyes off you at the Opera House, then the theatre. My friends couldn't identify you. Do you realize how much speculation you roused on those evenings? I stole a kiss at the apple tree. Only a few occasions, yet you dominated my mind."

"Actually, the day I fell into your arms at the theatre was not the first time."

He lifted an eyebrow at her. "No? When was the first?"

"I fell from the same apple tree into your arms when I was seven years old."

A momentary frown marred his features before enlightenment came. "Do you mean to tell me you were the dirty little ragamuffin who knocked me flat on my back?"

Judith's eyes sparkled as she nodded. "You kissed the tip of my nose."

"It was the only clean spot on your face!"

"Yes, you told me so."

"And you told me your name was Judith. That's it! That's the thought that has nibbled around my brain since I saw you at Grillon's! I knew I ought to know your name, but I didn't know why because I remembered our meetings at the Royal Academy and the theatre. We didn't exchange names either time."

"It hurt when you didn't recognize me later at the theatre," Judith confessed. "I thought of the boy who looked like a Greek god. I daydreamed about you, so I vowed to forget you and never think of you again when you didn't remember me."

"It's my turn to confess. I didn't remember the tiny little girl, but I often thought of the blue-eyed schoolgirl. She rode beside me in battles."

That left her speechless: a rarity, Richard knew.

To lighten the atmosphere, he risked teasing her. "You can understand I didn't connect the filthy little urchin with the beautiful girl you became. However, considering all your hoydenish behaviour I've observed since, I should have made the connection."

Judith smiled but relapsed into silence.

Richard voiced something, which had puzzled him throughout the weeks since they met. "Tom Hinson was with me when I saw you at Grillon's Hotel and the inn at East Leah. Yet you were in East Leah an appreciable time before he told me there was someone that he wanted me to meet. He didn't tell me who. Truth be told, I accepted his invitation only to get away from my estate problems for a few days. He didn't tell me it was my bewitching, blue-eyed beauty whom I longed to meet."

She lowered her eyes but admitted she hadn't noticed Tom at either place. "I only saw you, the god-like boy, now a man."

He tilted her chin upward. "I'm pleased to hear that, but I don't understand why he waited so long before telling me where I could find you."

Judith explained. "I met Hope soon after I moved there. Tom was too busy for afternoon visits, and I didn't go out in the evenings during our early weeks at the Manor."

He casually cradled her hand in his own. "Since I found you, I have been unable to stay away. Your face interferes every time I look at another woman. They must think I'm touched in the upper works."

Richard didn't know what had upset her, but something had at the mention of another woman. Jealousy? His heart leaped. Perhaps there was still hope for him.

"Do you realize your eyes turn from blue to gray when you're angry? Of late, I've seen them gray more often than blue." He studied her averted face. "Nonetheless, all our time together hasn't been spent quarreling. There have been times when our minds functioned as one. I found those times encouraging. Do you think you could learn to care for me?"

Judith's head snapped up.

The normally suave duke took a deep breath, steadying his voice. "The simple fact is you are lodged in my heart for all eternity. Will you marry me?"

The gray eyes turned blue. Judith slowly shook her head, while she continued gazing at him. "You could marry anyone you please. You must know any number of females who would make you a comfortable wife and conform to your every wish. I could never meet your expectations. I wouldn't even try."

Her self-knowledge amused him—conformity was the last thing he would expect from Judith Elizabeth Ainsley—but he quickly sobered. "If I wanted a milk-and-water miss for my duchess, I could take my pick from the bevy my mother parades before me. No, I want one young woman who keeps me on my toes wondering what harebrained thing she'll do next. Also, you don't giggle."

She laughed but only for a moment. "I don't know what to say. We seldom meet without quarreling. Besides, I haven't considered marriage."

"Yes, I know." Richard hesitated, knowing he was risking everything. "My darling, you haven't given any thought to marriage because you're so wrapped up in misery that there isn't room for anything else in your life."

Those bewitching blue eyes turned stormy gray yet again. Judith opened her mouth, her intention clear. Annihilation. Richard couldn't allow her temper to explode, surely saying words she would regret later, so he forestalled her.

"Judith, I believe we could be happy together. However, you can't admit my love into your heart until you empty it of the hurt you harbor against your father. There isn't room for both. Surely, you can understand: one cancels the other. Would you rather hurt than love?"

"He lied to me. He lived a lie, which proves he's totally without honour!"

Again, he faced the risk of losing her. "Does that not mean you too are without honour?"

Her shoulders stiffened. "Whatever can you mean?"

"Your whole life between the ages of fifteen and twenty-one was a lie, so how can you condemn your father?"

She stared at him in silence for a long moment, then raised her stubborn chin. "That's different. My father's lies forced me to live this way. The dishonour is all his."

"Did you answer my question with honesty?"

Lady Judith Elizabeth Ainsley rose to her full height and raised her haughty nose into the air, preparing to give him another sample of her temper.

Before she could speak, he also rose and towered several inches over her. He cupped her face between his hands and gazed into the stormy eyes before lowering his lips to hers in a gentle kiss, which deepened when her lips grew soft. Drawing away, he again brushed his lips against hers and then spoke in a ragged voice.

"I will leave you now to think over what I said." With a quick bow, Richard strode out the door.

Judith sank back onto the sofa. Richard's husky voice had melted her until a different reaction set in. How dare he take advantage of her with another kiss? How dare he think she would marry him after saying she was without honour? He was interfering again. What right did he have to say her heart was full of hurt? Not hurt—hatred. She had every right to hate her father. She did.

"I hate him." Her hands clenched when the words shattered the quietness within the house. No, I don't. The knowledge came in a flash as her hands relaxed. I want to hate him, yet I don't. He lied to me. He cheated me out of happiness for several years. So, why don't I hate him?

Because I love him.

Childhood memories flashed through her mind. She'd been happy. At least she had believed she was happy, so it was the same thing. Since moving into the Manor and seeing how the children played together, she realized she should have had friends her age. The only one she could remember was Sybil. Their friendship didn't last long because Sybil's father forced her into an unfortunate marriage with an old man. At the same time, her father had promised he would find her a husband of her generation even though he denied it now.

Memories of the earl's devious behaviour returned Judith to the present. Bitterness welled through her. Renewed anger threatened the precarious balance she'd achieved when she realized she didn't hate her father. What should she do? If she released hatred entirely, she would have nothing to sustain her.

You would have Rochdale's love.

Susanna hovered about ten feet from her.

You've realized you love your father, so why don't you admit you love Richard too?

Did you bring us all together here?

With the help of their angels, yes, I did.

Why?

I told you before. The two people you love most in the world also love you. I knew you would realize it, if you had no outside distractions.

I don't know what to do now.

Yes, you do. Susanna faded into nothing.

Yes, Judith knew. She wanted her old relationship with her father. She wanted Richard. That simple, so she must approach them. This was what Susanna had meant about the sequence of things. If her father had not acted the way he did, she wouldn't have purchased the Manor. If she hadn't purchased the Manor, she wouldn't know Richard. If she had not been abducted, she would not have found her father, and she wouldn't have realized her love for both men. Judith fought that acknowledgment for a moment but then let it wash away her hurt.

<> <> <> <> <>

"Father?" She found him in the kitchen.

Ainsley straightened his gaunt body, nervously rubbing his hand across his thinning hair. Her eyes locked with the eyes so like her own. Through her sudden tears, she saw the pleading expression. With a cry, she threw herself into his arms holding him as he rocked backward. His tears mingled with hers.

"I love you, Father." Judith helped him into a chair, then sank down beside it, her pleading eyes gazing into his. "Can you forgive me for trying to hate you, for being dishonest with you?"

He stroked her hair and raised her face toward his. "Kitten, I'm the one who must apologize. I treated you badly by not trusting you. I'm pleased you had the gumption to defy me. I hope you can forgive me."

She gazed into his eyes through the mist of tears clouding hers. "I'm surprised at how easily I can, Father. I suppose it's because no apologies from you are truly necessary."

With a smile, he brushed away her tears.

She worked up her courage to speak again. "Father, would you object if I marry Richard?"

"I would be delighted, Kitten. In my view, no man is worthy of you, but Rochdale comes closer than anyone else of my acquaintance. Has he asked you?"

"A few minutes ago, he did. I thought you heard."

"I'd just come inside from my walk when you came into the kitchen."

"You approve?"

"Yes." He shot her an amused smile. "This is not your primary concern, I know, but have you considered your management skills are exactly what Chadwick Park needs?"

"My obsession with owning the Manor left no room for his estate needs." Judith's eyes gleamed. "It will be quite a challenge—after I convince him his duchess will not sit in her boudoir doing needlework."

"My daughter, the duchess!" He chuckled. "Do you remember what your Mama thought about that rank?"

Her mother's face flashed into her mental vision. "I was ten years old when she informed me that I must learn to curtsy because I might meet a duchess someday. The idea amused me. I didn't understand why she held duchesses in such awe but decided I would never stand in awe of anyone."

"She taught you well in the niceties of life."

"We had daily lessons for a time, not only in the various degrees of the curtsy but also forms of address and the other details social life requires. I objected to the two hours she insisted upon each day. Yet during those few weeks of my childhood, we developed a level of friendliness we haven't had since. I wish it had lasted."

"My fault," Monford admitted. "I owe her an abject apology too. When we return home, I'll go to the Dower House and apologize."

"She won't be there," Judith told him with a grin. "You know how much she hated everything about the Dower House."

"Where is she?"

"At Warminster. Remember, you gave her the house."

"I remember executing the conveyance deed, but she doesn't have sufficient funds to live there."

Judith pushed aside remembered bitterness of his satisfying her whims. That was in the past and best forgotten, but forgetting would require time. The hurt had lasted for too long to disappear on the instant.

"Yes, she does."

He stared at her a moment before his frown cleared. "Ah. You supplied her with the necessary money."

"I invested funds in her name," Judith conceded. "She's independent of us. I hope you will allow her to keep her status at Warminster. Now, I want to find Richard."

She left the earl lost in thought.

Judith turned the corner of the house and saw her love leaning against a fence, staring into the distance. She walked until she stood about three steps from him and peeked around him to see what enthralled him. A calf on wobbly legs took a few steps, then returned to her mother's side. Judith cleared her throat.

Richard didn't turn.

"If I moo, will I get your attention?"

He turned, his face lightening. "Judith."

"Yes."

The duke raised startled eyebrows and favored her with a questioning smile. "Yes, what?"

Her lips curved into a wide smile as she teased him. "Forgotten already! You did make me an offer of marriage, did you not? Is the offer still open? Can you bear to marry an infuriating, independent, shrewish hoyden who admits she's devious?"

She held him off with an outstretched hand. "I must warn you—I will probably continue to play games with children, climb trees after kittens, and splash in brooks. There are any number of other things I will do that will need apologies."

He pulled her into his arms. "That will keep you in practice. To answer all your questions at once—yes!"

After a few satisfactory moments of mutual bliss, he ventured a necessary question. "I realize you're an independent lady and have reached your majority. However, would you object if I acted like an old-fashioned male and approached your father for permission to marry you?"

"I would have sent you away with a flea in your ear if you had said that when you asked me. However, I've made my peace with him. He has already given me his blessing." Judith gave him a teasing smile, "Besides, all Ainsleys, male and female alike for two hundred years, at least, have wed at Ainsley Park. I am not sufficiently independent to risk the consequences of not only marrying without my father's permission but also failing to have the ceremony in the chapel there."

He answered with another kiss. Judith ended it with a gasp for air before she confessed with a twinkle. "In reality, you never had a chance to marry anyone else."

"Why is that?" His lips twitched while he waited for her next impertinence.

"Because I decided to marry you when I was seven years old, even if you are prettier than I am," she told him. "I even told you so."

"I believed our marriage was my idea," he admitted. With another smile, Richard gathered Judith in his arms again.

<> <> <> <> <>

Susanna smiled too. She had finished this job and could hope for a long period in heaven's quietness before God sent her to another human, perhaps a less recalcitrant one.

Historical Notes

A prevalent belief holds that, until the current era, a woman could not inherit an English noble title held by a man. My research revealed this is a fallacy. *Wikipedia* lists 119 women holding titles *so jure* (in her own right), beginning in the fourteenth century and continuing. (https://en.wikipedia.org/wiki/List_of_peerages_inherit ed_by_women.) For these notes, I chose one which supports *An Independent Woman*.

In the year 1702, Queen Anne created the Duke of Marlborough title for John Churchill, the first Earl of Marlborough (1650–1722). In historical texts, unqualified use of the title typically refers to the first Duke. The dukedom name refers to Marlborough in Wiltshire. In 1703, his son, who was also named John, Marquess of Blanford, predeceased him.

In 1706, Parliament passed a special Act to prevent the titles' extinction. According to this Act, when the first Duke of Marlborough died in 1722, the Marlborough titles passed to his eldest daughter Henrietta (1681–1733), now the second Duchess of Marlborough (https://en.wikipedia.org/wiki/Henrietta_Godolphin,_2n d_Duchess_of_Marlborough). Upon Henrietta's death in 1733, the Marlborough titles passed to her nephew, Charles Spencer (1706-1758), who became the *third* Duke. Note there was not a second Duke. The title passed from John, first Duke of Marlborough, thence to Henrietta, second Duchess of Marlborough (following her mother), to Charles, third Duke of Marlborough. (https://en.wikipedia.org/wiki/Duke_of_Marlborough).

The Napoleonic Wars began in 1793 and ended in 1815, with a brief peace in 1802. I use the final year.

Shipping difficulties between France and Russia prompted Napoleon to launch a massive invasion of Russia. This ended in disaster for France. Encouraged by the defeat, Austria, Prussia, Sweden, and Russia formed the Sixth Coalition and began a new campaign against France. The coalition defeated Napoleon at Leipzig, hastening his fall from power. He abdicated on April 6, 1814. The victors exiled him to Elba Island and restored the Bourbon monarchy.

On the evening of February 26, 1815, Napoleon, with a small number of soldiers, escaped from Elba Island. He arrived in Paris on March 20th, marking the commencement of what was contemporarily labeled the Hundred Days War, which included his final defeat at Waterloo.

On July 15th, he surrendered to the British at Rochefort and was exiled to the remote Saint Helena Island in the South Atlantic Ocean. The Treaty of Paris, signed on November 20, 1815, formally ended the war.

After several failed attempts at escape, Napoleon died on May 5, 1821, at age 51, most likely from stomach cancer. Rumours persist that an unknown person poisoned him. His initial burial site was on the island.

However, his remains were returned to France in 1840 and placed in St. Jérôme's Chapel in Paris until his tomb was completed in 1861. His last resting place is in a sarcophagus in the crypt under the dome at Les Invalides.

Sources

https://www.thebristorian.co.uk/the-past-today/napoleonescapesfromelba#:

https://www.historyextra.com/period/modern/hundred-days-napoleon-elba-exile-escape/

https://www.nam.ac.uk/explore/battle-waterloo#:

https://www.napoleon.org/en/history-of-the-two-empires/articles/napoleon-and-saint-helena-1815-1816/

https://blog.nationalarchives.gov.uk/end-conflict-napoleons-surrender-hms-bellerophon/#

https://www.britannica.com/place/United-Kingdom/The-Napoleonic-Wars

https://en.wikipedia.org/wiki/Napoleon

Select Glossary

Almack's: Assembly rooms on King Street in London, which held exclusive subscription balls each Wednesday night of the Season. Only those deemed worthy by the fastidious patronesses were awarded vouchers to enter. Said patronesses could be fussy about which ladies were allowed to attend but reportedly weren't quite as discriminating about the gentlemen allowed to enter such hallowed halls.

Batman: An orderly assigned to a military officer, often retained by the officer after leaving the military.

Bedlam/Bedlamite: The term comes from the name of a hospital in London: "Saint Mary of Bethlehem," which is devoted to treating the mentally ill, beginning in the 1300s.

Bluestocking: A lady with an unfashionable interest in intellectual and literary pursuits, often with a scientific bent.

Dowager: The widow of a peer. The term was added to a widow's title when she received the dower house and the new heir married. It was seldom used in speech unless it was to differentiate her from the wife of the new peer. Normally, the term only appeared in writing, such as letters and legal documents.

Dower House: Usual place for the mother or mother-in-law to reside when a new heir moves into the main house.

Foolscap: Writing paper. The name derives from the watermark of a jester's cap.

Fop: an ostentatiously dressed gentleman who spends too much time and money on his looks, often thought of as excessive and even effeminate.

Footman: a male servant, usually wearing a special uniform called "livery," who worked in the home and waited on the family. Often, he was the servant who might deliver a message or follow the lady as she shopped to protect her and to carry her packages.

Jointure: A financial provision for a widow. The amount is negotiated based on the portion she brought to the marriage and is generally established as part of the marriage settlement.

Laudanum: A mixture of brandy and opium used to treat pain or to aid sleep.

Leg-shackled: Married.

Marriage Mart: The usual reference is to Almack's, where young ladies went in search of a husband.

Missish: an adjective for a girl who is naïve and inexperienced in society and tends to be silly.

Modiste: A fashionable and quite expensive lady's dressmaker, often French (or pretending to be).

On dits: Gossip

Paper skull: Lacking in intelligence.

Pistols at Dawn: Dueling was based on a code of honor, not to kill the opponent but to restore honor by demonstrating a willingness to risk one's life for it.

However, too often dueling was the result of anger. Although frowned upon in 1815, possibly bringing flight out of the country, dueling only became illegal in 1854.

Season: The social "Season" began in early spring after Easter and lasted until the end of June. The Season typically matched Parliament's schedule. Originally a way to amuse the families of the men who served in the House of Lords and the House of Commons, it became a social event.

Set down: a sharp response to an impertinence.

Special license: A license obtained from the Archbishop of Canterbury that grants the right to marry at any convenient time or place. Only people of influence could obtain one and then only in rare circumstances.

Subalterns: lowest military rank, usually new recruits.

Thatch-gallows: Dishonest men who preyed on innocent females.

Tittle-tattle: Gossip.

Toadeaters: People who try to gain approval by praise, flattery, etc.

Ton: Fashionable Society. *Ton* comes from the French word *bon ton*, which means good manners, good breeding, etc.

Tinderbox: a metal box holding something easily flammable and a flint and steel for striking a spark.

Upper Rooms: A place for assemblies in Bath, England, near Circus and Bennett Streets. It consisted of four social rooms: the Card Room, the Octagon Room, the Tea Room, and the Ballroom.

West Indies: The West Indies is a generic term used to cover the islands located in the Southern portion of the Atlantic Ocean near South America. The West Indies, for a time, were a major source of income for the powers in Europe, including Spain, England, France, and the Dutch.

Whitehall: Military headquarters. Became known as the War Department in the 1850s.

Books by Peggy Lovelace Ellis

Suspense
The Mysterious Face

Regency Novels:
An Independent Woman (Standalone)

Regency Heart Series
The Uncertain Heart
The Merry Heart
The Divided Heart

Short Stories
Silver Shadows, Stories of Life in a Small Town

Anthologies
Challenges on the Home Front, World War II (Second Edition)
A Beautiful Life and Other Stories
Lest the Colors Fade

Your opinion matters to me, so if you enjoyed *An Independent Woman*, please spread the word by posting a review on Amazon, Good Reads, Barnes & Noble, and other sources to which you have access. Reviews are enormously helpful to the reading community, and your support really does motivate me to keep writing. Thank you!
♥ Peggy ♥

www.ingramcontent.com/pod-product-compliance
Lightning Source LLC
Chambersburg PA
CBHW071357300726
48976CB00006B/1914